MURDER YOU WROTE

AN INTERACTIVE MYSTERY

One Story. Twenty Writers. Your Choice.

L.J.M. Owen Ed.

First published by Clan Destine Press in 2023

PO Box 121,
Bittern Victoria 3918
Australia

National Library of Australia Cataloguing-In-Publication data:

Editor: L.J.M. Owen

MURDER YOU WROTE

ISBNs: 978-1-922904-54-6 (hardback)
978-1-922904-52-2 (paperback)
978-1-922904-53-9 (eBook)

Cover art and internal illustrations: Judith Rossell

Design & Typesetting by Clan Destine Press

www.clandestinepress.net

Dedication

This book is dedicated to every reader who loves a good mystery, and to every person who is working on improving their reading skills. You were in our thoughts every step of the way.

It is also dedicated to hard-working furry supervisors around the country who put in extraordinary hours to ensure their humans had company while creating this book. A special mention of my own Loulou, the sweetest little kitty who ever did live, and her incredible bravery during her chemo journey this year.

CONTENTS

HOW TO READ THIS BOOK

A note from L.J.M. Owen

Murder You Wrote: An Interactive Mystery is a traditional murder mystery. Set in an isolated manor in the Tasmanian countryside, it is the story of a detective investigating the death of a famous author. It differs from a classic mystery though, in that you are in the drivers' seat. Let me explain…

You are the detective

Throughout this investigation, you – yes, you the person reading these words right now – become the detective. Your case is the body in the library.

As the detective, you choose which clues to follow. You can track a lead, a hunch or a suspect and create your own pathway through the book.

At the end of each chapter you can choose to turn the page and read straight on, or you can pick a different chapter from a Where to Next? list of options. At the end of some chapters, this list includes an option to find out what really happened in the library. But beware! Once you know, it will change how you read the book.

If you reach the end of the book and realise you didn't find all the clues, try going back to the beginning and choosing a different pathway through the chapters to see if you can piece together the solution to the mystery.

A challenge

For those of you who enjoy a challenge, there is one special pathway through this book where you can collect all the clues you need to solve the mystery in just ten chapters. If you think you have found this path, and want to know if you are correct, you can email a list of the chapters and clues to me at ljmowen@gmail.com for the solution.

Twenty writers, one story

This book is a novel anthology. It contains one long story, making it a novel. It is also a collection of stories and story ideas from a group of writers, making it an anthology.

Each writer has their own way of telling a story. This means you may notice different styles of writing as you read various chapters. Some have a more historical flavour, some are darker and some are quirkier.

Reading anthologies is a great way to discover new authors. If you particularly enjoy a chapter, perhaps turn to the biography section at the end of the book to see if that writer has other books available for you to read.

Suitable for emerging adult readers

In Tasmania, and in some other regions of Australia, less than half the adult population is functionally literate. Many of these adults are working to improve their reading skills. They enjoy the same stories as everyone else.

To make this book suitable for avid mystery readers and accessible to emerging adult readers, it has been edited to an average Flesch-Kincaid readability level of around 80 out of 100, or grade 5.

In terms of language, we opted for modern usage or the Macquarie dictionary. Thus 'a historic' not 'an historic', and 'verandah' not 'veranda'.

A mentoring anthology

This book began as a mentoring project for emerging Tasmanian writers. Established authors helped unpublished writers to develop their story contribution. If you enjoy this book, please tell your family and friends to read it and please give it rave reviews online. This will help the new writers find their own readers and future fans.

Good luck with your investigation,
L.J.M. Owen
Commissioning Editor
Murder You Wrote: An Interactive Mystery

CHAPTER ONE

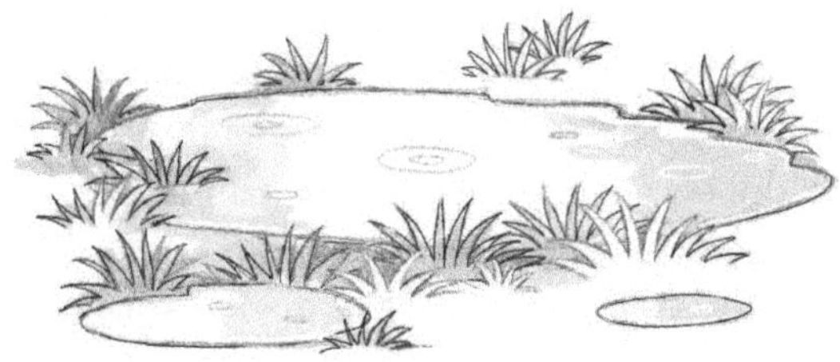

Your Body in the Library

Z.E. Davidson

In which you, a retired police detective, arrive at a convict-built manor house on the edge of the Huon River for a crime fiction writers festival.

THIS YEAR, THE HUON VALLEY CRIME WRITERS FESTIVAL IS OFFERING YOU the royal treatment. You didn't expect to hear from them again, given what happened last time. Perhaps it's hard to find retired police detectives who are willing to share trade secrets with eager mystery writers.

You are staying in a historic sandstone manor on the banks of the Huon River. The festival volunteer who drops you at the front gate wishes you a good night. You thank her, zip your jacket against the driving rain and begin dragging your luggage up the winding gravel path.

Warm yellow light spills from the manor's windows, guiding you through sodden spring gardens. You startle a small, dark creature in the bushes as you pass by, causing it to thump away through the undergrowth.

You're looking forward to the festival starting tomorrow morning and you can't wait to meet some of the writers you're staying with tonight. But you feel a spurt of apprehension as you knock on the front door. These festivals add a certain excitement to retired life – though hopefully not quite as much as last year.

After some confusion about which of the cool white bedrooms is yours, you stow your cases in the Huon pine-trimmed wardrobe. You place your pyjamas on a pile of woollen blankets on the end of your wrought iron bed, then head to the sitting room to join the other guests.

In front of the fireplace, resplendent in a crisp white suit, is the famous Shao T. Mann. You're eager to introduce yourself to the author of the bestselling Detective Carl Kuphem series.

Shao's waving a crystal tumbler of whisky in the air as he talks to an admiring young man. You recognise him from the festival program as Hudson van Daemon, one of Tasmania's homegrown crime fiction writers.

At twenty-five, Hudson has just released his second novel. Dressed in a red flannelette shirt, long cargo shorts and hiker's boots, he's the only one who stands to greet you. You've done a little research on him – on all of them, in fact – and know his only skirmish with the law was to protect old growth forests.

Bruce Tossington-Smythe, another crime novelist, sits across from Shao. You know that Bruce recently divorced for the fifth time and he is the only person in this group with a police record. He's leaning back in his chair, letting the occasional drop of whisky fall from his lips to the collar of his otherwise pristine tuxedo. Every now and then he snorts in disagreement at Shao.

Bruce barely inclines his head when you say hello.

Critics often compare Shao and Bruce's work, mentioning that they were at university together. While you can see some similarities, Bruce's books don't have the cleverness and wit that you enjoy in a Detective Carl Kuphem story.

The beautifully made-up woman clutching Shao's arm is his American wife, Jasmine Quill. With big hair, gold jewellery and coral lipstick stretched over fluorescent white teeth, she flashes you a smile when you offer to shake her hand.

Again, you've done a little research. It's a recent union, a third marriage for them both. Of the two, she is far more academically qualified.

The fifth and final guest doesn't appear until it is time for your pre-dinner guided tour of the manor. A sharply dressed woman in a pale yellow trouser-suit and black-edged glasses, who explains she's been resting to rid herself of a headache.

The three men acknowledge her, while Jasmine continues chatting with the festival volunteer. 'Here she is, Mann's editor extraordinaire,' Bruce says.

You've never seen Shao's editor before, not even a picture. She doesn't smile when you introduce yourself, whispering so as not to distract the volunteer who has ushered you all into the manor's tiny museum to guide you through the exhibits.

She shakes your hand and responds with a crisp, 'Paige Hybrough'.

Her name isn't in the acknowledgements of Shao's books. 'Have you worked on the Kuphem series long?' you ask, handing her some colonial kitchen item that is being passed around.

Your question is more than polite small talk – you're genuinely interested in your fellow guests. If you'd paid more attention at the last of these writers' gatherings, perhaps you could have avoided certain newspaper headlines...

'We've known each other for thirty years,' Paige answers. Her eyes slide toward Shao, who is now deep in conversation with Bruce and Hudson about a display of vintage books.

Paige pulls a fountain pen from her handbag and scribbles on the back of her left hand in red ink – is she taking notes? She sees you looking. 'I'm always losing pens, so I bought this special one to ensure I don't leave it behind.' Her turn of phrase, for a moment, is like Shao's famous character Carl Kuphem. She is his editor, after all, so that makes sense.

Shao points at one of the books in a glass case and says something, making Bruce laugh. Hudson, between them, flushes beet red and steps back.

You can't decipher Paige's expression as she stares at the trio.

'When did you start working on the series?' you press, as the seven of you enter the manor's library. It is a stunning wood-panelled room filled with built-in bookcases, wingback armchairs, soft warm lamps and a crackling fireplace. The floor is criss-crossed with richly patterned oriental carpets, similar to the other rooms you have toured.

The volunteer picks up a convict ball and chain set and passes it around. This one, unlike the set in the museum, sits on an open bookshelf above a desk in the library. You note how unwieldy it is as you place it back on the shelf above the leather inlay desk.

'I've worked on all of them,' Paige answers, drawing you back to your conversation with her.

Years of editing Shao's books and not one acknowledgement? You point at the towering boxes of books on the desk, labelled as copies of

Shao T. Mann's latest Detective Carl Kuphem investigation, *High Time*. 'Including this one?' you say.

Jasmine interrupts your conversation. 'They've announced that dinner's served,' she purrs. She smiles at you, then turns sharply toward the dining-room door, as though Paige isn't standing beside you.

The dinner, consisting of course after course of local produce, is delicious. But with each new bottle of wine, the mood at the table deteriorates.

Harsh words echo across the high ceiling, chandeliers and display cabinets of blue-and-white china as Bruce and Shao argue about sales figures, reviews, and who will win this year's Devil in the Detail Award – the festival's annual prize.

You try several times to discuss the weekend's program, and each of the writers' latest books, to no avail. Hudson and Paige both express interest in your past as a police investigator, but the only topic everyone is happy to listen to you talk about is fingerprinting.

You think about the Pelican case in your room and the kit of forensic tricks inside you brought to show the audience tomorrow. Next to it is a small satchel containing a copy of your first attempt at a book – another reason you accepted the invitation to this year's festival so soon after the fiasco of last year.

Bruce and Shao begin arguing again, this time dragging Hudson into their squabble. Jasmine largely ignores them, interrupting only to correct Bruce when he gets one of the plot points from Shao's third novel wrong.

'Even I knew that,' Hudson snaps.

Sitting next to you, Paige mutters, 'They should leave him out of this.' She's not so much talking to you as thinking aloud.

Shao helps himself to a third serving of dessert, unperturbed.

Bruce insults another of the Carl Kuphem books, and the verbal sparring begins anew. You aren't impressed by the bickering, self-indulgent mood of the evening.

The remaining festival volunteers clear the table and say they will pack the dishwasher then head to their own homes for the night.

After dinner you put aside your annoyance and seek out Shao in the manor's library, where he is pre-signing books for tomorrow's crowds.

This may be your only opportunity to speak to him alone, his poor behaviour this evening notwithstanding.

Exiting the library shortly after 8.30 pm, your interaction with Shao leaves you shaken.

You're eager for this day to end.

Just twelve months ago you'd been at the centre of an incident dubbed by the media as the 'Coppers' Clash'. You told yourself that this year everything would be fine, but you now regret staying in the same house as these combative, secretive people.

You push last year from your thoughts, and remind yourself you only need to stay here one more night. Then you can return home.

Teeth cleaned, pyjamas donned, you knock back enough sleeping pills to stun a horse. After years of late night shifts poring over case files you now suffer from unrelenting insomnia.

You drift off to the soothing sound of rain on the corrugated iron roof, but your dreams are filled with shouting and the sound of running feet.

It's barely sunrise when you're woken by a series of screeches and bumps outside your window. Dim sunlight seeps through the wet windowpane as you hold your breath, listening.

A series of barks and the sounds of something heavy thumping on the roof tells you it's possums. Noisy creatures.

The room is so cold your breath fogs in front of your face. You're sure you left the hydronic heater on the wall turned to high when you went to bed, but it seems to have switched itself off during the night.

What time is it? You grope for your phone on the bedside table. You find it and the screen comes alive, a blinding flash in the darkened room.

You've got notifications for a missed call and two messages. One is from your partner, wishing you a good day at the festival. The second is from the festival organisers. This text is a lot longer than your partner's and gives you pause for concern.

You curse at yourself for having the phone on silent. The organiser's message tells you what you now confirm by peering out the window – the river is up and you're stranded. The rain last night caused severe flash flooding, you read, cutting the roads in every direction. You're stuck on the grounds of the manor house until the waters recede.

But there's good news as the house has plenty of supplies: food, wood, battery-powered lights, and a generator for the hot water heating system and general electricity.

You pull up the number of the festival's panellist wrangler. Surely there's something that can be done about this? Even as you tap their number to call back, the signal bars in the top right-hand corner of the screen collapse to zero.

No phone, then. No internet either.

You clamber out of bed and dress in your warmest clothes, layering a puffer jacket over two jumpers, then go in search of your fellow guests.

Entering the corridor outside your room you hear clangs and soft cursing coming from the kitchen. To your surprise you find the editor Paige standing over lit logs in the woodfired stove, sucking a corner of one thumb.

You raise an eyebrow and she responds with, 'Country girl. I'm all over this off-grid stuff, except I burned myself. Coffee won't be long.'

She's wearing black pyjamas with white piping at the edges and a matching robe and slippers. It's refined and stately…and is that mulberry silk? Paige must be earning a pretty penny as Shao's editor.

A huge figure looms in the doorway to the corridor. Still clad in his red flannelette shirt, long cargo shorts and boots from last night, Hudson's carrying an enormous axe over his shoulder, looking for all the world like he escaped from the Lumberjack song.

'Generator's going now,' he says. 'It's connected to the hot water heater and a few power point circuits, I'd say.'

'Well done, you,' Paige says.

'And there's plenty of firewood,' he continues. 'Enough for a few days.'

Surely he's wrong. 'A few days?' you ask.

He shrugs, making the axe bob up and down. 'Tasmanian weather, what can I say?'

You stare first at him, then Paige. 'How have you both swung into action so quickly?'

They smile, almost in unison. 'It's just what you do,' they chorus.

'Jinx,' Hudson hoots. 'I'm not sure about Ms Hybrough here, but I grew up spending summers in our shack by the beach,' he says, glancing at her. 'We lived off the land during the holidays, so I'm used to all this.'

You can't interpret the look Paige is giving him. 'Me too,' is all she says. Then, 'Coffee's almost done.'

'You grew up here too?' you ask her.

'Yes. Would you like a cup?'

She makes a show of carefully wrapping the percolator handle in a thick oven mitt before pulling it from the stovetop. She clearly doesn't want to discuss her Tasmanian past.

'Thanks,' you say as she pours you a mug. 'You're a lifesaver.'

Hudson sticks his head in the pantry. 'There's plenty of food. How're your cooking skills?'

'I do a mean bacon, eggs and fried bread,' Paige replies. Is it the light, or are her eyes glistening?

'I need a well-cooked egg and a hot coffee,' Bruce announces as he stumbles into the kitchen, yawning. 'Why is this place so bloody cold?'

Paige doesn't acknowledge him; Hudson's face flushes red.

'There's been a blackout,' you say.

Bruce glares at you and grunts. There's a flask in his hand. Drinking already? No, you realise, as he turns it upside down and tries to jiggle a final drop from it.

Bruce has run dry. He's in the same suit he wore to dinner last night, though it's now crinkled and creased. You wonder if he slept in it. He's lost his tie somewhere and has draped a footy scarf in its place.

You, Paige and Hudson get to work, while Bruce sits at the table and watches. He doesn't offer any assistance and you can see that this annoys Hudson.

Bruce does summon the words to thank Paige when she hands him a plate of breakfast. His eyes linger on her as she walks away, but she doesn't seem to notice.

At the table with her meal in front of her, Paige lets the sleeve of her dressing gown trail in her eggs. She seems distracted, as though she's tussling with some kind of internal debate. She notices her sleeve, curses, then glances at the doorway to the corridor as she blots egg white from her robe.

You almost don't recognise Jasmine as she hobbles into the room and takes a seat opposite Bruce, hunching as though she's in pain. She's in a drab black dress you wouldn't have imagined a woman like her would even own, let alone wear.

Her face is grey and her hair a lank mess. Only her gold earrings have retained their lustre overnight. 'Why is it so cold?' she demands.

You repeat everything the volunteer told you. She looks increasingly outraged as you speak.

'This is unacceptable,' she croaks, her throat apparently raw. 'I need to go to a drugstore.' She glares at Paige. How could it be the editor's fault? 'Are you telling me there's no hot water? I've been sick all night with food poisoning. I need a shower, maybe a weak tea.'

You feel sorry for her. You walk to the stove, pour hot water from the kettle onto a tea bag in a cup and give it a few jiggles.

Despite looking weak, she jerks the cup from your hand. A hard look in her eye gives you pause.

'Is anyone else ill?' you ask, as Jasmine cups her hands around the tea for warmth.

A chorus of shaking heads from other three.

'Is Shao ill, too?' you ask her again.

'No idea,' Jasmine says.

You frown. 'What do you mean?'

'He didn't come to bed last night. Probably stayed up working and fell asleep over that damn fool electric typewriter of his. Or heard me being sick and stayed away.'

After your conversation with Shao last night you can easily believe that he would be uncaring toward an ill spouse.

Bruce snorts. 'I wouldn't've come to bed either, after the way you screamed at him last night.'

Jasmine tsks and turns her head away from him.

Hudson's earlier cheerfulness has soured. 'You haven't seen him since last night?' he asks. You're aware of a new, sharp note in his voice.

Jasmine shakes her head. 'He'll sleep anywhere.'

'If my books were that boring I'd fall asleep writing them, too,' says Bruce with a sneer.

Paige snatches up her plate and moves to the kitchen sink, depositing her dish with a clatter. 'What did I say?' demands Bruce.

Jasmine glances at Paige's back with a look that is pure poison.

'Let's see if there's anything in the first aid kit that might help,' Hudson says, standing up. 'Then I'll check the generator has plenty of fuel. The house should be warm again in no time.'

Jasmine gives him a wan smile.

You walk to the stove to refill your cup. 'Someone should let Shao know what's happening,' you say.

Hudson is outside checking the generator; the other three avoid your eyes. The stillness in the room screams at you.

Today, with a little more insight into the character of Shao T. Mann, you can understand why they might not be enthusiastic to speak to him. 'I'll go then,' you say.

You cross the manor's dark, rich red foyer to the library and tap on the wooden door. There's no reply. You see the door is slightly ajar, so you push it open.

At first, you can't see Shao. There's no-one sitting at the desk. Then you notice the books on the floor. Several boxes have fallen, spilling their contents in a drift of pages and spines.

Shao T. Mann is, indeed, still in the library.

In fact, he is still in his chair…

…which lies on the floor, surrounded by the fallen books.

You step closer. A gash on his forehead has created a small pool of blood, which has soaked into the carpet beneath him.

You check his pulse. The skin on his face is cold, his splayed hands are candle wax grey. You try to lift an arm, but he's stiff.

Kneeling beside the body you close your eyes and carefully inhale the RMS – the rigour mortis scent. It can sometimes aid in establishing approximate time of death. This, together with the stiffness of his limbs, and the feel of the flesh on the back of his neck suggest he's been dead around ten or eleven hours. He must have died sometime around 10 pm last night, not long after you'd taken your sleeping pills.

Your mind whirrs. The house is cut off from civilisation; who knows when you'll be able to notify the authorities or get a forensics team out?

You pull a small spiral-bound notepad and biro out of your jacket pocket. Old habits die hard.

As meticulously as you can and without disturbing the scene, you scan the room and begin taking notes.

One of the chair legs is broken in half. And, visible among the drift of bright yellow books, the convict ball and chain lies on the floor near Shao.

The desk is cluttered with more books that are the same as those on the floor – Shao's latest release, *High Time*. An Olivetti electric typewriter takes centre stage and, beside it, an emerald antique hardback with green page edges.

Next to the typewriter are a red fountain pen, a small plastic bag and – strangest of all – a small swarm of enormous, dead ants.

There's something in the plastic bag.

You reach out to nudge it with your biro, but brush against the typewriter. You jump back with a yelp as it gives you a nasty shock. It must be plugged into a generator-powered circuit.

The item in the plastic bag looks like an orange gummy bear.

A copy of *High Time* has been mutilated. The cover lies open, revealing a small compartment hacked roughly from the pages.

You take one step back, then another. There it is: your clichéd, straight-from-Agatha-Christie-style body in the library. But what else are you looking at here?

When you came to the library last night, as part of the tour and to see Shao, you'd clocked the typewriter, the boxes of books and the ball and chain set. You're certain he was in the same black lacquered bamboo chair, but you don't remember the vintage green book, the red fountain pen, the plastic bag, the mutilated copy of *High Time* nor the dead ants. You would especially have noticed the dead ants.

Your instincts kick in.

There's no way to call for help. Even if you could, there's no particular urgency here compared to the umpteen emergency service calls most likely happening across the region. There must be many folks and animals stranded by floodwaters.

Whatever happened here, you need to preserve the scene and begin collecting evidence.

First, you turn off the radiator on the library wall. When Hudson started the generator at first light, the hydronic system began reheating the house. Heat, more than anything, will make Shao T. Mann's body decompose.

Next, you will need your Pelican forensic kit. You'd packed it with investigation paraphernalia, ready to show the contents to festival goers this weekend. Looks like it will be getting a workout instead.

You walk quietly to your room, grab your forensic kit and return to the library door. You can hear Bruce complaining about something or other, so are reassured the four other guests are still in the kitchen where it's warm.

Quickly, with years of practice, you glove up, photograph as much as you can with your phone, dust for prints and examine the body.

You pause as the irony of the situation hits you.

You were determined to avoid making the newspaper headlines this year, but now you're trapped in a 200-year-old country manor house with a body in the library, a bizarre death scene and – if Shao's demise was unnatural – four suspects in a homicide.

Why do these things keep happening to you?

Your tasks of recording the scene complete, you close the library door behind you. You turn the large, old-fashioned key in the lock and slip it into your pocket, then feel your heart rate rise.

You find the others in the kitchen and the adjoining sitting room. The crackle of the fire in the sitting room's grate, and a low, murmured conversation between Paige and Hudson, are the only sounds.

As tactfully as possible, you tell all four of them that Shao T. Mann has died.

You offer your condolences to Jasmine, at the same time as observing everyone's reactions to your news.

Shao's widow is strangely quiet, merely nodding when you tell her of her husband's demise. She doesn't cry or scream or beg for you to be wrong. Perhaps she's feeling too ill to comprehend what you're saying.

You see the colour drain from Paige's face as her eyes dart to Hudson, who looks stricken.

Bruce grunts, then attempts to swig from his empty flask.

None of them speak. If the peculiar scene in the library hadn't stirred your suspicion that one or more of the other houseguests had a hand in Shao's death, their behaviour right now does.

You stress that no one should enter the library at this stage, not even Jasmine. You then ask for their cooperation to establish what has happened.

Paige swallows hard, seeming to push away a tear, then offers to make another round of coffee.

Jasmine stumbles from the kitchen to the sitting room and slumps on a velvet sofa. She stares into the fire, mute.

Bruce goes in search of a whisky bottle, promising to return.

And Hudson sits on a chair at the kitchen table, biting his lower lip.

Then you feel it, that tingle of anticipation – the beginning of a new investigation.

Did Shao die of natural causes or because of foul play?

And who of his four companions had reason to harm him?

How did he end up in the middle of a library floor surrounded by books, a broken chair, and a ball and chain? And what about all the items on the desk? Could a malfunctioning typewriter, an eerily green vintage tome, a small plastic bag containing a single gummy bear, a mutilated brand-new book, an expensive-looking pen or those dead ants have played a part?

You're the only one here qualified to piece together what happened.

By observing the scene, interviewing your four potential suspects, and carefully examining the clues, you can solve the puzzle of Shao T. Mann's death.

Who will you question first?

Shao's wife Jasmine Quill?

His editor Paige Hybrough?

His old rival Bruce Tossington-Smythe?

Or the new kid on the block, Hudson van Daemon?

Where to next?

Choose from option 1, 2, 3 or 4.

1. Read on to Chapter 2, *Third Time's the Charm* by Livia Day, to question Jasmine.
2. Skip to Chapter 3, *Skeleton in the Closet* by Natalie Conyer, to question Paige.
3. Skip to Chapter 4, *The Nice Guy* by David Owen, to question Bruce.
4. Skip to Chapter 5, *An Impatient Youth* by Elaine Kelso, to question Hudson.

CHAPTER TWO

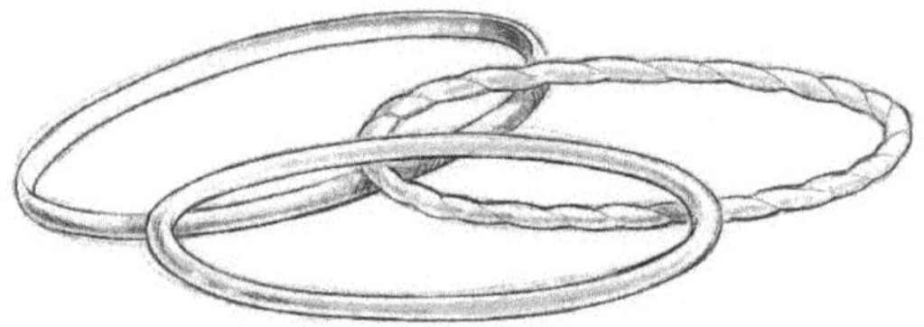

Third Time's the Charm

Livia Day

In which you question Shao T. Mann's wife, Jasmine Quill, regarding her relationship with her husband.

JASMINE, THE NEW WIDOW, APPEARS TO BE NOWHERE IN THE HOUSE. YOU GO from room to room, searching for her. Her belongings are strewn across the 'Hartz' suite she shared with Shao. If she has tried to run, she's done it without any kind of preparation.

You have the death of an internationally famous writer to explain, and that means talking to everyone – but there's a reason you usually start with the spouse. When it comes to a suspicious death, you can't afford to overlook the obvious.

It makes it a little too easy on you when they run. It almost always means they're guilty of something. Then again, you've been in this crime-solving game too long to look a gift horse in the mouth.

As it turns out, she hasn't run anywhere. Or at least, she hasn't gone far. You find her on the sandstone verandah outside her bedroom, staring at the sodden gardens, her hand curled around the stem of an enormous wine glass full of water.

Black doesn't suit her, though she's piled on enough gold jewellery to brighten the long dress she's now wearing, in her role as widow to the murdered writer. It doesn't look like the kind of dress that's useful for dinner parties – there's something overly dramatic about it, like she knew when she packed it she'd need a dress for weeping.

Right now, though, Jasmine is dry-eyed, standing slightly hunched on the verandah with a stack of books balanced on the wrought iron railing in front of her: paperbacks of various titles by Shao T. Mann. Much read, much loved copies, by the looks of it. Faded and battered around the edges, some of the spines a little creased.

She clears her throat. 'I always take a walk at this time of day,' she says as you step onto the verandah. 'My constitutional, Mumma called it.'

She couldn't go for a stroll today, you think, even if it wasn't raining. You wonder why she's standing on what must be a sore foot.

She doesn't look in your direction, as if she doesn't give a damn who has joined her. 'Do you know the boardwalk down by the riverside? It goes for kilometres, spectacular views. One of the best reasons to stay around here. Whenever we get hotel details for a festival that's the first thing I ask: is there anywhere decent to walk?'

As you draw closer you can smell her, the moisture-heavy air enhancing all scents. A hint of mint from cleaning her teeth, old hairspray, and a tinge of bile; you assume that is her breath from being ill. 'A chance to escape a house full of writers?'

She responds with a short, rough humpf. 'You'd best believe it. I suppose the boardwalk's underwater right now.'

'That's floods for you.'

'Look at that.' She points to a spiky grey-green silver banksia tree, still dripping from the recent downpour. It's covered in the usual bright yellow cone-shaped flowers, but there are also splashes of pink against the green.

As you look closer you realise they are pink galahs, dozens of them, all gathered in the same tree to drink from the wet leaves.

'You'd never see a sight like that back home,' says Jasmine with a sigh. 'Pink birds. They're kind of goofy, but they'll probably try to kill you like everything else in this godforsaken country.'

As you move closer to the verandah railing, you notice something odd down on the grass – a whole lot of scattered, soaked-wet pages. What has she been doing?

'Do you know what you'll do now?' you ask. 'Do you have anyone to be with here, or will you return to the US?'

Jasmine looks at you like you're crazy. 'Go home? To the loving arms of my family? No, Sugar, I don't need the aggravation. My life is here. My life is this.' She waves her wine glass around, letting a little water splash out. 'Writers festivals. Books.'

'You're not a writer.'

She gives you a filthy look, as if you insulted her. 'I'm a reader. You think that's not more important? Without readers, none of these scribblers would make a buck, that's for sure.' She winces for a moment, her body tensing. After a moment she relaxes, then thrusts her wine glass toward you, her hand trembling slightly.

'Shao didn't drag you to these festivals. You genuinely enjoy them?'

She gives you a wan smile. 'Nothing I like better than hearing folk talk about books.'

'Especially Shao's books?'

'I'm his biggest fan.' It sounds like something she's said before, but it means something different now. Her smile fades. 'Was his biggest fan. They should put me on those panels. Sometimes they ask me, y'know, but it's always something stupid like "What's it like living with a writer?" I could talk for hours about plots and twists and characters. But no one ever asks me that stuff.'

She picks a book off the top of the pile next to her, looking thoughtful. It's *High Road*, the first Carl Kuphem mystery. Not your favourite, *Hell or High Water*, but you've seen it for years in the bestseller lists, in bookshops. Reprinted and reprinted and reprinted forever.

'This is a first edition,' Jasmine says. 'Signed *To Jasmine, my greatest fan*. Ha!' She leans over the verandah and throws the book onto the wet grass.

Dozens of galahs erupt from the banksia tree, taking to higher perches in the trees near the river, scattering away from the lady throwing books in their general direction.

'Oh, you'll get a kick out of this one,' says Jasmine, reaching for the next book. *High Wire*, by Shao T. Mann. '*For Jasmine, who loves my books more than I do*. What a joke.' She throws that one over the side, too.

The galahs eye her suspiciously from their safe distance.

'You're angry,' you say. It might seem obvious, but finding out what happened in a murder case isn't always about asking the right questions. It's also encouraging people to vent their frustrations, their secrets. If you give them the right kind of space, sometimes you don't need to ask questions at all.

Jasmine clutches her stomach. You drag a heavy metal chair closer for her.

'I'm fine,' she mutters.

You're still holding the wine glass, so put it on a nearby wrought iron table. 'It's normal to be angry at a loved one when they die unexpectedly.'

'Oh yeah?' Jasmine's lipstick is smeared, her streaked mascara lending her a slightly tragic air. 'It's also normal to be angry when you find out your whole life's a lie.'

That sounds ominous. 'What do you mean?'

'Come on. An ex-detective like you, surely you know already?'

It's always a gift to an investigator when a potential suspect thinks you know more than you do.

'My husband was a goddamn fraud,' she says.

This is interesting stuff. Plenty of writers are accused of fraud, but rarely by their own wives. 'What kind of fraud?' you ask.

She gives you a slow, sad smile. 'You know how we met? It was one of these damned festivals. I was travelling around America with a friend, seeing the sights. Checking out the birthplaces of our favourite authors, or spots that inspired our favourite books. When I saw Shao T. Mann was signing in Boston, I was ecstatic. He was the author who made me fall in love with crime fiction. And then when I saw him at that table – well.'

'You liked the look of him?'

'He looked exactly how he'd always described Carl Kuphem,' she says, pinching the bridge of her nose. 'My favourite detective had come to life, right there in that bookshop. I gave him my number when he signed my book, and the rest is history.'

A bitter laugh escapes her lips, not what you'd expect from a recently widowed woman reflecting on how she met her husband.

They'd married quickly. You know that much already. A whirlwind overseas romance; he had previously divorced twice, she had been widowed twice. It occurs to you to wonder how her first two husbands died. Two's a coincidence, three's a pattern…

She seems more comfortable talking about Shao's detective than Shao himself. 'For you, he was Carl Kuphem come to life?'

'I thought so at first. Much was familiar, all his quirks. Like I knew him already. I adored Carl, adored having a version of him in my life. After a while I figured out Carl was his better self, though. More romantic, more…virtuous. I suppose it makes sense,' she adds. 'Now I know he never wrote the books at all.'

It's astonishing to you that Shao didn't pen the Kuphem series – it's amazing what famous authors can get away with. 'What do you mean he didn't write the books?' you say, needing her to keep talking.

'Carl wasn't his inner hero. He was my husband seen through rose-coloured glasses.'

How fresh was this news for her? 'Jasmine, when did you learn that Shao wasn't the author?'

Her face closes over. 'Why does that matter? You gonna arrest me for being duped?'

'Bruce said you were yelling at Shao last night. Is this what you were arguing about?'

She pouts. 'He never used to talk to me about his books while he was writing them. I always got mad about it – no one loves his characters more than me. Why not listen to my ideas? Have a freaking conversation, you know?'

'He didn't ask your opinion?'

'He never seemed interested in what I thought.' Another book from her pile spins out over the railing. 'You know how many writers would kill to have a wife who even reads their books?'

'But you did. Read them, I mean.'

'Of course. If I could've swapped my actual husband for Carl Kuphem, I'd have done it in a heartbeat. I finally got to read his latest, *High Time*, yesterday, and…'

'And?'

'I couldn't believe he was going to betray his readers like that.'

'The book wasn't any good?'

'Oh, the book was fine. Except he did the one thing that no reader could ever forgive an author for.'

'Cliffhanger ending?'

'Worse,' Jasmine says grimly. 'He killed off his detective.'

Her words hang between the two of you for a moment. As an avid reader yourself, you understand the wall of anger from fans that Shao would face once *High Time* was released this weekend.

Would Jasmine, Shao's greatest fan, harm her husband over this? 'You argued with him about killing off Carl Kuphem?'

'It wasn't even a good death,' she says. 'It was a whole lot of nothing. And it would have ruined his career. So yeah, I went to give him a piece of my mind. And guess what? It was the first he'd heard of it.'

Ah, and we return to the fraud. 'He hadn't written the book?'

'He hadn't even read it.'

That is an extraordinary thing. Writers who don't write their own books – that must happen every day. But surely most of them at least ran their eye over the manuscript, so they knew what questions to expect when it was released?

Before you can interrogate Jasmine further about her fight with Shao, you hear a knock on the glass door, and Paige pops her head through from the bedroom. 'Hello, Jasmine,' she says in a voice that's surely meant to be sweet, though she's strained around the eyes. 'How are you doing? You seemed quite unwell at breakfast?'

Jasmine whips around, glaring at the other woman. 'You! What do you want?'

'I just–' Paige starts, but before she can speak, Jasmine limps toward her then veers and goes straight past her and inside. You hear two doors slam then the sound of someone being noisily sick. There goes the last of that coral lipstick.

Paige disappears from view. You wait.

'Oh,' Jasmine remarks when she hobbles back to the verandah a few minutes later, her face washed and makeup reapplied in what could only be described as a feat of optimism. 'You're still here.'

'Me and my questions.'

'You should be asking them of Paige, not me,' she snaps. 'What kind of person spends decades running around after a man, writing his books for him, taking no credit? She must be mad.'

'How do you know Paige wrote the Kuphem series? Did Shao tell you that?'

'Well, sure,' says Jasmine. She peers at the last few paperbacks resting on the verandah railing but doesn't bother to throw them over. She nudges them, watching them tumble to the wet grass below. 'Eventually.'

'What was he doing when you went to the library? And what time was that?'

She gives you a strange look you can't interpret. 'About nine, and the usual. Sitting at the desk, under the shelf with that ball and chain we all looked at yesterday, messing around on his stupid typewriter. I swear he spent more time fixing it than typing anything.' She stops. 'Well, of course. He never typed a darned thing. Anyway, I'd throw that machine off the verandah if I could. He took it to every festival. The number of times I banged my foot on it in the night because it was shoved into the corner of some hotel room.'

'And you asked him why he had killed off Kuphem?'

'He didn't understand what I was talking about.' She shrugs. 'Once he did, though, he was distracted. Didn't really care what I thought or how I felt about it. I guess he never did.'

'And how did that make you feel?'

Jasmine attempts to charm you with a coy smile, though given her current appearance and general smell, it has the opposite effect. 'I was shocked, of course, to realise that not only was my favourite character going to die, but the man I married had lied to me every day about who he was. And this woman he employed was really the creator of Kuphem.'

'Did that make you angry?'

Her face is carefully neutral. 'Wouldn't anyone be?'

You suspect there is a seething, roiling cauldron of rage beneath her calm exterior. 'How did you leave things with Shao?'

She looks at you, as if surprised you asked the question. 'I walked out, passing Hudson on the way.' She's speaking more deliberately now, as if she has remembered that you're a trained detective. 'I was going to find Paige, give her a piece of my mind. I wanted to see the look on her face when she found out I knew her dirty little secret.' She looks at you. 'How did I not know? She was always there, every day, conspiring with him to keep me in the dark, her and her stupid red pen.'

'And did you confront her?'

'I couldn't find her, and then spent the rest of the night throwing up, as you know.'

It's not exactly an alibi, but if she's faking being ill she's committed to it hard. Her eyes look bloodshot beneath the new layer of mascara. 'Did you see Shao again last night after that?'

'No.'

Every part of her body language screams that she did; you would bet your retirement pension on it. 'What was Shao's state of mind when you spoke to him?'

'He gave as good as he got, if that's what you mean,' she says. 'But after a while he became quiet. That's when I left, since he wasn't even bothering to speak to me anymore.'

She sighs, collapsing back into the chair, looking twenty years older than she did when you first met her yesterday. The past twenty-four hours have not been kind to Jasmine Quill.

'I suppose you'll inherit Shao's estate?' you ask her.

She scoffs. 'Oh honey, what estate? The books, sure, if he was smart enough to get Paige to sign her rights away. But the house is mine. Most of our assets are in my name.'

'Surely there's money in being a successful author?' You had assumed, like others might, that Shao and Jasmine lived on his money, not hers. She didn't seem to have any occupation other than following him around to book festivals.

'Oh, the money came in. But it always ran right back out again. He never could manage it, or hang on to it. Come to think of it, he must have been paying Paige off all these years. Makes sense there was less money than there should have been.' She shrugs, as if she hasn't already considered it.

'Do you know what you'll do now?' you ask.

She turns sharp eyes on you. 'You asked me that before. Like, have I planned out what my life's gonna look like now my husband's dead? No, I have not. But I tell you what; people are going to be interested in what happened here. And I bet I could find someone in the media to interview me about the true story behind Shao T. Mann and his books.'

'It's not a good idea to go public before the police have closed any investigation,' you warn her. 'It could affect any trial if someone is accused of harming your husband.'

'Hmm,' Jasmine muses. 'Wouldn't want that.' She sits forward and looks at you. 'If anyone should be suspected of harming my husband last night, it's Miss Paige Perfect. She's obviously lost it, she must have, in order to kill off Carl. You should tell your police friends that.' She sits back in her chair again. 'But Paige isn't the only one who can write a book. I could call my own story *The Real Carl Kuphem*. Then they'd invite me to festivals in my own right. Wouldn't they?'

She seems to slip into a reverie, perhaps fantasising about being on stage at writers festivals in the future. You decide to leave her to it, as you have much to ponder.

In your room, you jot your thoughts in your notepad. There are hints that Jasmine is both furious and insincere. You are sure she was lying about not seeing Shao again last night.

Did she have a reason to kill him? You've handled enough investigations over the years to know that, in cases of possible homicide, the husband or wife of the victim is generally the prime suspect. In cases where there's an obsessive fan, they might be second on the list. In this case, Jasmine is both.

She discovered last night that her husband had tricked her into marrying him under false pretences, that her love for him and the fictional Carl Kuphem was based on a lie, that her fictional hero was dead, and that the ostensible editor Paige was behind it all. The way Jasmine gritted those shiny white teeth of hers, barely restraining her fury when the other woman appeared, well, if Paige had been killed last night you'd mark Jasmine as the prime suspect for that, too.

Hell hath no fury like a woman scorned.

Where to next?

Choose from options 1 or 2.

1. Read on to Chapter 3, *Skeleton in the Closet* by Natalie Conyer, to question Paige.
2. If you need to know more about Jasmine's visit to the library at 9 pm, jump to Chapter 14, *The Jig's Up* by Jack Cainery.

CHAPTER THREE

Skeleton in the Closet

Natalie Conyer

In which you question Shao T. Mann's editor, Paige Hybrough, on her relationship with her deceased employer.

YOU STAND ON THE STRETCH OF WRAPAROUND VERANDAH OUTSIDE YOUR ROOM breathing in the cold, bracing air. You have a view of the bay, of green trees and misty, rolling hills. It's undeniably beautiful but you don't register any of it. You're looking inwards, trying to make sense of what you saw in the library.

Your years in forensics taught you to be ultra-observant, to remember everything. You're famous for it. Yet nothing in that library – that potential crime scene – made sense. Your inner eye focuses on the fountain pen sitting in the middle of the dead ants. You realise you've seen it before.

You open your eyes. Time to interview its owner.

You find Paige Hybrough in the sitting room, deep in conversation with Hudson van Daemon. She doesn't notice you and you pause for a moment, taking her in.

Last night she told you she'd been Shao T. Mann's editor, employed solely by him for the past thirty years. By your calculations she's mid-fifties and she's still an attractive woman.

Light breaks through the clouds outside and streams through the window, catching her silver cap of hair. She's changed out of her silk pyjamas and wears a smart, tailored cream wool jacket over a black polo neck jumper and tailored black pants.

She's one of those women who always looks as if she's on her way to a board meeting, even here in rural Tasmania. It's not just her clothes; it's her upright posture and her air of self-possession.

Right now, she looks anything but composed. Her eyes are red-rimmed. Grief? Or something else?

You walk up to her. 'Paige,' you say, 'I need to ask you about Shao's death.'

'Can't this wait?' Hudson says, angling his body as if to protect her. 'Can't you see she's upset?'

'Until outside communication is restored,' you answer, 'I'm the only person here with a police background. My experience has taught me that the sooner an investigation begins, the more likely it is that the truth will out.'

Hudson exhales deeply then sits down. Paige pats his arm to calm him. There's a connection between them, though you don't yet know what. Your reputation hangs on noticing what other people miss and there's something here, something tugging at your brain…

You try again. 'Paige, I need to ask you some questions.'

She stares out the window, blinking as if the light hurts her eyes. 'Can we go for a walk? I've learnt that, at times like this, fresh air helps.'

'I think it's soggy out there,' you say. 'I'm wearing suitable footwear but you…' You indicate her low-heeled shoes.

'I brought a pair of Wellington boots,' she replies. 'Give me a minute to fetch them.'

You meet her at the front door. You've both put on rain jackets – Paige's is classic black with cream detailing – but the mizzle is so fine you both leave the hoods down.

The path through the garden is lined with dripping purple bushes which release a rich minty smell as your legs brush against them. The Huon River pours past the front of the manor house grounds, considerably broader than yesterday.

You make for a walkway that crosses a nearby inlet, leading to another part of the manor's extensive gardens. It's wet but not submerged. For a while you walk in silence, working out how to approach the interview. 'Forgive me,' you ask, 'but is anything the matter?'

Paige stops dead. 'Anything the matter? You mean apart from the death of the man I…I worked for, the man I…' She stops herself from saying more.

'You seem unwell.'

She sighs. 'I have terrible tension headaches. I've suffered from them since I left home for university. I know if I take ibuprofen as soon as the headache starts, it doesn't last long, but I can't find…'

You remember meeting her yesterday. 'And you had a headache last night?'

'Yes, before dinner.' You've crossed the walkway and are trudging through a stand of trees, moving uphill, away from the ground left waterlogged by the storm. Paige changes the subject. 'Would you mind if we keep going? There's supposed to be a platypus in a pool up here. I've never seen a platypus in person, ever, and I'd love to see one.'

'You're a nature-lover, then?'

'I am.' Paige's eyes light up. 'I particularly love the smaller animals, the timid ones. Last time I came home, I saw an eastern barred bandicoot. Beautiful, just beautiful. But I know they're endangered. It's so sad, the way we're treating our planet.'

It strikes you that you're trying to determine if this nature-loving woman might have acted to end the life of another person, which seems at odds with her behaviour today. Years of policing have taught you to assume nothing, however. 'Paige, did you go to see Shao last night in the library, after dinner?'

She nods. 'When I work on a book… I mean when Shao… In any case, when we work on a book, we meet every night after dinner. Met. Last night I went to the library and we had our usual session.'

Paige Hybrough is a bad liar. She'd make a terrible poker player. Her pace has quickened. She won't look you in the eye. She leads you through squelching mud along a tree-lined lane which ends at a wire fence surrounding a large pool. The overcast sky has turned the water silver-grey. That and the dark reeds which border the pool give the scene an ominous air and, although the water is calm, you have a sense of hidden depths beneath.

Paige comes to a stop by the fence, hands in the pockets of her rain jacket. 'Here,' she says. 'This is the pool. Yesterday, before the storm, I came here and waited, but no luck.'

She's avoiding the question. You press the point. 'Tell me what happened last night in the library.'

'We had dinner together, all of us; but you know that, of course. You were there. I guess we finished coffee at, what? About eight-thirty? I went to my room, made a few notes.'

You glance at her arms, now covered by her jacket. 'On the back of your hand?'

She pulls back her lips in a grimace. 'Bad habit, I know.'

The pen on the desk in the library this morning drifts across your mind. It looked exactly like the one Paige used to make notes during dinner last night. You make a mental note to ask her about it later, when she is used to the rhythm of your questions.

'Well, Shao and I arranged to meet at nine-fifteen, and I was a minute or two late. I saw him going into the library as I left my room, but when I got there he was talking to Hudson.'

'Who was going into the library? Shao or Hudson?'

'Shao.'

'Did you hear what they were talking about?'

Paige's eyes swivel away and fix on the water. Is she about to lie? 'Not really.' After a beat she continues. 'When Hudson left, I went in, we discussed the latest book. After the meeting with Shao ended I went back to my room, had a shower and an early night.'

Her eyes are back on the water. You know she's hiding something and you need to find out what it is. Meanwhile, above the trees the clouds are darkening. More rain's on the way and you'll have to turn back soon. There's not much time, so you go for a nerve. 'Well then,' you say, 'if that's all you can remember, I'll move on to my next interview. Let's return and I'll have a little chat with Hudson. Given the state in which I found Shao, I wouldn't be surprised–'

Next to you, Paige's body tenses. She turns, eyes wide, hands grabbing for your rain jacket. 'No! Leave him alone.'

Why is she so protective of Hudson? She's facing you now and suddenly you see it, what you missed earlier when Paige and Hudson were together. It's in the set of the eyes, the shape of the nose, the curve of the jaw.

As a forensic investigator you were trained to notice minute variations in features, to look past age and colouring and see the shape of the bone, the nuance of muscle. 'You're related,' you say slowly, as understanding dawns.

Paige gasps, then blushes.

Ah, a deeply held secret. 'You're… Are you his mother?'

Paige's body sinks in on itself. Then she heaves a great breath and, to your surprise, she smiles. 'I need to sit down,' she says.

There's a fallen tree behind you. She sits; you join her. Eventually she says, 'You have no idea what a relief it is to admit it. Or how hard it is to be so proud of someone and not be able to say, *That's my son.*'

'Does Hudson know?'

'No. And he must never know. You can't tell him.'

'Why not? Who is Hudson's father?'

She doesn't answer. Suddenly there's a splashing noise. Paige jumps to her feet, points. 'Look.'

At the edge of the pond, underneath a clump of reeds and twigs, you see a black shape. It's the size of a large cat and at first it could be anything. Then it lifts its head and yes, it's a platypus, hard at work burrowing into the bank, its flipper-like tail guiding and splashing. A few seconds later it dives, vanishes. Ripples spread; the water grows still.

Paige steps up to the fence. 'It's a sign,' she whispers. 'Yesterday, when I waited here, I thought to myself, If I see a platypus it'll be a sign that everything's going to be okay. Childish, I know, but here, in the middle of this…' She looks up at the tall eucalypts, the misty air '…I believed it. I saw nothing, and then it was as though, seeing my plan come to life, but so messily, it felt as though my world was falling apart.'

My world was falling apart? What does she mean? Suddenly, things fall into place. 'It's Shao, isn't it? Shao T. Mann was Hudson's father.'

She lowers her chin. Overhead, the clouds are more ominous.

'Paige, if you don't come clean I'll have no choice but to tell Hudson. Believe me, I'll do it.'

Paige can see you mean what you say. She shoots you a look of pure venom. You're taken aback. For the first time you realise she is capable of malice. How far would she go to keep her secret safe?

'Okay,' she concedes. 'I'll tell you what happened. But this must stay between us. Promise?'

'I can't promise anything. It all depends on what I find out.'

'At least you're honest.' She nods to herself and gives a heavy sigh. 'To understand, you have to know the whole story.'

You're side by side on the tree stump in the drizzling bush. Paige Hybrough straightens her back, begins. 'I grew up here in Tasmania. My father was a miner, my mother a housewife. They loved me very much, but they didn't understand me. To them, girls were meant to be wives or, at most, secretaries. I didn't fit the mould. I was quiet, bookish. When I won a scholarship to go to Sydney University I thought they'd be proud; instead they tried to stop me going. They told me uni was no place for someone like me. They said people like us should know our place.'

'For once I disobeyed my parents. I went to university and oh – it was wonderful. Full of beautiful, confident people who believed the world was waiting for them. Meanwhile I believed what my parents had told me, that I wasn't good enough and that I had no right to even be there. I tried to make myself invisible, cowering in the back row of the lecture theatre, watching other students chat and flirt with each other.

'There was one in particular that caught my eye, a boy. Beautiful and with an air, you know, an attitude, as if he'd be up for anything. He looked dangerous. All the girls were in love with him, and the boys wanted to impress him. Everyone wanted to be near him.'

Paige trembles. 'Shao, of course. I fell hard for him. I thought about him day and night. I was too shy to talk to him, but when I heard him say he was enrolling in Creative Writing 101, I signed up as well and managed to worm my way into the same tutorial. It was the bravest thing I'd done in my whole life.

'There we were – Shao, his friend Bruce Tossington-Smythe, and me. I'd written before, but only for myself. Poetry, a few short stories. Now I had to submit my work and have it read by others. To my amazement, they liked what I wrote. The tutor said I was talented, that I had a future. I didn't believe her, of course. How could that be? Didn't she know I wasn't good enough?

'But it had the desired effect. Shao noticed me. He sought me out. I already knew he intended to be a great writer – he'd told everyone – and now this flash of brilliance wanted to spend time with me. With me.

'We became lovers, of course. We kept it secret because Shao wanted it that way. Made it more exciting, he said. By this time he was editor of the university magazine and that, together with his social life, kept him busy. So when he asked me to do an assignment for him, I agreed. Then there was the next one, and the next… In the end I did most of them. I helped others too, like Bruce, but I did the most for Shao. It was a small price to pay for his love. I dreamed of the day he'd appreciate me, tell the world he loved me as much as I did him. And then I fell pregnant.'

'That must have been a shock.'

'We'd just graduated. Shao was overseas on the obligatory post-university trip when I found out. I didn't tell him about Hudson.'

Her voice breaks; you give her a moment to collect herself. 'I was savvy enough to know that if I told him then I'd never see him again,' she continues, stifling a sob.

'Instead, I went to my mother – my father had passed by then – and she asked family friends, a childless couple here, to take him in.'

Paige stands again, arches her back and returns to the fence, leaning on it with her elbows. You follow. She continues in an almost sing-song voice, the cadence women sometimes use to relate something painful.

'They – the friends – made a deal. They would raise Hudson as their own son, provided I stayed out of the picture. Hudson was never to know he was adopted. They didn't want him torn between two mothers, they said, so that was the condition.' She lifts a shoulder, a gesture of helplessness. 'I accepted. What else could I do?'

'It must have been terribly hard for you.'

Her jaw tightens. 'Don't pity me. I was luckier than some. I saw Hudson grow up – from my car outside the playground, the sidelines of a footy match, the back row at award ceremonies. I sent him presents too, on birthdays and at Christmas. He thought they were from my mother, who he saw at the shops sometimes.'

'You never met in person?'

'Not until yesterday.'

Her words hang between you both. You gather yourself. 'Go on with your story.'

'A year after Hudson was born,' Paige says, 'Shao knocked on my door. He was back. He made a production of having missed me and said he'd written a book, a great one. Would I like to have a look?

'I knew he was asking me to edit it. Part of me realised his pure selfishness, but part of me was still in love with him. I read the book and, make no mistake, it was terrible, awful. I had to rewrite it from scratch.

'You know what happened next. *High Road* was an international success, on the bestseller lists for a year. I wasn't mentioned in the acknowledgements, and I managed to convince myself it didn't matter. Coming from money, Shao never paid attention to percentages or contracts, so I also acted as his manager and ensured I was compensated for my efforts.'

That explains her expensive outfits and belongings.

She shakes her head in wonderment. 'Shao was a marketer's dream – a charming, handsome, devilish golden boy. The trouble for him was his publishers screaming for the next book. So he came to me with the offer that changed my life. I would be his editor. What he meant was I would be his secret ghostwriter.'

'How could anyone stand to be that self-sacrificing?'

She turns to face you, smiling slightly. Inclines her head. 'I loved him,' she says simply. 'He made promises, told me it was just for a while, and that he needed me. If I had qualms, I buried them. I kept hoping he'd love me as I loved him, that I'd tell him about Hudson and we'd live happily ever after. But time went by and nothing changed. Looking back now I can see he was a user plain and simple, someone who stole indiscriminately from others.'

'Stole?'

'Shao pilfers…pilfered…anything he wanted. I don't think he thought of it as stealing. When he was younger, I think his parents paid off anyone who complained and he never learned to understand or respect boundaries.'

'His parents were wealthy?'

She nods. 'His parents were, his wives too. Of course he should have been independently wealthy because of the Kuphem books, but somehow he frittered it all away.'

It sounds to you as though Shao T. Mann's life was built around an attitude of entitlement and connections supported by his charisma.

And that apart from being a hollow figurehead he hadn't contributed anything of significance to the world.

'The longer it went on, the harder it was to leave,' Paige continues. 'We had a life together, I told myself, even if it wasn't entirely what I wanted or deserved.

'After university, Shao moved on to other lovers, girlfriends. None of them were serious, not even his first two wives. That is until he came back from America with Jasmine in tow. He introduced her to me as his third wife and the true love of his life – to me – his lifetime companion and the mother of his child.'

Paige falls silent. When she speaks again, her tone is bitter. 'We might not have met before this weekend, Hudson and I, but he's here because of me. Via his mother I sent him copies of every one of Shao's – of my – books. He adored them. Carl Kuphem became his hero and that's why he decided to become a writer. Ironic, isn't it?'

'Genetic, perhaps?'

She has that look again, that elemental hatred. Like the pond, she's calm on the surface but churning underneath. You consider the decades of anger and resentment built up inside her and wonder if they boiled over last night. You see, again, the books flung around Shao's body.

'What did you do?'

Paige glances at the sky. 'It's starting to drizzle again,' she says. 'We need to go back.'

'Not until you tell me the truth.'

She lifts her chin. 'About eleven months ago when Shao received the invitation to this festival, I saw Hudson was invited too. I knew from reading the publicity for his first novel that he had somehow found out that he was adopted, but that he was happy and held no resentment. It changed everything for me, made me re-examine the last thirty years.'

'And?'

'And I decided to make a change.'

She falls silent again.

'What kind of change?'

'I decided to leave Shao and try to be in Hudson's life, in whatever capacity he'd accept. So I decided to kill him.'

'Him? Him who?'

Paige smiles. She's teasing you. 'Kuphem. Shao was so arrogant he didn't bother to read the books I wrote on his behalf anymore, not until they were published, and sometimes not even then. I killed Carl Kuphem, the hero of all Shao's novels – my novels; the man I created to be everything Shao should have been.'

For all her accomplishments, Paige avoided confrontation to a destructive degree. 'What did you think would happen when he realised what you'd done?'

'If Shao had bothered to read the manuscript before it went to the publisher, even once, things might have been different. But he didn't, and I didn't care anymore. I was maintaining everything as normal, waiting to see how long it would take him to understand what I'd done.'

Surely she expected some retribution from Shao for such a monumental betrayal of their arrangement? 'He was signing copies of the book last night,' you say. 'How much longer could it have been?'

She shrugs. 'Sometime this weekend, I assumed. I'd planned what I'd say, but then…'

'Then?'

'Last night, when I went to meet Shao, and heard him talking to Hudson, he said he'd help him break into the international literary world. For a moment I thought that finally, finally Shao was ready to do something selfless for someone else. I was wrong. In the next breath Shao insisted Hudson should write for him and described ghostwriting without using the word. And when Hudson asked about me, Shao told him not to worry, I was leaving.'

'Just like that?'

'He'd obviously finally read the book and knew what I'd done, and moved on in the blink of an eye.' She sounds defeated. 'How could I have wasted my life on that man?'

'Do you remember exactly what Shao said?' you ask.

'Something about my not being in the picture any longer. I knew from the smugness in his tone that he'd figured out some way to get around me.' Her voice cracked. 'Thirty years of my life, gone. Just gone.'

'Surely that was one of the best outcomes for you, though, that Shao would just let you go?'

'You don't understand! He was going to do it all over again to Hudson. Condemn a gifted young author – his own son, if he'd only known – to living in his shadow. Hudson would have to deny his own essence, subordinate himself to that wicked man.'

A flash of lightning punctuates Paige's use of the word 'wicked'. Even the weather here seems offended by Shao's character, or lack of it.

'What did you do about it?'

'I went in as Hudson left and Shao was putting something down on the desk. I confronted him, told him I'd heard what he said to Hudson and that I was never going to let it happen.'

'And?'

Paige frowns. 'Actually, he didn't say much, which took the wind out of my sails. He said he wasn't feeling well, and asked me to make him a cup of tea so we could talk.'

'And did you? Make him tea, I mean.'

'Yes. I often did when we met like that, and I wanted him to listen to what I had to say. But once I brought him the tea, all he did was drink it in silence, then handed me the cup and turned his back on me.'

'What happened then?'

'I tried to persuade him to leave Hudson alone. I begged him. But,' she has a strange look in her eyes, 'he just sat there, ignoring me. So I grabbed my handbag, took the cup and saucer, and left. I thought I'd be able to talk to Hudson instead, warn him against working for Shao.'

'But that's not necessary now.'

'No.'

'And did you see Shao again last night?'

She tilts her head to one side. 'No, but I heard him and Bruce having a row when I went for a shower shortly afterwards. They were so loud Jasmine had come out of her room and into the corridor. Then we saw Bruce rush out of the library. He was angry, so angry I don't think he noticed us. He stomped into his bedroom and slammed the door, hard. Surely you heard it as well?'

'I was fast asleep,' you say, raising your hood.

'And that was the last thing I ever heard of Shao, him and Bruce arguing.' It's started to shower again, but Paige doesn't seem to notice. Raindrops, perhaps tears, course down her cheeks. Her hands are balled into tight fists, knuckles white.

This woman had devoted her life to a narcissistic man who she'd witnessed trying to trap their secret son into a life as his ghostwriter, casting her aside in the process. That would be enough to tickle most people's murder bone. What of this brilliant, dedicated, quiet woman?

Enquiries are pending…

Where to next?

Choose from options 1 or 2.

1. Read on to Chapter 4, *The Nice Guy* by David Owen, to question Bruce.
2. If you need to know more about Paige's night, skip to Chapter 7, *Bear Attack* by Karen Brooks.

CHAPTER FOUR

The Nice Guy

David Owen

In which you question Shao T. Mann's rival, Bruce Tossington-Smythe, regarding his long-term enmity with the dead writer.

BRUCE IS GUILTY ALL RIGHT. GUILTY OF HAVING SWAPPED HIS ASSIGNED GUEST room – 'kunanyi' by name, a local Aboriginal word for Mount Wellington – with yours, 'Heemskirk', a mountain on the western Tasmanian coast. From what you could see, your originally-intended bedroom had a significantly nicer view.

He could at least have waited until you arrived and asked you politely to swap. Instead, when you were shown to the last available room, you found yourself standing in kunanyi holding a confusing envelope from the festival director that read Welcome to Heemskirk.

Over dinner, Bruce summoned the courtesy to confess that, on arrival, he'd unpacked his belongings in Heemskirk and used the bed for a nap before ripping open the Welcome to kunanyi envelope. He figured you wouldn't mind the swap since the rooms were all the same.

You suspected that he knew what he was doing. Irked, you'd tucked the unopened Heemskirk envelope in a pocket and wondered at the rudeness of some.

You decide now is the time to prod more confessions from Mr Tossington-Smythe.

Desultory light pushes through the deep bay window of the peacock-blue sitting room adjoining the kitchen. You huddle around the fireplace with Bruce, Jasmine, Paige and Hudson in the mix of navy velvet sofas and red Victorian armchairs that fill the space.

After what happened at last year's festival, it's unfortunate that you've found yourself in a contentious situation again. You had delivered a talk on forensic matters to a large audience of attentive crime fiction enthusiasts. You warned against crime-deducing graphology – handwriting analysis – as an overblown pseudoscience, advising authors instead to rely on trained and accredited Forensic Document Examiners for accurate work.

The audience was enjoying it until an older fellow in the front row stood abruptly and began criticising you for slandering a fine profession and shaming all crime fighters.

He wouldn't stop talking, so you had to fight back to maintain your dignity and reputation as a festival guest. He swore. He pushed a horrified organiser aside. He happened to be a renowned forensic officer from Queensland who specialised in graphology and had made a special trip from Townsville to be at the festival. Eventually two big football players from the Huon Valley, partners of passionate mystery readers, convinced him to take a break and enjoy the fresh air of the countryside. But the damage had been done. The media gleefully headlined it the 'Coppers' Clash'.

Perhaps it wouldn't be so bad this time. You might even redeem yourself by explaining the circumstances surrounding Shao T. Mann's death before the authorities can arrive.

You're thinking about the scene in the library: the way the body lay in its flung-out position, the broken chair, the awry ball and chain and the books strewn everywhere. That suggested vigorous final moments and a hard fall. Leaping in agony out of the chair as if electrified? A brain injury from the contusion on his forehead? Did someone inflict the ball and chain upon Shao's head? Or else a typewriter, a box of books, or some other implement? He was insulting enough to rile someone to violence, of that you are certain. Or did he die from some other internal cause, as yet unknown?

'I say,' Tossington-Smythe is at his best, brutally hungover, 'with Mann gone, surely I'm next in line to receive this year's award?'

Paige, Jasmine and Hudson all speak at thc same time: 'Excuse me?' 'I beg your pardon?' 'What?'

Bruce smiles, though you think it fake. 'Indeed. Though, between the four of us shortlisted authors, well, three…'

Everyone in the room makes noises of agreement. There were some scandals even in the writing world too upsetting for discussion this early in the morning.

'…I should be in with a chance,' Bruce continues. 'The latest Kuphem was pretty ordinary.'

'I don't think so,' Paige sighs in long-suffering indignation.

'Of course, you wouldn't,' says Jasmine.

'Don't they tell you ahead of time if you've won?' Hudson says. His ultra-calm tone makes you suspect he already knows the answer and is making a point.

'I imagine they'll award it to my husband posthumously,' says Jasmine. A second later she scowls at Paige.

You decide to get this conversation on a track that is useful to you. 'As you know, I'm concerned there may have been foul play involved in Shao's death. And you, Bruce, in my professional opinion, most definitely have some questions to answer.'

'Get knotted,' he says amicably, flicking the end of his Collingwood footy scarf. 'I know of nothing other than the ribbing and debates of last night, people coming and going, booze spilling everywhere…the usual pre-festival nerves. But come on, you know about all that.'

'No, I don't know at all,' you say, without adding that you were asleep through most of it, knocked out by your habitual sleeping pills. 'I have some questions for you before I return to the library to conduct more tests.'

Jasmine takes a sharp breath, in response to your words or internal discomfort from her illness, you're unsure.

Bruce's heavy jowls move about awkwardly, his eyes rove. You've seen that kind of involuntary physical reaction countless times in your career. It implies unease for sure, but guilt? Roving eyes would never stand up in a court of law, so you disregard it.

'Oh, rack off,' he says, as amicably as before. 'You see, Mr so-called detective, sure you're a retired cop, and yes, we're all playing along because we're stuck here with a dead body. You may reasonably be the one to investigate, but legally that doesn't mean a thing. So when you say you have questions for me to answer, that annoys me greatly.'

Swinging his bulk extravagantly around in his chaise, Bruce points two loaded fingers at Jasmine and says, 'Why'd you do it, darl?'

His foetid whisky breath from last night seems to have flowed into her airspace, making her flinch. Or is it something else? 'You're a pig,' she says, 'a truly abominable pig of a man.'

He guffaws, throwing back his head. 'Oink,' he exclaims mockingly.

Jasmine turns away from Bruce toward you. 'More tests?' Jasmine asks. 'What tests have you already done?'

'Forensically reliable ones.' You pointedly leave it there.

Shao's widow shifts to staring out the sitting room window, seemingly still uncomfortable.

'I saw you with a case when you first arrived,' Hudson says. 'I wondered what could be in it; too small for an overnight bag, too large for a manbag…'

You nod, acknowledging his sharp eye and enquiring mind, and wonder if he is also nervous about what you might find. 'It's called a Pelican forensic kit case, which I've stocked with the latest tests available as well as all the classics.'

You shift your attention back to Bruce. 'Okay, Bruce,' you continue, 'help me put together your part in last night's events. You were with us through dinner, during which you polished off three? four? bottles of wine.'

Bruce favours you with a scowly nod.

'You remained in the dining room finishing a whisky after the others departed.'

'Several,' says Paige.

Did Bruce's demeanour just soften a touch?

'Until…' you prompt him.

'Around nine I heard Harridan Quill over here going at it hammer and tongs with her old man.' Jasmine tsks her disapproval of Bruce's words. 'Then my heart pill alarm went off and I went to my room to take it.'

'When was that?'

'It's set for 9.25 pm every day.'

'And then you…?'

'Went to my room, took the pill, heard a strange thumping.'

'I heard that too,' Hudson says. 'Coming from your room, a bumping and scraping sound.'

'Working yourself up to confront my husband, Bruce?' Jasmine says, clearly trying to retaliate for his harridan remark.

Bruce glares at her. 'Tosh! That sound kept waking me up all night long.'

'Or you were trying to hide whatever you used to hit him,' Jasmine says.

'Probably possums,' says Hudson.

They certainly were around, you thought, remembering them galloping across the roof to wake you just a few hours ago.

'Why would I hit Mann with a possum?' Bruce asks, seeming genuinely bewildered.

'No, I meant–'

Unusually for Tasmania, bright lightning flashes into the room, and thunder booming overhead has everyone ducking. A chorus of nervous titters echo around the room.

'I figured I'd best apologise to Mann for verbally roughing him up at dinner,' Bruce says. 'Went to see the old boy in the library.' He glares at Jasmine. 'Without a weapon, furred or otherwise.'

'At which point you began screaming at him,' Jasmine says.

'That's an exaggeration,' he says.

'No mate, you really let it rip,' Hudson says. 'I knew – well, Planet Earth knew – you guys were the best of rivals, but last night was over the top.'

Paige mutters something unintelligible. She is now sitting erect and motionless in her armchair, statuesque, her expression hard to read.

On you plough. 'You went to see Shao at half nine to apologise for provoking him at dinner. And?'

Bruce squints with the effort of remembering through his alcoholic haze. 'I paused at the library door and cleared my throat. He was at the desk, didn't turn around when I went in, but I knew he'd heard me.'

He pauses.

'And then?'

'And then nothing. He sat there facing the other way, grunting, burping. I thought he was either sozzled or deliberately ignoring me, even though I came bearing a peace offering.'

'What kind of peace offering?'

Bruce brandishes his flask. 'A tipple of my Lark whisky, Para 100 II Rare Cask Release, a mere snip at one thousand dollars a pop, dear boy.'

'And?'

Bruce flashes you an annoyed grin; he must have expected the price of the whisky to prompt a reaction of some kind. 'He continued to ignore me, so I yelled at him for being a self-centred, no-talent git, which also had no effect. Gave up and left.'

'Was that the last time you saw him?'

'I might have gone back again, 'bout ten.'

'How much was still in the flask by then?' Paige says.

Bruce smiles at her, almost shyly. 'Not a lot, I suppose.'

Paige somehow straightens further, sitting even more primly, while Bruce looks disappointed.

'Why did you go back?' Hudson asks in your stead, sitting forward with particular interest in the answer.

'Not that it's any of your business,' Bruce scowls, 'but to apologise for having shouted at him the last time. Okay?'

Again, you saw all the signs that this man was lying. 'And did he accept this apology?' you ask.

'He ignored me, again.'

'And then?'

Bruce yawns. 'And then nothing. I walked out.'

'Staggered out, I imagine,' Jasmine says.

'Here's the problem, Bruce,' you say. 'You were apparently the last one to see Shao alive. You were already upset with him for ignoring you earlier, had half a vineyard on board, and you've been arrested in the past for your violent temper.'

After last year's debacle, you'd asked some friends still on the job to run a check on your fellow panellists for this year's festival. Only Bruce came back with a record, some priors for drunk driving and disorderly conduct.

'What? That's ancient history.'

'Five arrests, the last of which was last year. Hardly old news,' you say.

'Storm in a teacup,' Bruce says, barely chastened. 'You'll note I broke things, not people.'

'Who's to say you weren't so drunk last night that you crossed the line?'

'This is ridiculous,' Bruce says. 'Steady on. Mann drank a bit less than

I did, maybe, but not much. I've had a heart attack or three. He probably had one of those.'

You'd briefly considered that a shock from the typewriter, the same that you'd received this morning, might have caused Shao to have a heart attack, but it was far less of a shock than an electrified fence. Besides…

'Not sure that explains the scene in the library this morning.'

'What scene?'

But you're the one asking the questions. 'Tell me what the library looked like when you arrived last night?'

Bruce shrugs. 'Same as yesterday afternoon. Mann sitting in that bamboo chair pretending to be a king, piles of his books and that bloody typewriter on the desk.'

'And when you left for the second time?'

He shifts in his seat.

'As far as I can tell, Bruce, you were the last person to see Shao last night. So how did he, his books, and a number of other items go from vertical to horizontal? What did you use to cause such carnage?'

Bruce's nostrils flare. You're silently thrilled. Bruce, shiny in the guilt headlights, may say more than he intends, helping you unravel the rat-cunning puzzle in the library.

'It was that bloody typewriter of his,' he says.

Paige gasps. 'You hit him with it?'

He deflates a little. 'No, it gave me a shock. The rest is a bit…hazy…'

Hudson snorts.

'I stepped back, hit something with my hip, saw that Mann was on the ground, pissed as the proverbial, and there was no point talking to him, so I left.'

Jasmine pitches forward, her hand clamped over her mouth. She stands quickly, swaying, says, 'I'm still sick from last night, I must…'

She limps from the room and a moment later you hear the bathroom door in her suite close loudly and the toilet seat bang up.

'So,' Bruce stands, 'arrest me for getting an electric shock, or move on. I need some kind of drink.'

You might not have had that flare-up with the retired Queensland cop at last year's festival if you'd done a bit of homework, found out the type of people likely to attend a crime writers festival, prepared for trouble. This time you'd cased the joint, as it were, like a good former detective and now hopeful crime writer. And you'd made some interesting discoveries, in particular regarding Bruce Tossington-Smythe and his age-old feud with Shao T. Mann.

Even though Bruce had a clear motive – rivalry-fuelled revenge being one of the oldest and most reliable motives in the book – all was not as it seemed. Yes, he was jealous of Shao's success, and possibly jealous of Shao's closeness to Paige. And yes, there were multiple witnesses who heard him screaming his head off at Shao in the library. Even a defence lawyer might have a hard time persuading a jury to dismiss such heated and puzzling interactions.

And you couldn't ever rule out the possibility Bruce became so inebriated that he crossed the line from hitting things to hitting people; after so many years of public slanging matches and personal humiliation, why not? It was the perfect opportunity, too – how often had they slept in the same building? But…

You follow a stumbling Bruce to the kitchen. He's making himself a coffee, his hungover hands trembling.

'What do you want now? Why don't you leave me alone?'

You lean against the stove, watching him dunk a coffee bag. The percolator on the stove must be empty.

'The thing is, Bruce,' you say, 'because of the natural intrigue of your feud with Shao, I did some homework.'

'And?' He tosses the dripping bag in the pedal bin and spoons in a heaped sugar, auto-tremble hand stirring the teaspoon clinkety-clink-clink in the fine china cup.

'I used a spreadsheet. Old habit. To check the dates your novels and the last half dozen Kuphem novels were published. Then the dates of your publicly reported slanging matches. And guess what, Bruce?'

No more stirring. He knows what's coming. He keeps quiet.

'About every four to six weeks before one of your novels came out you found a way to needle him. Either a newspaper article or radio interview or podcast about how crap the last Kuphem was.'

'Coincidence!' he proclaims.

You push yourself languidly off the stove and move around to stand directly in front of him. 'Shao T. Mann was your guaranteed publicity machine. You wind him up, he flies off the handle. Your new book is released with the word controversial in the cover quote and impressive early sales do the rest. Game. Set. Match.'

'Once a cop, always a cop.' He looks at you and you see the acceptance in his rheumy eyes. 'On a bloody spreadsheet. That would be laughable if it wasn't so, so…' He stops, sighs deeply.

'Difficult to contest in a court of law?' you suggest.

He holds the cup in both hands and takes a mighty gulp. Then he says tiredly, 'As Mann was my free publicist I had no reason to get rid of him, so there goes your motive.'

'You agree that you used him?'

He nods. 'And I've got a few more books in me, why would I want to kill my publicity machine?' Bruce grins a little. 'Obviously, I didn't do anything to him.'

You take a punt on what Bruce might actually have been yelling at Shao about last night. 'But he had cottoned on to your malpractice, hadn't he? He'd worked it all out; that you deliberately, maliciously preyed on his name for personal profit. And he was going to reveal it all at the festival, thereby humiliating you and murdering your literary career. So you got in first by murdering him.'

Looking down, Bruce Tossington-Smythe closes his eyes, grimaces. 'Hardly.'

'You were jealous of his literary success.'

He snorts.

'Jealous of his awards.'

He scoffs.

'Jealous of his relationship with Paige Hybrough.'

His façade of self-assurance and superiority slips for a second. You've struck a nerve; he has feelings for Paige. How deep do they run?

'I want to make this an Irish,' Bruce says, holding up his cup of coffee then wandering off in the direction of the dining room liquor cabinet, which he had helped to drink dry the night before.

You let him go and decide to return to your room and add to your notes. You ponder as you wander.

You had also considered that Bruce might have another sound motive to attack Shao – revenge. Thanks to some old connections in the force, you learnt that the particularly scathing reviews of Bruce's latest novel may have had the persuasive and powerful hand of Shao T. Mann behind them.

You weren't surprised at the poor reviews per se, given the novel's clunky title: *Foul Play Underground.* Its daft premise – that a person alone in Hastings Cave died when a large stalactite fell from the cave's roof and just happened to pierce them straight to the heart, then conveniently melted – didn't help the book either. But you were surprised when you read the Carl Kuphem novel published the year before *Foul Play Underground.*

Murder in the High Cathedral was a well-received murder mystery set in and around Mole Creek, northern Tasmania, with key action taking place in Marakoopa Cave and its fabulous Great Cathedral filled with millions of glow-worms. The fact that Shao's novel so obviously riffed off the title of T.S. Eliot's famous 1935 play gave the usual Kuphem best-selling numbers a nudge even higher. And with the Eliot well out of the seventy-year copyright window, there was no chance of being pinged for plagiarism.

You, and probably everyone else, could fairly assume that Bruce wrote *Foul Play Underground* to feed off the success of the earlier-published Kuphem novel, then Shao struck back by arranging a string of crushing reviews to suppress Bruce's sales.

You enter your room still ruminating, free-associating. The unopened guest envelope welcoming you to Heemskirk pops into your mind. You retrieve it from the pocket of last night's outfit. As you slit the envelope open, you consider this scenario: if, at half past nine last night, Shao had told Bruce he wouldn't fight with him publicly anymore – crippling Bruce's notoriety and media presenc – and would instead arrange damning reviews of anything Bruce released – a second blow to Bruce's career – what more motive for murder would a writer need? Bruce also entrapped himself by admitting that he noisily and without explanation returned to the library later in the evening.

Hmm. Bruce was already jealous of Shao's success, awards and relationship with Paige. How did he react when his publicity machine, Shao, turned on him for the Foul Play transgression? Add four bottles of wine and a flask of whisky to the mix and that might have pushed Bruce into a murderous rage when Shao appeared to ignore him for the second time.

You ponder the possibility of Tossington-Smythe as a blackout drunk killer. as you distractedly read the note from the festival director:

Dear Festival Panellist

Welcome to the Huon Valley, and your room, Heemskirk.

We hope you enjoy your stay in this idyllic rural homestead. No traffic jams or partying neighbours here, just gardens, the river and our spectacular wildlife.

As the guest in this particular room, we ask for your indulgence as a special mother living beneath Heemskirk cares for her latest litter – our resident Tasmanian devil has her den right under your feet. You may hear the occasional thump, bump or screech; it's nothing to worry about.

You make your way to the verandah outside, then descend four steps to the gravel driveway lined with Tasmanian flax lily, a low-growing perennial with strappy leaves and violet flowers.

You walk slowly along the grass back towards the room Bruce took, the Heemskirk, eyes down. There's a neat, black, devil-sized hole right through the tangled flax, leading directly under the building. Hudson was right about the possibility of creatures making the noises heard. There's even a lone, fresh, tube-shaped scat at the entrance, as if to conquer any doubts you may have held. As ever, a devil in the detail.

Where to next?

Choose from options 1 or 2.

1. Read on to Chapter 5, *An Impatient Youth* by Elaine Kelso, to question Hudson.
2. If you need to know more about Bruce and the Olivetti typewriter, skip to Chapter 8, *A Certain Type* by Jason Franks.

CHAPTER FIVE

An Impatient Youth

Elaine Kelso

In which you question Hudson van Daemon, up-and-coming Tasmanian crime writer, on his interaction with Shao T. Mann last night.

YOU STAND ON THE VERANDAH OUTSIDE YOUR ROOM AND CONTEMPLATE THE investigation in front of you. None of your four potential suspects was as affected by your announcement of Shao T. Mann's death as you'd normally expect. Given the way the deceased behaved last night you can understand why that might be the case, but some of the remaining guests are also displaying signs of dishonesty. Or, at the very least, of concealing something.

A flash of grey in the garden behind the manor breaks your concentration. After watching the dense row of native trees for a few moments, you realise it is teeming with birds. Forest ravens are swooping at flocks of squabbling blue fairy wrens, as yellow and grey honeyeaters dart among them.

You pull out your notebook and begin jotting down your thoughts on this morning's events. Circling his name, you decide to talk to Hudson.

The young writer appeared to be uncomfortable when you mentioned Shao at breakfast, but last night seemed in awe of the bestselling author – at least until Shao's rudeness dulled his enthusiasm. Could there have been a clash between the two of them after you went to bed? You decide to find out…in a minute.

You gaze across the lawn behind the sandstone mansion, through the fine mist of continuing drizzle, to the Sleeping Beauty mountain range to the north. You take deep breaths, the cold, humid air bracing but full of wonderful scents from the bush.

'I think we're stuck here for a while,' a voice says behind you.

Startled, you turn around.

Hudson moves to stand next to you, rests his forearms on the wrought iron railing, then gazes out to the mountains on the other side of the river. The colour and pattern of his shirt reminds you of a picnic blanket your family used to have when you were a child – the memory gives you the first true smile you've had today.

'I think you're right,' you reply.

'I'm itching to get out of here, though. I need to stretch my legs.'

'A few turns around the garden won't cut it?'

'Nope. I need to be out there,' he says, a sweep of his arm taking in the surrounding hills.

'I'm going to visit the Kermandie marina while I was here,' you say, 'stroll along the boardwalk. I've heard it's a beautiful walk. Don't think I'll get there now.'

Hudson's face lights up. 'Oh, I love the Kermandie. The whole of Port Huon, really. There's a magical quality about it on the right day.'

You nod. 'The outdoors here are fantastic.'

'Outside is the only place I am – I dunno how to describe it – really me, I guess.'

You find it interesting that someone who writes for a living could struggle to find the right words, but you understand.

'I do my best writing out there,' he says, pointing at Sleeping Beauty.

The logistics of this puzzles you. 'You write in the bush? Do you take a laptop?'

Hudson chuckles and taps the side of his head. 'Nah, I do it in here.'

'And you remember what you wrote when you get back home?'

'It's more I mull over the plot and the characters. Walking gives me the space and time to work on how it all fits together.'

That makes more sense.

You turn to look at Hudson more fully. He may be resting his forearms on the balustrade but his shoulders are tense. His hands are clasped together but you can see the fingers of one hand are faintly drumming on the back of his other hand. Despite his patina of calm, he seems to be uncomfortable again.

'This weekend certainly isn't turning out as expected,' you say. 'Have you been to many festivals before?'

Hudson shakes his head. 'You're only invited to these things if you have a new book out,' he looks at you, 'or some kind of expertise to share, so I've only been invited to them for the last year or so.'

'Your first novel did well, didn't it?' You're interested to see how he responds to flattery.

He puffs out his chest, and the drumming stops. 'It won the…'

Your focus wanders as Hudson reels off his awards. His debut work had feature displays in bookshops for months, and he was interviewed on every mainstream media channel.

'So now you're worth inviting?' you ask when he has completed his list.

Grinning for the first time in your conversation, Hudson says, 'You got it.'

'It must've been satisfying to receive so many accolades for your debut novel. I can't even fathom such instant success.'

'I worked really hard on that manuscript,' Hudson says flatly, the smile disappearing. You notice the drumming is back.

'I'm sure you did.'

'Yeah?'

You nod slowly, for emphasis. 'It's impressive that your first book – a really good one in my opinion – was so successful. That's not a common experience for novelists.'

The drumming pauses.

'Sorry, it's just that I've heard that *instant success* comment a lot over the past year. People have no idea how hard I worked to make it happen. I've dreamed of being a novelist since I started reading Carl Kuphem as a kid. I used to get them as birthday presents. So when someone suggests I don't deserve the success, it makes me–'

'Angry?'

'Yeah. Heartbroken, maybe. I wrote my soul into that book.'

'By others, do you mean other authors?'

Hudson turns towards you. 'Yeah, like those two old so-and-sos last night.'

'Shao and Bruce?'

'They couldn't help themselves from trying to draw me into their petty, pathetic rivalry. But they were also attacking me. Bruce, I can kind of understand. He's not the most popular of authors, you know? But Shao?'

Hudson slumps with a sigh and turns to face you, resting his hands on the wood behind him.

'That one hurt, huh?' You could empathise.

'Remember how I said I got Shao's books as presents as a kid?'

'Yes.'

'I wanted to be a writer because of those books. I loved the stories, but also the success of the series and its author. I wanted to be Shao. He made a name for himself with such consistent success. That's what I want…wanted.'

'To be him, to replace him?'

Hudson shakes his head. 'Not replace. But to have him recognise me as his equal, as someone who could sit alongside him on the bestseller lists. With my own work, of course.'

Why wouldn't it be with his own work? 'Of course.'

Hudson looks uncomfortable, as he did earlier at breakfast. 'I spent a long time finding my voice,' he says, 'I couldn't write like Shao even if he wanted me to. I mean, even if I wanted to.'

You decide to prod what is obviously a sore spot. 'Why would he want you to write like him?'

'Like I said, I grew up on his books, and last night I told him that.'

Hudson looks down at his feet, thinking for a long time, his fingers drumming on the railing once more. You watch wrens and honeyeaters dive and play in the bushes as you wait.

'I thought he was who I wanted to be,' he says.

'What changed?'

Hudson's large, sturdy frame stiffens, and he falls silent again.

The air is thick with static and ozone, as if another storm is about to be unleashed. This one isn't bringing rain, though.

'I'll leave you to it then,' you say, intending to look into something else that is troubling you about the scene in the library.

Before you can leave, Hudson lets out a long, slow sigh. 'No, it's…I suppose I should tell someone, especially if things might get messy.'

Is he wrestling with his conscience? 'If you become a suspect in an investigation, you mean?'

You aren't usually so direct, but you're a little tired.

'I wouldn't have put it so bluntly, but yes.'

'What changed?'

'He wants…wanted…me to be him.' Hudson mumbles the sentence.

'Did you say he wanted you to be him?'

Hudson nods.

'Isn't that what you wanted, too?'

'No, you don't understand. Before all the snide comments he and Bruce were flinging around last night, he'd already agreed to talk to me about my career after dinner. And I was, I dunno, in awe of him enough that I still went.'

'That's understandable,' you say.

'Only he was even more of a jerk.' Hudson's voice catches in his throat. 'A lazy, manipulative, hypocritical windbag and I wish I'd never met him.'

You realise Hudson feels deeply hurt.

He takes a few breaths before continuing. 'He was there with that giant stack of books beside him, like he was saying, *Look at me and my success*. I said something like it's great to finally meet you, and he said he knew it was.'

Shao obviously had his spiel for emerging writers down pat. 'Remarkably conceited, isn't it?'

'It got worse,' Hudson says. 'Then he then said that even though I'd shown promise I was not going to make it internationally without his help.'

You're certain you know where this is going, but you want to hear it directly from Hudson. 'Did he mean as a mentor?'

'That might have been worth the grief of putting up with his ego. But no, he wanted me to write his books. He said he'd stick his name on the cover and we'd split the profits.'

'A collaboration?'

Hudson snorts. 'No, not a collab. An unacknowledged ghostwriter. He reminded me he sells a thousand times more books than me, so my paycheques would be huge, but that he was good at public appearances and promotion so I wouldn't have to worry about any of that. I'd do all the work and he'd take all the glory.'

Shao, you suspect, didn't have many songs on his playlist. Stealing from others seemed to be his go-to move. 'That doesn't seem fair, or honest,' you say.

'It could be a good deal, with the right person, but I refuse to have any of my work associated with someone who treats…treated…other people like that.'

Hudson is shaking slightly. From remembered shock at Shao's suggestion or from anger, you can't tell.

A flutter of white catches the corner of your eye and you both turn to see a disturbed curtain in Paige's bedroom. Is she listening?

'That's why your attitude to him changed so significantly?'

'How could it not? He wanted me, *me*, to pretend to be him. His books are great, but…' Hudson looks at you, wide eyed. 'Were they his books? Was this going to be the first time he did this to someone?'

You wonder how much he has pieced together. 'What do you think?'

'I asked him about Paige, figuring that as she edits them she would know if someone else wrote one, but he said she wouldn't be in the picture anymore, and I didn't know if that meant she knew what he was planning to do and objected, or if he was firing her, or…'

Hudson is becoming more agitated.

'What did you tell him?'

'I said there was no way someone who's won as many awards as I have would ever stoop to writing his drivel.'

'You used those words?'

Hudson waves a hand at you. 'I don't know exactly what I said. It was something like that, probably with more swearing.'

You can't help but smile at that. 'I know I would have replied with some choice phrasing.'

Hudson chuckles. 'I bet you heard some doozies in your time as a cop.'

'I've noted a few inventive insults from perps in my notebook.' They'd made their way into your manuscript. 'So you said no. How did Shao reply?'

Hudson shrugs. 'I don't remember. I'd lost it by then so I yelled at him and left.'

'Shao didn't follow?'

'Nah. Well, ah. It's a bit of a blur, I don't remember the exact order of things, but he did go red in the face at first. Said he needed a quick break to take in my response. He went out, came back a minute or so later. I hadn't changed my mind, so there was nothing left to say.' He frowns. 'In fact, I think at the end he even turned his back on me, like he was dismissing me.'

'As if you were his naughty child?' You watch for any reaction to the suggestion.

'I'd like to have seen him try and discipline me.'

You share a laugh at the thought; it was good to lighten the mood. 'Did you see Shao again last night?'

'Eh, kinda,' Hudson replies.

'What does that mean?'

'After I calmed down I went back to see if he would apologise, but apparently he was already fast asleep at the desk. Seems like conflict meant nothing to him. All that yelling would keep me up for hours.'

'Is that really why you went back?'

He looks caught, a man not used to lying who was about to try. 'Well, I…' He leans toward you. 'Look, can I tell you something you can't repeat? I don't know if it still matters, but could you keep it to yourself just in case?'

Your interest is piqued. 'I can keep my mouth shut when I need to.'

Hudson nods. 'Yeah, figured you'd be the best person to share this with. I was going to receive the Devil in the Detail Award this weekend.'

'Congratulations!'

'But I think Bruce and Shao both thought they were going to get it.'

'Do you think that's why they were cruel to you last night?'

'Yeah. If they each thought they were getting the award, they both seem like the type who would crow about it, especially Shao.'

'How do you know you're winning it?'

'The organisers told me.'

'Well, congratulations. Another feather in your cap.'

'That it is. And I may have thrown it in Shao's face if he hadn't been passed out, farting in his sleep.'

Had Hudson really gone back to the library to reconcile with Shao, or had he gone there to retaliate in some way? You'll circle back and ask more detailed questions, put together a timeline of people in and out of the library.

The more you learn about Shao T. Mann, the more of a creep he appears to have been. The arrogance of the man seemingly knew no bounds.

You hear a door open at the far end of the verandah and Paige emerges, rubbing her arms in the chill. 'Hey, you two. Want to come in for a cuppa?'

'That sounds great,' says Hudson.

'Come on then,' says Paige, an oddly proud smile on her face.

'I'll just be a minute,' you say, intending to write more thoughts in your notepad.

'Thanks for listening,' Hudson says.

'See you inside,' Paige adds.

You note their similar gait as they walk away.

You scribble in your notepad then return to staring into the depths of the garden. A pair of the same forest ravens you'd seen earlier settle in nearby treetops, cawing. You wait for them to fly away, then head inside for that cuppa.

Where to next?

Choose from options 1 or 2.

1. Read on to Chapter 6, *The Old Ball and Chain* by Sarah White, to question Jasmine about the convict manacles.
2. If you need to know more about Hudson, skip to Chapter 9, *Green with Envy* by E.K. Cutting.

CHAPTER SIX

The Old Ball and Chain

Sarah White

In which you question Shao T. Mann's wife, Jasmine Quill, regarding the antique convict ball and chain you found on the floor of the library, next to her husband's body.

DESPITE HOW UNWELL SHE IS THIS MORNING, YOU FIND JASMINE IN THE garden. You know she enjoys the outdoors, even if she finds the untamed Tasmanian landscape a little more wild than she anticipated. But, you think, surely she should be resting?

You want to speak to her again. Your first conversation with her did not go as you expected. There was something about her version of events last night that did not sit well with you. And you're curious as to what she knows about the convict ball and chain she mentioned – the one you found beside her husband's dead body.

Jasmine is standing at the edge of the multitiered sandstone fountain, captivated by the water as though the ground around her isn't flooded. She's still dressed from head to toe in black, her bright outfit of the previous evening a distant memory, and has shifted the weight of her body onto her undamaged foot.

She senses your presence. 'I'd like to remind you that I'm entitled to a lawyer,' she says, without turning. Her voice is soft and melodious, the sharper edges from earlier this morning smoothed over.

A rescue boat first might be nice. 'You're entitled to one, of course,' you say, wondering if she is aware of how jarring the American insistence on a lawyer is to the average Australian. Here, it's often perceived as an admission of guilt.

She turns her head away. 'I'd prefer not to talk until then.' Her accent is strong, and the vowels are drawn out long and slow, easily recognisable as someone from southern USA. 'After all, you're not really a detective anymore, right?'

Even if you're not officially investigating the death of Shao T. Mann – that will come later, with members of the local police force – you can't resist the temptation of trying to have a neatly packaged explanation for the crime scene ready and waiting for them. Old habits die hard.

'It's true that you don't have to speak to me again,' you say, ignoring her dig about not being a detective. As if anyone ever stops being a detective. That would be like suggesting a writer stop writing, or a reader stop reading. Unnatural.

'My husband just died,' Jasmine says. She adds a delicate sniff. 'I don't know why you're here bothering me. As I told you before, I'm sure Paige will be able to answer any questions you may have. She seems to have managed everything else about my husband's life. She likely managed his death, too.'

Your impatience gets the better of you. 'Jasmine, your husband is dead, in what appear to be suspicious circumstances.'

She ignores you.

'A murderer may walk among us.' You throw this into the conversation to see how she responds; she stiffens, then seems to force herself to relax. 'Until such time as communications are restored, we have to work as a team.'

'You are being provocative.' She sighs. 'I find it coarse.'

'My apologies,' you say. You chastise yourself for failing to realise that an appearance of civility could be important in a situation like this.

Jasmine brushes your apology aside. 'I suppose you already have your suspicions as to what happened.'

Some rustling in a native rosemary hedge further down the slope captures your attention.

'What was that?' she asks, turning awkwardly to look at where the noise came from.

Probably a snoozing pademelon unhappy about being disturbed by human voices. 'I'm sure it was nothing,' you say, 'and yes, I suspect your husband's death wasn't straightforward.' You do have your suspicions, but there are multiple possibilities as to the mode of his death, and the method.

The ball and chain on the floor beside Shao's body is an obvious possibility. The gash on his head, the way the edges were torn, suggests he was struck by something hard and blunt. That Jasmine asked about it earlier, despite not having seen the scene, is certainly suspicious.

She has turned her back on you and is now looking at the ever-rising water slowly creeping up the banks of the Huon River.

'For example, you mentioned the ball and chain earlier,' you say.

Jasmine delicately clears her throat and turns to face you. She twists a large gold ring on her finger, her face twitching for a second. 'That is true,' she says. 'I've thought back over last night, about the way each of us reacted to the ball and chain when we were passing it around during the tour. I feel I should draw your attention to how interested in it Paige was. You were there, you must remember?'

It was true that you had been there. But according to your recollection Paige was no more interested in the ball and chain than anyone else. 'It's curious that you recall that detail. What made you think of it?'

'Well,' Jasmine sighs. She seems annoyed that you haven't jumped on her suggestion. 'Do you think it was used maliciously?'

Jasmine is implying that Paige used the ball and chain to attack Shao. In your experience, that could mean that Jasmine herself had thought of using it to hurt her husband, possibly in retaliation for the pain he had caused her. 'Anything is possible,' you say.

'And you've taken fingerprints?' she asks, continuing with her own line of questioning.

There is an unexpected persistence in her interrogation. It is, after all, you who is supposed to be interviewing her. 'Should I request a lawyer?' you say, tongue in cheek.

She ignores your attempt at levity.

'Yes,' you say, 'I examined a few items for fingerprints.' And more. You have quite a few tricks up your sleeve, well, in your Pelican case.

'And did you find any?'

'Many.' You remember the interest in fingerprints last night at the dinner table.

'And what did they tell you?' She raises her hand in front of you. She seems particularly interested in the pads of her fingers, though you note a rash covering most of the palm.

'Nothing as yet. But cases are rarely solved by straightforward things like fingerprints. Sometimes you have to dig a little deeper to reveal the truth of what happened at a scene.'

'Nonsense,' she says, closing her eyes and shaking her head.

'Is it?' you say. 'Take for example the ball and chain in the library, and the second set in the museum. Their very presence in the manor suggests that they belonged to convicts who were associated with the property.'

'Y'all told me that this place was built by those wretched souls, so that seems obvious.'

'However, the convicts who wore those punishment devices were not given liberties like working on building sites.'

'I don't understand,' she says.

'The convicts who wore a ball and chain were under much harsher punishment elsewhere, they wouldn't have helped to build this manor. They would have been condemned rapists and murderers, the worst of the worst. The prisoners who built this house would have been convicted of lesser crimes with much shorter sentences and comparatively more freedom.'

'And no ball and chain?' she asks. She turns her face up to the sky, which highlights streaks in her make-up, the colours and shadows reminding you of a modern surrealist painting.

'No. They would have used hammers and chisels to dress the sandstone,' you say, watching her carefully. 'The ball and chain in the museum, and the one in the library, are there because it's expected. It's also misleading.'

'Is it?' she asks. She startles at a scuffling sound, this time on the wet gravel behind you. You both turn to look, but see only a flicker of leaves in the bushes.

'Coming to a convict-built house, wouldn't you expect to see a ball and chain on display?' you ask. 'It makes sense, it fits expectations.'

'I am afraid that you've lost me,' Jasmine says, her southern drawl particularly heavy now. 'I don't see how the ball and chain being in the museum or the library under false pretences has anything to do with it being used as a murder weapon.'

Why is she so insistent that the convict artefact was the cause of her husband's death?

You locate the three other guests – your three other suspects – lingering on the verandah, all spread out, not speaking to one another. It's as though they don't want to be alone, or perhaps, no one wants to be in the house with a dead body.

You pat your pocket, checking again for the key you used to lock the library door. You can't risk an overly eager writer disturbing the scene. You learnt at last year's festival that crime writers make the worst kind of investigators: they know just enough about processes and procedures to think they can solve a mystery. If you didn't take precautions to protect the scene, they might bumble about and ruin the evidence.

Jasmine sits carefully beside you on a painted wrought iron bench at one end of the verandah. It is covered in comfortable cushions matching the colour of the blue velvet ones inside. She glances at the others, none of whom are looking at her. You think they would understand that death isn't contagious.

She is playing with her ring again, removing it from one finger, placing it on another, then back again, before clenching her fingers and shaking out her hand. She lets out a long shuddering breath.

'Are you feeling worse?' you ask, noticing a light sheen across her forehead.

'Last night was dreadful,' she says. 'I don't think I slept a wink.'

'Do you feel better or worse today?'

'Oh, Sugar, my heart has been racing all morning,' she says, placing her hand on her chest. The light catches on a necklace. 'Now my fingers are tingling. It's a strange one, must have been the salmon.'

You consider her symptoms. Nausea. Heart palpitations. Tingling fingers. It could be food poisoning, but it could be something else. There's little you can do to confirm that right now, though.

'I think you'd feel better if we figure out what killed your old man,' Bruce says from two seats over, his voice reverberating between the sandstone floor and corrugated iron roof of the verandah.

Here we go, you think, crime writer come to save the day. You notice Jasmine is holding her breath. Another wave of nausea?

'Pretty sure it'll turn out to be a heart attack,' he says.

You shake your head. 'We won't know for certain until...' you were about to say autopsy, but want to be sensitive, 'he's examined by medical people, but it didn't look like any heart attack I've seen before.'

'Then,' Bruce makes a popping sound and points a finger at you, 'had to be the ball and chain.'

Had he and Jasmine been cooking something up?

'It's like Jasmine said to me earlier,' he continues.

You see her close her eyes at his bluntness. If she had been whispering in his ear, trying to influence him, it hadn't gone quite according to plan.

'It's obvious,' he says. 'Mann was on the ground, wound to his head.' He looks at you for confirmation. 'The only real question is, which one of us was wielding it?'

And they're off; you sigh to yourself. Amateur Sleuths R Us.

'The ball from a ball and chain is not quite a balanced sphere,' Hudson says, scratching his jaw. 'With the heavy chain and manacle, even the lightest of balls would take a ridiculous amount of strength and practice to wield accurately. I'm not sure I could manage it myself.'

That accords with your attempt to hold it yesterday, during the tour.

'You've thought this through,' says Bruce.

'Unless Shao was already on the ground,' Hudson says, 'using the ball and chain as a weapon doesn't make sense. No, if someone wanted to use it, they'd have to position it to fall on the intended victim from above. The weight alone could cause a brain injury that would kill on impact.'

'Whose fingerprints did you find on it?' Paige asks quietly.

You see Jasmine's upper lip curl in a shadow of a sneer.

'All our fingerprints will be on it,' you say, 'as we all handled it yesterday. Mine will most likely be the clearest, as I put it back on the shelf. And I don't have the equipment on me to analyse fingerprints, only to take them.'

That wasn't exactly true, but you didn't want them to know all the tricks you had up your sleeve. 'But, if it fell from the shelf where I put it, it couldn't have hit Shao, it was too far to the left.' In your mind, you picture the library when you visited Shao last night. 'It would have hit the typewriter instead.'

You notice Jasmine clenching her fingers again.

One bench over from Bruce, Paige lifts her head, pinning the other woman with her eyes. 'This situation has all the hallmarks of a story you once told, Jasmine,' she says.

Jasmine has closed her eyes and is drawing shallow breaths.

'What story?' Hudson asks.

'A professor Jasmine knew died from being struck in the head with a rogue cannonball from the Revolutionary War,' she frowns. 'It fell from a display shelf above him.'

'It's uncanny, if that's also what happened to your husband,' Bruce says.

'Particularly after you had a fight,' Paige adds.

You notice Jasmine doesn't deny Paige's accusation. A repetition of a history always piques your interest. A set up? Given how angry she was with Shao, she might have been happy for him to die. But did she take action to make that happen?

Jasmine's shoots a glance of pure hatred at Paige. 'How easy it is for you, the writer, to take your little story and pop it into a convenient narrative to insinuate I murdered my husband. Wasn't it your pen that was on his desk? He wasn't happy with you, did he betray you too? Make a mockery of your life together? Destroy your future together?'

Bruce and Hudson both look lost. Paige doesn't respond. She merely pushes herself up from her bench and leaves the verandah. Both men watch as she goes.

You glance at Jasmine. You make a mental note to ask her privately how she knew Paige's pen was found on the desk, and to find out if any of the others remember seeing it there.

Hudson looks at Bruce and says, 'Interesting you think it was the ball and chain.'

'You think it was something else?' Bruce says.

Hudson smiles an innocent sort of smile. 'Haven't you been in this game longer than I've been alive?'

'What is that supposed to mean?'

'Only that if you really knew crime, had really seen crime scenes, you'd know your idea about the ball and chain was wrong. Unless you were trying to mislead our friend here.' Hudson gives you a barely noticeable wink before he stands, turns, and follows Paige.

This isn't the first death that's occurred here. No. A plaque in the museum says that the sandstone floor was first bloodied in the colonial era – a guest attacked by an enemy masquerading as a friend, just over there, on the other side of the verandah, said to haunt the building still. You look closely, noticing a small, rusty stain on the stone. Over 150 years later and the victim's blood is still there.

You suspect the authorities were more easily contactable in that case, despite the long ride to reach the nearest police constable.

'Oh Lord, what a morning,' Jasmine says. 'I really need to get out of this place.'

'Isn't there some way for us to contact those festival people?' Bruce says. 'Surely they won't simply leave us here with a dead body.'

Jasmine stiffens beside you.

'If the authorities knew there was a body here, things would be quite different,' you say.

'Yes, well, a real detective would have this sewn up by now.' He huffs, before heading back inside.

You pat your pocket once again. The key to the library is still there, though you wouldn't put it past these writers to be able to pick a lock.

'Do you think we'll have telephone reception again soon?' Jasmine asks.

It's like she read your mind. 'I can't say.'

'I really do feel like I should call my lawyer.'

She seems to have relaxed, though. A decision made? Or a cessation of her discomfort?

'I sense that the history of this place is quite dark, don't you agree?' she says, changing the topic.

'Why do you say that?' you ask. You know you should be redirecting the conversation, or chasing down the others and checking what they're up to.

'I feel an undue affinity to places of crime, the kind that involves complex puzzles with lots of clues. The kind where the bad guy is captured and held responsible. Not the kind of crimes that the poor souls who built this house committed. I suspect they were quite desperate.'

What is she talking about? 'Desperation sometimes leads to drastic action,' you say.

'Yes, it does. Sometimes people do things in the heat of the moment but later regret their actions, left alone, so far from home.'

You realise she could be speaking of herself now, not merely a convict transported to the other side of the world. You wonder what it is that she regrets.

A bright blue superb fairy wren appears on the flagged sandstones in front of you. He prances and dances about, calling to his friends.

'Well, look at that pretty bird,' says Jasmine. 'I saw a little family of them in the wattle tree last night.

As Jasmine chatters on, you nod distractedly, staring at the small flock of fairy wrens now flitting through every crevice and piece of furniture on the verandah. You can see how someone might think this place is haunted, built as it was by forced labour and stained with the blood of at least one murder. The thumps and bumps above and below the house at night, the sounds of movement in the garden when no-one was visible, the antique items everywhere, could be interpreted as the ghost of a convict wandering the grounds.

You, however, have your feet planted firmly in reality. You wonder at Jasmine's quick mood changes, her desire for a lawyer, her insistence that someone killed Shao with the ball and chain and a story she'd already told Paige about that same thing happening, and how – how – she knew Paige's pen was on the desk in the library this morning.

Ms Jasmine Quill is not a straightforward spouse, that's for certain.

Where to next?

Choose from 1 or 2.

1. Read on to Chapter 7, *Bear Attack* by Karen Brooks, to learn more about the plastic bag containing a gummy.
2. If you need to know more about Jasmine's night, skip to Chapter 10, *The Last Leg* by Allison Mitchell.

CHAPTER SEVEN

Bear Attack

Karen Brooks

In which you question Shao T. Mann's editor, Paige Hybrough, and discover more about her deceased employer.

YOU STAND ON THE FRONT STAIRS OF THE MANOR AND WATCH THE GREY clouds divide to reveal a small patch of blue. A shaft of morning light strikes you. You're in the spotlight, as if the land and the overflowing river below are an audience and you are a player in a performance on a stage. But who's the hero in this production? More importantly, who's the villain? You mock yourself for such flights of fancy. You've spent a little time with other bookish sorts, and already your imagination is in full flight. It's unsurprising though, considering you suspect someone in this house of foul play.

Your four suspects – the American wife, the underappreciated editor, the young writer, and the rival – all have potential motive and means. It's like an episode of *Death in Paradise*.

You pinch the bridge of your nose as tiredness washes over you. It didn't help that the bloody possums started jumping from the roof onto the verandah outside your room before dawn. They must be the size of baby elephants in the Huon Valley given the noise they made.

You give your body a shake, roll your shoulders. You need to be alert, to think clearly, with all your little grey cells firing like Agatha Christie's detective, Poirot.

Still, the shock of finding a man – who for years had been your literary idol – dead in a collapsed chair only hours ago hasn't quite left you.

The moment telephone connections are restored you'll call the police, hopefully to gift them a watertight explanation of what occurred in the library last night.

Settle down, Inspector Barnaby, settle down.

And to think – you'd put this type of work behind you, believed it over. What were the chances your old life would beckon you again so soon?

You blame the festival. Why oh why did you agree to present here again? They sent the invitation to this year's festival one month after last year's 'Coppers' Clash'. Why were you so eager to attend again given what happened?

Your ego wouldn't let you say no. You wanted to be heard, seen, needed once more. You also wanted to mingle with writers, editors and publishers, talk with them, pick their brains. You wanted a sense of what it was like to be part of their mysterious, selective world.

Still, it's not a complete hardship being here, even with a possible homicide to solve. The place is stunning. From your vantage point on the steps you pan around, taking in the lovely old building behind you with its iron lacework and golden sandstone. Wrought iron benches with plush blue cushions rest at intervals along the wide verandah for guests to sit on and admire the view.

You look across the sodden garden grounds towards the Hartz Mountains, rising slate-blue along the southern horizon, mirroring the Sleeping Beauty range behind you. Nearby, the river rushes to sea. Closer, a haze of lilac and ruby flowers explode from neatly trimmed bushes, while the swollen purple clumps of Tasmanian pepperberry bushes populate the perimeter like intruders.

One thing missing though is butterflies. Had someone used chemicals in this garden, polluting the air and the soil? You frown. You're thinking more about the idea of poison. Shao's wife, Jasmine, had been quite ill after breakfast. Something she ate, or was it guilt making her sick? Or was the culprit something much simpler, some kind of toxin? That's what you need to find out.

You release a long sigh and re-enter the maroon-painted foyer, making your way past portraits, vivid landscapes, vases of flowers atop sideboards and a glass bowl of crisp-looking apples. You pick one up as you pass. A dark hole in the flesh indicates a worm has burrowed its way inside. You quickly replace it, turning it over so the spoiled bit is hidden.

Isn't that what everyone else here is doing too, hiding things? None more so than Shao's editor, Paige Hybrough. While she'd revealed a great deal to you on the walk you took together earlier, you sense there's more. There are grave inconsistencies in her account.

You pass the door to the library, still locked, the room kept cold – best to preserve the crime scene. Not that anyone is currently about; the house is quieter than a morgue.

You stifle a grin at the gallows humour, hard to shed after years on the Force. Between that and the books you immersed yourself in, you were able to function well in your previous role – excel, even. The irony that a potential murder committed at a crime writing festival has you hunting the responsible party isn't lost on you.

You're eager to continue your conversation with Paige. Not only was she the real talent behind Shao's literary success, she'd killed off Shao's hero in the current soon-to-be-released novel. You loved the Carl Kuphem series as much as any fan; you're not sure you can forgive her for that misconduct against the series' readers.

She is also the proud mother of Shao's child, none other than Hudson van Daemon. Paige overheard an outrageous proposal Shao made to him, which would both render her redundant and diminish their clever son. Shao had attempted to kill two birds with one self-serving stone. If that isn't motive for retaliation, you're not sure what is.

Then again, if the list of suspects includes everyone Shao lied to, conned, denigrated, and offended, then you should include yourself as well. And not only because your literary idol was a fraud.

He was also a complete bastard.

This is on your mind as you enter the sitting room. It's empty. You glance at the grandfather clock ticking in the corner, then cross to the window. Gazing across the grass towards the car park you see someone. They are walking up to the manor from the lake that appeared overnight at the bottom of the grounds. You recognise the cream jacket and black-and-cream Wellington boots. Paige.

The wind is strong. As the bushes sway, you see a second figure: the flash of a red shirt. Is it Hudson? Was Paige confessing her past to him? You'll learn soon enough.

You sink into a high-backed chair and face the door. Time to compose yourself, to push what happened last evening when you first met Shao T. Mann out of your mind. But it's hard to forget that after a few minutes in his company you were overcome with the urge to kill him.

After dinner, Shao had adjourned to the library to sign books and fiddle with his typewriter. You'd returned to your room, grabbed your satchel, and headed straight for the library.

'What a wonderful evening,' you'd said under your breath with a broad grin while crossing to the library; you'd been so eager to spend some alone time with Shao, and here was your chance.

He was everything you'd expected: lean, hair greying at the temples, handsome and haughty. He sat at the desk with a high-end Parker pen in his right hand, having just signed a book in blue ink, while the other hand tapped a screwdriver against the Olivetti's keyboard.

You'd imagined this moment for a long time, considered how you would thank Shao for the many hours of pleasant escapism his books had given you. You wanted to tell him how, after processing a brutal crime scene, you'd retreated into his novels to forget the nightmare of fear, anger and violence that occupied your working days and nights. Because of this man's words, you'd been able to imagine a life after retirement and hold onto the hope you might get there one day.

You'd enrolled in writing courses, listened to authors talking of their successes and failures, sought advice, and worked hard at honing your fledgling craft until you had a complete draft of a novel. After the Copper's Clash at last year's festival, you'd briefly hesitated to accept their invitation this year. But when you learned that Shao – the person who'd inspired you to be a writer – was also invited, you agreed. At last you'd be able to thank him in person, tell him what his books meant to you. It had inspired you to dig in and put the finishing touches on your first manuscript.

In the library you'd stopped a short distance behind Shao's antique bamboo chair, cleared your throat, and held out your hand. 'It's a pleasure to meet you, Mr Mann.'

Shao didn't say a word. He didn't even look up from the typewriter.

Uncomfortable now, wondering if the man was hard of hearing, you shifted feet and transferred the satchel to your other arm. The thickness of your unpublished manuscript in the satchel made you self-conscious.

What if he thought you'd brought it to show him? You felt hot. You wished you'd left it in your room.

'Hello,' you said again, louder, withdrawing your hand. 'It's an honour to meet you, Mr Mann. I've long been an admirer–'

'You and every other wannabe,' said Shao with a nonchalant wave of his left hand, now devoid of the screwdriver. He then swivelled in the chair and swept you head to toe, thin lips curled, narrowed eyes dark as raisins. 'I had dinner with you. Are you after something more?'

Taken aback, it was a moment before you could answer. 'I'm…That is to say, I…' You'd never been lost for words before, not like this. You felt a lick of anger mixed with indignation.

'Come on now,' said Shao, snapping his fingers. 'Detective, are you in there?'

'Ex-detective,' you said. Honest to a fault.

'Ex. Of course,' drawled Shao. 'Not just a wannabe, but a has-been. Why the organisers invite people like you to these events is beyond me.'

'People like me?' A dangerous note entered your voice. In the past it had made cocky crims think twice.

'I recognise your type in an instant.' Shao clicked his fingers again. 'I can smell you, too.'

'Smell?'

'You reek of desperation.'

'Is that so?' you said with amusement. You'd never been desperate in your life. 'I'll make sure to change my deodorant.'

Surprised by his hostility and lack of civility, you suppressed your anger and decided to try and change the tone of the encounter. It certainly wasn't turning out anything like you imagined.

You sat in the chair behind you, momentarily losing your balance as you sank into the deep cushions. Your satchel slipped and the old zipper finally broke, typed pages spilling across the floor in a fan, some coming to rest against the polished brogues of Shao.

A familiar but long-forgotten sensation turned your blood to ice then began to burn. You felt your cheeks redden. You were at school standing before the headmaster once again, caught out for a transgression you never intended to commit. But like a character from George Orwell's *1984*, you were penalised for the very thought of it.

You pushed yourself out of the chair and onto your hands and knees on the floor to retrieve the manuscript. Before your fingers touched the nearest page, Shao stood and shoved it towards you with his shoe; the paper caught under his heel, scrunching and bending, your words twisted.

'My, my, what a cliché you are, ex-detective,' your former occupation an offence in his mouth, 'bringing an unpublished manuscript to a festival. No doubt you were hoping to foist it upon a published author, beg for advice, make a connection that might magically open the door to the publishing world and usher you in.'

You inwardly squirmed. His words were close to the mark.

'Let me tell you,' he continued, 'it takes more than you've got.' His hand swept over you and the pages on the floor. 'You're an imposter. A fraud. You don't belong here. But like every other pathetic soul who thinks they can string two words together, you believe you're a writer.'

He leant over, so close you could smell the red wine from dinner on his breath. 'I'll tell you what I told that try-hard Tossington-Smythe, and what I'll tell that upstart, van Daemon. Just because you write, just because you're published, it doesn't make you a writer. That takes qualities few possess. And I can tell just by looking at you that you don't have them.'

His eyes raked you as his foot ground your pages into the carpet, leaving a smeared imprint. 'Here's some advice for nothing: go home, ex-detective. Go and watch re-runs of Inspector Morse and Bosch. Stick to what you know.'

He fell back into his chair and raised a book to his face. The conversation was over. You stared at the cover of one of the books on the desk. His name was larger than the title, mocking you.

You wanted nothing more than to take that book and smack him with it – not once, but over and over. Who the hell did this jerk think he was? How dare he speak to you, to anyone, like that?

And how appalling that he'd casually crush your dreams like that for no good reason. You hadn't shared them with anyone before. To think, you'd lugged well-thumbed copies of his books all this way for him to sign. You'd even intended to buy more at the festival, gifts for your family and friends.

What infuriated you was that you misjudged him so badly. You prided yourself on your ability to read people – to see them for who they were, not the face they presented to the world. And yet here you were like a scammed pensioner having fallen for this man's pretence: his lyrical prose, his clever plots. You had marvelled at how he kept you turning the pages. That this turd of a man was the one to inspire you to try your hand at writing now turned your stomach a little.

No, you reminded yourself. It wasn't him. It was his books that inspired you. Now all you wanted to do was use one as a weapon against him.

Your hands balled into fists. You took a deep breath, released them, and picked up your pages as swiftly as you could, bundling them into your satchel. Whereas once you'd felt satisfaction at having completed your novel, a story based on cases you once worked, you were now plagued by doubt.

But what shocked you most was that, for all the felons you'd captured, interrogated, arrested, and put in gaol, you'd never felt the urge to kill one.

A low growl escaped your throat. Shao didn't even notice. Time to leave before you did something you'd regret.

You stood, bulging satchel hanging off your hip.

'I'm glad I met you, Mr Mann…' you said through gritted teeth.

He waved his hand in dismissal. 'You're not the first to say that.'

You felt a smile building. '…because if you're what it means to be a writer, I'm glad I'll never be one.'

He lowered his hand and sat in silence.

You felt a petty twinge of satisfaction. 'See you on stage tomorrow.'

Paige Hybrough enters the sitting room from the hallway, breaking your reverie. Does knowing she's the true author of the Kuphem novels give you permission to love them again? You think so – unless she proves to be a murderer. What then?

She flashes you a half-smile as you stand out of politeness and gesture to the chair opposite yours. At least she hasn't tried to kill your dreams.

'I'm glad you're here. I've a few more questions I'd like to ask you.'

'I'd have thought after everything we spoke about earlier there'd be nothing left to say.' She smooths her black trousers with elegant hands as she takes her seat.

'I need to clarify a few points. I'd still like to ascertain how Shao died.'

'You want to check that my story hasn't changed, you mean?'

Paige's earlier revelations posed as many new questions as they'd answered. Everything she's told you so far shows she had motive to harm Shao; more than one, in fact. She was a secret lover, mother, and author. She'd even killed off the beloved Carl Kuphem, her cash cow, in order to cut ties with the man.

Is it too great a stretch to think Paige would go a step further? First kill the literary protagonist, then the man who took credit for creating him?

She tilts her head to one side and winces, sucking her teeth a little.

'Headache?'

Paige nods slightly. 'I still haven't found my ibuprofen.'

You had revisited most public areas of the manor this morning. 'I might have seen it somewhere. What does it look like?'

'It's normally in my handbag, but,' She gives a tight smile. 'I know you're asking all these questions in the hope of some big confession, so here's one. I can't stand swallowing pills, so I take medication meant for children, those little orange gummy sweets that look like teddy bears. But I don't know where they are.'

The single gummy bear in a clear plastic bag on the library desk springs to your mind. 'What colour is the packet?'

She grimaces again. 'I don't like people to know I take painkillers, so I empty them into a plastic bag. That way it looks like I'm snacking.'

The plastic bag and single gummy were Paige's. 'What sized bag? Was it pretty full?'

'Yesterday I emptied two packets from the chemist at the airport into a little bag.'

'When did you last take some gummies? That might help you remember where you left them.'

'After I arrived yesterday, before dinner.' She smiles. 'I know you're trying to jog my memory, thank you. I'm sure I put them back in my handbag. I do lose them occasionally though, I'm not quite as fastidious with them as I am with my pen.'

The pen next to the bag and gummy bear on the desk in the library. 'The red Mont Blanc?'

'That's the one. I keep them in adjoining compartments in my handbag.'

You'll circle back to the pen later. For now, that little orange bear is in your sights. 'I think your plastic bag of gummies is in the library, Paige.' You watch her closely to gauge her reaction.

Her eyes widen. 'I didn't think I'd taken them out of my handbag last night, but that's good to…' Then she frowns. 'Oh. I can't get to them, can I? Maybe there's something in the back of a cupboard.'

'Are you sure you left the gummies there?'

She looks at you as in puzzlement. 'You just said I did.'

'I mean is there any chance someone else left them there?'

She shrugs. 'Shao was always rifling through my bag.' She smiles. 'It's so freeing to say that aloud. Shao was always stealing from me, so yes, it's possible he took them without asking. But he wouldn't have liked them, they were sugar free and he had a sweet tooth.'

'Might he have taken them as some kind of strange attempt to deny you painkillers when you might need them?'

She shakes her head. 'He didn't know they had ibuprofen in them.'

'Shao didn't know that?'

'No one did. I don't walk around announcing I take kids' medicine. What adult would?'

Something about the gelatine bears is nagging at the edge of your mind. If they contained ibuprofen, what quantity would someone need to ingest in order to hurt themselves? You lean forward to look into her eyes intently.

'Then why would he take them?'

Paige's hands are still. Faded red letters mark the back of her left one. 'He liked lollies? Or to annoy me?'

Shao had stolen her time, energy, career, a possible life with her son, her headache medication and – it occurs to you now – possibly her prized Mont Blanc pen. If he had spotted the pen while rifling through her bag for sweets, he might have taken it just as casually.

You don't want to disturb the crime scene, but think a second viewing of the library is in order before you question Paige any further. It crosses your mind that you may be enjoying this morning's return to life as a detective – taking fingerprints, noting clues and interviewing everyone in sight – a little too much. Then you remind yourself that it's your duty to assist where you can.

Despite her innocent appearance, you're aware Paige may have contributed to Shao's death – or even murdered him – and is now pretending to be unaware of the scene you met in the library after breakfast. After all, isn't this the woman who created one of the most brilliant literary detectives of the century? This is a woman who has not only kept important secrets for decades, helped build a literary empire and accrued enormous personal wealth; but she's also done it right under everyone's noses. If she wanted to commit murder she would be clever enough to plan to get away with it.

At least you now know what the orange gummy bear is and who brought it into the house. You'll have to attack this puzzle from another angle to determine if the gummies were involved in Shao T. Mann's death.

Where to next?

Choose from options 1 or 2.

1. Read on to Chapter 8, *A Certain Type* by Jason Franks, to find out more about the Olivetti typewriter in the library.
2. If you want to know more about the Mont Blanc pen, jump to Chapter 11, *Poisoned Pen* by Marion Stoneman.

CHAPTER EIGHT

A Certain Type

Jason Franks

In which you question Shao T. Mann's rival, Bruce Tossington-Smythe, regarding the green Olivetti typewriter in the library.

You find Bruce Tossington-Smythe on the verandah, slumped in a wrought iron chair, still attempting to coax one last drip from his empty flask. He's gazing out across the valley at a shallow peak that stands darkly behind a forest of bone-white gum trees. There's still a good six inches of water in the lowest parts of the garden, but the air has lost its staticky taste, so you're pretty sure the most recent storm has passed. Even so, the wind is bitter, and Bruce has rugged up with a heavy jacket and wrapped his black and white scarf around his neck. You'd never have picked Bruce for a supporter of the Magpies. Perhaps the man has some hidden depths. You certainly aim to find out.

He does not turn his head towards you, but you see his eyes skid past as he stifles a yawn. 'Mount Misery,' he says, looking again at the peak in the distance. 'You could only put that in a book if it was a real place.'

'It's a bit on the nose, isn't it?' you reply.

'You could still use it,' Bruce says. 'Make it the title of the book. Mount Misery. A bleak, literary crime novel full of damaged heroes, sympathetic villains and unspeakable cruelty. I wrote a couple like that. Didn't sell well, but I did get on the Miles Franklin shortlist.'

'Was it worth it?'

'It would have been if I'd won,' replies Bruce. 'That was the entire point of the exercise. But it ended in misery. Ha! The misery of writing those books and having Mann gloat when I lost. Or, at least, I thought that was misery.'

It seems that Bruce is warming to you, or at least needs to express his inner windbag, and you decide to let him go for it. You know from experience that if you can get a suspect talking like this they'll answer many of your questions before you can even ask them, alongside questions you wouldn't have thought to ask. All you have to do is nod and prompt him when he pauses.

'Sounds miserable enough to me,' you say.

'Oh, that was nothing,' says Bruce. 'That's the day-to-day of being a writer.' He reflexively attempts to sip from his flask again, and gives a ponderous sigh when he realises that no additional whisky has magically appeared inside it. 'Did you know they made a TV show out of one of my books?'

You shake your head.

'I'm not surprised. Nobody seems to know it was based on my book, my story,' he says. 'One of the streamers bought it. They cast Pecks McGluteus,' Bruce spits out the name of the actor, 'as my Detective Hiram Golgotha.'

You're not familiar with this particular character, but you have a good understanding of how precious writers can be about their pet protagonists. 'Completely wrong for the part?'

'Completely,' says Bruce.' They changed the story, and the title: *Crime of Theft*. No wonder nobody watched it, except the critics, who hated it. And you know the worst thing of all?'

You shake your head again.

'Nobody mentioned me. Nobody said, *The book was better*. Nobody even said, *Adapted from the novel by Bruce Tossington-Smythe...*' He trails off, stares out at the mountain again.

'Sounds like a truly miserable experience,' you say.

Bruce harrumphs. 'I thought so, at the time. But I cashed the cheque all the same, and I'm still here. I have my backlist and I have my career. But without Mann churning out his pulp on that bloody stupid typewriter of his, I'm not sure if it will be the same.'

To the casual observer, it might appear Bruce Tossington-Smythe truly regrets the death of his decades-old rival. But you recall he used his public spats with Shao to fuel his book sales.

It crosses your mind again that the Olivetti electric typewriter in the library is heavy and mobile, and Bruce is a big man. Shao's body does have a gash on the forehead. It is possible that Bruce used the typewriter – a symbol of his jealousy of Shao – to end the life of his rival. Despite his protests of innocence, you know from experience the quicksilver rages of the deeply inebriated, returning to seeming calm mere seconds later.

The nearest door rattles as the wind picks up again. You suppress a shiver. 'Bruce, as Shao was your bitter rival, and the circumstances of his death are suspicious, you must realise you're a person of interest?'

He finally looks up at you. Is that real grief in his eyes? 'So you keep saying. And of course I'll be seen as an aggressor,' he says. 'You know how mystery novels go? The innocent bystander always falls under suspicion to begin with. But I won't be found guilty at the end of this story.'

Bruce has swung to hangover maudlin and appears to be rewriting the events of the past twenty-four hours in his mind to cast himself as some kind of victim.

You clap your arms to your chest. You didn't wear enough layers to be out in this wind. 'You really are sad that he's gone?'

Bruce pulls the flask out again and looks at it forlornly. 'Yes, he was my rival, but I wouldn't be who I am without him.' He puts the flask back in his jacket and leans forward. 'If he hadn't copied my early work at uni, I wouldn't have known I had something worthwhile. When Mann outsold me he drove me to improve, to work harder, to be more ambitious. Without that rivalry I'd be nobody.'

'What did he copy, exactly?'

'When we began writing at university, my ideas were better than his. More dramatic. Better characters. That sort of thing. Then he began topping our class, but with essays and short stories that were essentially mine jazzed up with glamorous locations and beautiful people. It took me a while to get over his betrayal, but as he went on to become a bestseller, I realised I could be one, too.'

It is clear Bruce has no idea about the arrangement between Paige and Shao, even though it began when they were at university together.

He shakes a little and stands up. 'It's cold out here,' he says, 'and I need another drink.'

You follow Bruce back into the rich blue sitting room. The hydronic heating takes the chill off, and the wood fire adds cheer and the delicious aroma of smoke. You warm your freezing hands before the fire and feel pins and needles as the blood starts to circulate through them again.

Bruce goes to the kettle in the adjoining kitchen and makes himself another coffee. He spends a lot of time in Melbourne if the footy scarf is anything to go by, and based on what you know of him you're surprised he'd stoop to a coffee bag so quickly. His hangover must be starting to bite.

Jasmine is sitting at the table in the middle of the room with a tall glass of water. Her face is swollen and red. She keeps looking at her hands and you wonder if it's some kind of nervous tic that you hadn't picked up on earlier.

Bruce takes a seat across from her. 'You look ghastly,' he says over the rim of his coffee mug.

Jasmine scratches her hand. 'I'm not feeling any better yet.'

'There was something decidedly odd about the fruit salad last night,' Bruce replies. 'Those funny little purple things.'

'Purple appleberries,' says Jasmine. 'They're native here. Perfectly edible. It wasn't those; Hudson explained them at great length.'

'He does go on about the native flora, doesn't he?' Bruce says.

'I think it's charming,' Jasmine says. 'He wants to share what he knows. It's certainly more charming than Paige glowering at everyone while you and my husband take pot shots at each other over the whisky.'

Both Jasmine and Bruce go quiet. You decide now's the time to find out more about the Olivetti in the library. 'What were you saying before about Shao's typewriter?'

Bruce sets down his empty coffee and smiles sadly. 'Oh yes, that bloody thing,' he says. 'He used to lug it everywhere with him.' He reaches into his jacket again before remembering his flask is empty and his hand returns to his lap. His fingers curl into a fist. 'I never saw him write a damn thing on it, but somehow he managed to type one award-winning novel after another.'

'It's always broken,' says Jasmine, sounding bitter.

'It gave me a shock when I touched it this morning,' you say.

'So you know I'm telling the truth,' Bruce looks at his left hand, 'about last night when Mann and I were…talking.'

Well, shouting according to everyone else. At least, Bruce was; according to him, Shao ignored him.

'All I did was brush past it. Why did he lug it everywhere, taunting me?' His eyes widen. 'Do you think it was used to kill him?'

Is he acting to cover his actions last night? Or being melodramatic for effect? It's hard to tell with these attention-seeking types.

Jasmine sniffs again. 'Not likely,' she says, sounding husky. 'You'd have to completely rewire it if you wanted it to deliver enough voltage to kill a man.'

Bruce's brow creases. 'Did you read that in one of Mann's books?' I would think it'd need a little earth, or whatever you call it – somewhere for the current to go. A simple fix.'

Jasmine looks offended, as well she might. 'I'm not just a socialite with a trust fund,' she says. 'I'm a socialite with a trust fund and a master's degree in electrical engineering. My idiot husband was always trying to fix that stupid typewriter, but do you think he'd take my advice? I could have fixed it in one afternoon.'

Your brief encounter with Shao last night aligns perfectly with this additional insight into his personality.

'I think he kept it broken, always saying he had to fix it, so he had an excuse to escape meetings with his waste of space of an editor,' Jasmine continues.

'Steady on,' Bruce objects.

You wonder why Jasmine has still not told Bruce about Shao and Paige's sham? Hoax? What was it called when a man took credit for a woman's work? Tuesday?

'I heard her shrieking at him last night. She's the one you should be talking to,' Jasmine says to you.

You had taken your sleeping pills and heard nothing, of course. But you note that Shao's widow is again keen to cast suspicion on the other woman in Shao's life.

'Paige shrieking?' Bruce scoffs. 'I've never heard her shriek, not in thirty years. You, on the other hand…'

Tossington-Smythe really does have a soft spot for Ms Hybrough. You wonder if you can you use that to your advantage somehow.

Jasmine gets to her feet indignantly, but then has to brace herself on the table. 'Excuse me,' she says. She looks distinctly unwell again. She stumbles away through the sitting room door, favouring her hurt foot.

You wonder about her food poisoning. You ate everything she did, including the fruit salad – even the appleberries.

A few seconds later Paige's head pops through the door to the kitchen. 'I'm brewing a fresh pot on the stove. Anyone?'

You're pleased to see her. You want to find out what she knows about Shao's typewriter. You lift your empty mug. 'Yes, please.'

Bruce seems to perk up a little and also hands over his cup.

Paige returns with two steaming mugs, then moves to stand by the fireplace. She picks up the poker and aimlessly stokes the fire. Restless. Distracted.

'Where were we?' you say to Bruce.

'Mann's typewriter.'

'Jasmine and Bruce tell me that it's always broken,' you say.

Paige gives a long-suffering sigh. 'Since the day he bought it.'

'When was that?'

Bruce seems genuinely interested.

'The first Carl Kuphem novel had just won its first award and we were out celebrating,' Paige says. 'There it was, in the window of an op shop three doors down from the pub. He said he wanted it, that it would make him look like a proper writer.'

Bruce murmurs, 'Poser.'

'I thought he was joking, but the next day he went in and bought it.'

'Award-hogging git,' Bruce mumbles.

'Did you say something?' Paige asks sharply. It's obvious that she heard him perfectly well.

Bruce shuffles uncomfortably in his seat. 'No.'

'How did it break?' you ask.

'It came that way,' Paige shrugs. 'Never really worked.'

'Just like Mann,' Bruce says. 'It looked cool and made conversation but all it really did was take up space.'

Bruce can apparently be quite witty at times.

Paige ignores him. 'It went to every signing and every event he attended. It's in every author photo, every social media post.'

'It gets more credit than you do,' Bruce says.

Paige's expression warms briefly; she gives him an almost fond glance.

'And it's mentioned in every article about his bloody awards,' he continues, shaking his head. 'No way he won fairly all those years. He probably bribed the judges, knowing him.'

You watch as Paige's mouth forms a cool 'O'; Bruce clearly has no idea who he is insulting. But he is aware he's put a foot wrong again with the woman he…likes? Is in love with? You can't tell what his feelings toward her are, but they're clearly not reciprocated.

'Come on, Paige,' he says. 'The bestselling status, the awards, he could have bought it all. You know he could. It's no reflection on your editing skills; you could only work with what he gave you.'

It's like watching a man walk into quicksand, then struggle to reach the bottom.

'All the while showing off that bloody typewriter.'

Bruce's tone has taken on an angry edge. His obsession with the apparently effortless success of Shao's books, his jealousy of all that entailed, seems to be focused on the Olivetti. Is there merit to your idea that Bruce may have hit Shao over the head with it?

His countenance changes to sly. 'I've been meaning to ask you, Paige.'

'Hmm?'

'If Mann was only ever seen with that typewriter of his, but it never worked, how were his manuscripts typed up? Did he dictate them to you? Or did he give you handwritten notes?'

Paige is staring into the fire as though the smouldering embers hold the answer. She absent-mindedly twirls the poker in her hand.

'Paige?'

'Sorry, Bruce. What did you ask?'

'How it got on a computer, his amazing, award-winning work.'

You can't help but feel the sting of the sarcasm in Bruce's statement; you're certain Paige does.

'No idea. I didn't live with the man.'

Paige's voice has taken on an edge you recognise in quiet women who have been pushed too far.

Bruce yawns. 'That bloody ruckus under the house last night.'

You were annoyed by Bruce's room swap yesterday, but knowing that his selfishness saved you from an even earlier wakening is some compensation.

'I'm surprised you heard anything, being as drunk as you were,' Hudson says from the doorway. You get the impression that he's been lingering in the hallway for a while.

'Hello, Detective,' says the bare-shinned young writer, oddly hesitant as he crosses to the fireplace next to Paige.

'What can I do for you, Hudson?'

'You were talking about the typewriter.'

Is Hudson about to provide you with a lead? 'Yes?'

Paige hands the poker to Hudson who uses it to prod the embers in the fireplace. She smiles at him with what must be decades of longing. You're surprised the others miss it.

'What's going to happen to it?' Hudson asks. 'When the police get here, I mean?'

'The forensics team will inspect it, and they'll make a call as to whether it's evidence, along with other things in the library. If it's evidence, they'll keep it until after the trial.'

Hudson's eyes narrow. Does the prospect of having the typewriter examined concern him? Bruce wasn't the only person here last night with the strength to wield the typewriter as a weapon.

Speaking of the older man, he's shifting uncomfortably in his seat. 'Didn't we just conclude that the typewriter couldn't have killed Mann? That a shock wouldn't be strong enough to kill him?'

'You mentioned that Shao had a gash on his forehead,' Paige says, a sad note in her voice.

'Oh, yes,' is all the older man says.

'And if the typewriter turns out to not be evidence?' Hudson continues.

You wonder where he's going with this. 'Then it will go to Shao's estate. Presumably that's Jasmine.'

Paige nods.

'I see,' says Hudson, digesting this.

'Why do you ask, Hudson?'

Hudson looks at Paige, and Bruce, then back at you. 'Because I want it,' he says.

That isn't what you expected him to say; this young man is full of surprises. He couldn't suspect that he is Shao's son, could he?

Hudson shrugs, embarrassed. 'Okay, so it turns out the guy's a massive tool. But those books, they're still my favourites, still the reason I became an author. And that typewriter… He always said they were written on that typewriter, in every article and interview.'

You, Paige and even Bruce are too embarrassed to meet one another's eyes.

'I just,' Hudson pauses, 'I've always wanted it, ever since I first read one of his books and saw it there on the dust jacket. Do you think there's any possibility?'

'We'll see.' You aren't sure what to say.

He looks at you directly. 'After all this,' he gestures around him, indicating the stately home, the flood outside, and presumably the events of the last day, 'it'll make a hell of a keepsake.'

'A keepsake or a trophy?' You can't help but test his reaction.

He's quick to pick up on what you're implying. 'Come on.' He looks down, remembers he's still holding the poker, sits it next to the fireplace, then turns towards you with a cheeky look on his face. 'You understand, right?'

'I don't,' says Paige. 'How you could want anything from him is beyond me.' She stalks from the room, but you suspect in deep sadness, not anger.

'Yeah, me neither.' Bruce seems bemused. 'Mann was a complete tosser to you last night.'

'He wasn't the only one,' Hudson murmurs back at him.

Bruce shrugs. 'Fair.'

'I don't understand, Hudson,' you say. 'What are you asking of me?'

'If the cops don't take it as evidence, and it happens to disappear…' He laughs. It's a little forced. If you say no, he'll tell you he was only joking. 'If it were to disappear, would I be in trouble?'

He's asking if you would turn a blind eye to his stealing the typewriter. 'It will, of course, be Jasmine's property. I doubt she'll want to keep it though. Why not ask her? She seems to like you well enough.'

Hudson nods, biting his lower lip. 'Thanks, I will.' He leaves, presumably in search of Jasmine. You don't think she's in any condition to take visitors right now, but that's Hudson's problem.

'Listen, Detective,' Bruce stands, somewhat unsteadily, 'I may not remember everything about last night, but I do remember that bloody typewriter, origin of so many novels they ran out of awards for them. And I remember it shocking me.' Bruce shrugs. 'Now, if you'll excuse me, I'm going to try to find something decent to drink.'

Alone in the sitting room, you stare into the fire and review what you have learned. You can't be sure if the typewriter was used to cause Shao's death, but it seems emblematic of the man in many ways. All about style, of little substance and, if you'll permit yourself a pun, predisposed to occasional bouts of shocking behaviour.

Your attempt to rule out the typewriter as the murder weapon may have come to nothing yet, but the conversation with your four housemates has proffered more leads for you to follow.

You sigh and raise yourself from your comfortable seat.

Where to next?

Choose from options 1 or 2.

1. Read on to Chapter 9, *Green with Envy* by E.K. Cutting, to find out more about the vintage book.
2. If you need to know more about Bruce's night, skip to Chapter 13, *Too Many Books* by Carys King.

CHAPTER NINE

Green with Envy

E.K. Cutting

In which you investigate the antique green book on the desk in the library with the assistance of Hudson van Daemon, up-and-coming Tasmanian crime writer.

THE MORE YOU REVIEW YOUR NOTEBOOK, THE LESS SENSE YOU CAN MAKE OF the information available to you about the death of Shao T. Mann. No matter how you arrange the information you have, it won't settle into a recognisable pattern that explains the manner of his passing from the almost Cluedo-like set of potential weapons surrounding his body, nor the timing.

You are pacing the floor of your bedroom, wearing tracks in the tan and cream oriental rug that covers the room's dark floorboards. It's an old habit you used to employ as a detective when you couldn't move forward in a case.

You move to the bedroom's tall window. Wisps of mist hang over the hills beyond the sandstone manor's garden, and it feels like you could be standing in an ancient stone fort on the banks of a river somewhere deep in medieval Britain.

Staring out the warped panes of glass you see two pairs – no, a flock – of ravens settle in the monkey puzzle tree outside. The ravens seem to be circling the house and garden unable to settle in one spot, similar to your thoughts.

Okay, one foot in front of the other then. Pick a line of investigation and return to asking questions. You open your notebook again.

Your eyes are drawn to a line of three question marks next to your notes about the emerald green vintage book on the library desk. Sitting close to the Olivetti typewriter, you're sure the book belongs to the manor's collection and is probably supposed to be on display somewhere. This prompts further questions: where is it meant to be, who took it to the library, and why did they take it in the first place?

You seem to be getting along best with Paige and Hudson, so decide to go in search of them hoping to find one or the other. A quick knock on their bedrooms doors – 'Ossa' and 'Adamsons' – reveals no-one.

Next you head toward the kitchen and adjoining sitting room. As you pass from the corridor of bedrooms into the foyer of the homestead, you notice the door to the museum is ajar. You step up to it and peer through the ruler-width gap, spotting some naked calves poking out from beneath long cargo shorts. Bingo.

You push the door open further and enter the room. It is cluttered with costumed mannequins, 3D models, examples of agricultural equipment, taxidermied critters, and shelf upon shelf of books, paraphernalia and other items from the colonial era. Hudson stands in front of the section devoted to local buildings and infrastructure.

'I'm fascinated by antiques, aren't you?' he asks without lifting his head from a model of a bridge. You read the display tag: Huonville Bridge, original design, 1876.

'Quite a feat of engineering to build that in remote Tasmania in the 1800s,' you say.

'They certainly built them to last back then.' Hudson taps a picture of the finished bridge. 'But did you know they used lead paint? It leached into the water and poisoned so many people that they had to create a new reservoir for the town.'

You shake your head sadly. 'Humans, hey?'

Hudson turns to face you, crossing his arms. 'You're here to ask me more questions about last night, aren't you?'

You shrug. 'Guilty as charged.'

Hudson walks to a display of stuffed creatures and bends to look a pademelon in the eye. 'Poor thing.'

You follow him. 'I need to ask you about books.'

'Who's to blame if a book falls on your head?' Hudson says.

You're confused. Is Hudson telling you something in code? Something that relates to what occurred in the library last night?

'I don't know?'

'You only have your shelf to blame.'

You groan playfully, but to keep the repartee going offer one of your own. 'Why are writers always cold?'

He grins. 'Why?'

'Because they're surrounded by drafts.'

'Ha!' he says. 'Hang on, are you a writer too?'

After Shao's behaviour in the library last night you don't feel comfortable discussing it, but connecting with Hudson could lead him to reveal more information.

'Tinkering with it. Not yet published.'

'Given your background, and that you're here, I guess it's crime fiction?' he says.

You throw your hands up in a 'you got me' gesture. 'It's trite, but as an ex-detective it's what I know best. And they say write what you know.'

'Well, at the very least the forensics should be accurate.'

'They'd better be or I'll be pilloried by my ex-colleagues.'

'Well, I'll be at the front of the queue at your first book signing,' Hudson says with a smile. You hadn't anticipated such generosity of spirit from him. It makes you feel considerably better about your dishevelled manuscript.

Sauntering past walls of black and white photos as you talk, faces stare out at you, unsmiling. People in heavy layers of wool clothing labour in fields and orchards long since ploughed over. In some photos, the profile of Sleeping Beauty rises in the background. In others, the flat expanse of the Huon River, alive with boats and barges transporting apples around the world, feeding the British Empire.

You stop to peer at the apples in a display of over a hundred local varieties, and a wall-sized collage of colourful, iconic apple box labels behind.

'When Tasmania was world famous as the Apple Isle,' says Hudson.

His gaze shifts to a set of shelves in the nearby corner of the room. A sign declares it contains work from local authors. He points to a book on the end of the top shelf.

'That's mine.'

'I've read both of yours, actually. They're excellent.'

'Thanks! Which is your favourite?'

'Probably the first,' you say. 'It has a great sense of place. I'm looking forward to reading one a year from now on.'

Hudson slumps a little. 'I don't know if you'll be doing that.'

Hang on, what? Did Hudson do something to Shao last night and is thinking he'll be caught? No, no, don't get ahead of yourself here.

'What do you mean?' you ask.

'My first book was a huge success, sure, but it took years to write. Now, there's this expectation that I write another one every year. And it has to be better, and longer.' His voice rises higher and higher as he speaks, as though his throat is constricting.

'But I have to work a part-time job to actually pay the bills, so some weeks there's almost no time to write.' You notice his hands clenching. 'And then there's the crap I take from readers and reviewers and other authors, and I have to smile through it all.'

You're not sure where this is going, but you want him to continue. 'I had no idea it was like that,' you say.

'I've only released two books and already I'm tired of being a writer. It's so much work, takes so much energy. And for what? I don't know how some people do it their whole lives.'

His voice drops to a conspiratorial whisper that carries across the room. As a writer, Hudson would make a terrible spy. 'Not that I would ever do it, but I can actually see the appeal of Shao's offer: write books, get well paid for them, never have to do any publicity. But, argh!' He slams his fists onto a display table, rocking its exhibition of old pressed tins. 'It's ridiculous that I'm even considering giving up. What is wrong with me?'

You realise that beneath his calm naturalist exterior, Hudson is a powder keg of emotion. Did he lose control of himself in the library last night?

'Some days I just want to become a park ranger and leave this publishing stuff behind.'

Early in your career on the force, when you were showing signs you might snap from the pressure, you recall a Sergeant pulling you aside and levelling with you. 'Hudson, I'm going to tell you something a wise person once told me in a rough moment. It's not meant to be discouraging, but it is worth considering.'

He takes a deep breath, puts his hands to his sides, and turns to look you in the eye. 'Okay.'

'You don't have to do it.'

'What?'

'You don't have to be a professional writer. You might have always wanted to write, you might enjoy writing for its own sake, you might be great at it. But if the life of a professional writer makes you miserable, it's okay to walk away.'

'But I fought so hard to get to this point, and there are so many people expecting me to keep going. And I keep winning awards. I am really good at it.'

'And yet, you're not happy,' you say. 'You only get one life, don't spend it doing something that makes you miserable out of a misplaced sense of obligation.'

Hudson gnaws at his bottom lip. 'No one has ever said that to me before.' He looks calmer, a little less anxious. 'I'll think it over. Thank you.'

You continue to peruse the bookshelves, giving Hudson time to collect himself. In the middle of the bottom shelf is another display box with a few pairs of white cotton gloves beside it. This one is labelled "Arsenic coated book, 1850s".

The box is empty.

'Is this what you, Bruce and Shao were looking at yesterday?' you ask.

'Yes.'

You crouch to read the accompanying explanation of the missing book aloud. 'Published mid-nineteenth century, bound and covered with a pigment known as emerald green or Paris green. Contains arsenic.'

Well, that can't be good.

You continue reading. 'Paris green was used on wallpaper, confectionary wrappers, and as rat poison in the Parisian sewer system. When damp and infected with mould it releases arsenic gas, and as a result tragically killed many children and older people.'

Goodness.

'It was also used on books to discourage burrowing insects. Some took it a step further and used it to protect secrets written in private diaries and journals.' You look up at Hudson. 'Did you read this yesterday?'

'No, Shao and Bruce were making crude jokes about,' he blushes, 'well, it doesn't matter. No, I didn't read that yesterday.'

You continue reading aloud. 'Beyond painting its cloth covers with Paris green, the edges of this book's pages were painted with pure arsenic. Turning the pages with bare fingers could lead to micro cuts impregnated with arsenic, or if a person licked their finger to turn the page multiple times, they would ingest arsenic. Arsenic also absorbs through the skin. In the case of this book – a secret diary with a built-in defence mechanism – reading enough of a person's private thoughts could kill you.'

'You'd really have to want someone to suffer to use arsenic. It's a terrible death,' says Hudson.

From your training you know that Hudson is correct. Arsenic poisoning can result in blisters and open wounds, vomiting, diarrhoea, intense pain, tremors and eventually death. It's now imperative that you know how it made its way to the library. 'Hudson, time to level with me: did you put a book on the desk in the library last night?'

'You mean the book missing from this display case?'

'Obviously. What other book…' You meet his eyes and he blushes. At this moment you would take any bet that Hudson van Daemon was responsible for the other unexpected book on the desk, the mutilated copy of *High Time*. You will come back to the mutilated book in time – for now, your focus is on the deadly antique green one. 'As far as I can tell, the book missing from this display case appeared on the desk in the library while you were there.'

'How do you know that?'

'It wasn't there at 8.30 pm when I was in the library. Jasmine didn't see it at 9 pm. You've said it wasn't there at 9.10 pm. But Paige says it was there when she walked in, just after she passed you on the way out. Shao left you alone in there for a minute, you had an opportunity to place the book on the desk.'

'No. I can say honestly I did not put a book, any book, on the desk when I was in the library around ten past nine, including when the old man popped out for a minute.'

The way Hudson speaks tells you he is playing semantics, withholding certain information by using his words both precisely and deceptively. But it's not quite the time to challenge him on that, not yet.

'Okay, if the book wasn't there when you were in the library with Shao, but it was when Paige walked in, only Shao could have put it on the desk.'

'Playing devil's advocate,' Hudson says, 'Paige could have put it on the desk while she was in the room and be lying about it now.'

You nod slowly. 'Yes, that's true, any of you could be lying.'

Hudson looks at you with narrowed eyes. 'Including you. Who's to say you didn't go into the library after all the rest of us had gone to bed, kill the old man yourself, then spend all morning trying to set one of us up to take the fall?'

You smile at him. 'Now you're thinking like a detective.'

He relaxes a little. 'Why do you care so much about when this book appeared in the library?'

'Because if Shao left the library in the middle of an argument with you to steal this book, he had to have a specific reason for doing so; especially since he must have known it was coated in arsenic.'

Hudson's face drains to grey. 'Do you think he was actually that desperate? That he decided to kill himself using the poisonous coating on the book after I said no to helping him? Was that a cry for help?'

You think about the scene in the library – every part of Shao's body, his face, his fingers – and what you've learnt about the man. 'It can't be ruled out at this point, of course, but there's nothing to indicate suicide. I do think this deadly diary might be crucial to unravelling this mystery, though.'

It is time to double back. 'Why did you lie before when I asked if you'd put a book on the desk?'

'Ah.'

'Come on, Hudson, what are you hiding?'

'I told you before that I returned to the library last night.'

'Yes.'

'The green book was on the desk then, for certain. I don't think it was there the first time – I mean I'm pretty sure I would have noticed it – but I was filthy at Shao, distracted, so I couldn't swear in court that it wasn't there the first time.'

'Is that why you're hesitant, worried about having to testify?'

He stares at you blankly, possibly overwhelmed by the events of the day, but you'll take that as a yes.

He snaps out of it and moves over to a stuffed bird in a display case, trying to distract you both from the topic at hand. The bird looks like one your driver nearly hit yesterday when you arrived at the manor. You decide to give him a break from questioning.

'Did you know these little creatures are the fastest runners in the state?' Hudson asks.

You peer at the description. 'Tasmanian native hen?'

'A.k.a. the Tassie turbo chook.'

Outside the museum windows, which sit on the same side of the manor as your bedroom, the ravens are still cawing.

'They're everywhere here, just like the crows.' Hudson grins at you again. 'Hey, what did the passive aggressive raven say to start an argument?'

'I don't know, what?'

'Never mind.'

Where to next?

Choose from options 1 or 2.

1. Read on to Chapter 10, *The Last Leg* by Allison Mitchell, to find out more about the chair.
2. To learn what happened in the library at 9.40 pm last night, jump to Chapter 19, *Dazed and Confused* by Alison Alexander.

CHAPTER TEN

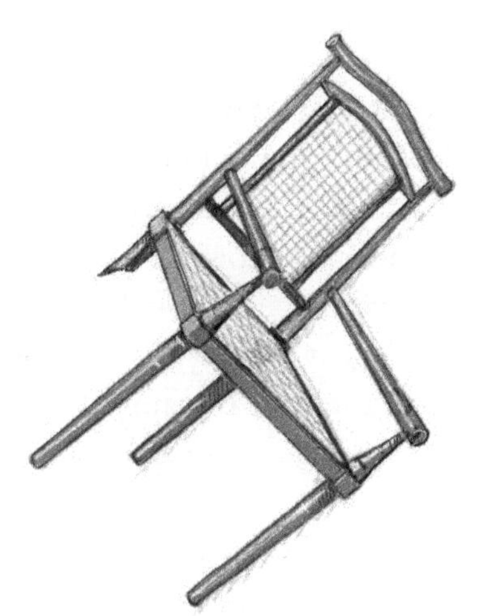

The Last Leg

Allison Mitchell

In which you question Shao T. Mann's wife, Jasmine Quill, regarding the broken leg of the chair you found, on the floor of the library, containing her husband's body.

YOU PUSH THE VELVET NAVY CURTAINS IN THE SITTING ROOM AS WIDE AS THEY will go, but it has little impact on the gloom.

The day started strangely, but well. You enjoyed mucking in with the other early risers to get the fires going and breakfast made. Being cut off from the rest of the world in a fine historic country homestead with an interesting library and a warm fire has its appeal. Unfortunately, that appeal evaporated when you discovered Shao T. Mann's body.

Outside, the mist-shrouded garden is alive with a chorus of frogs. And the pile of Shao's books Jasmine flung from the verandah earlier is almost under water now.

You have been prepared for something like this to happen for a long time. You had wanted to lead an investigation into the murder of a famous Australian in just such a setting. But your intention was that it be fictional – a made-up story for a legion of enthusiastic mystery readers – not discovering the dead-in-suspicious-circumstances body of Shao T. Mann.

Before meeting him in the library last night with your manuscript in tow, you wanted to ask Shao about a plot in one of his early novels where the victim was strangled with the Jolly Roger. The culprit had visited a replica pirate ship in the Caribbean, and the flag's fibres were a perfect match to fibres found on the culprit's tuxedo. The science Shao had described in the book was ahead of its time.

What a shame that after two minutes in the man's company you'd wanted nothing more to do with him. How ironic that he was now the focus of your every thought.

You look at the tray of cake on the low wooden table in front of you, and hope the four remaining houseguests join you in front of the now blazing fire. You particularly want to talk with Jasmine again – not that she is likely to be enticed by cake at the moment. But she does seem to feel a need to be around others, even if she doesn't particularly like anyone else in the mansion.

The widow's limp intrigues you. You're certain she is lying about how she acquired it, and about how many times she visited her husband in the library last night. The image of the broken leg of the bamboo chair keeps floating through your mind.

The three other guests drift into the room.

Hudson heads straight for the cake and cuts himself a huge slice, then takes a seat in a firm-looking chair near the window. Noticing your gaze in the reflection, he gives you an awkward nod.

Paige sits on the sofa nearest Hudson. She stares off into space as if dazed, or perhaps deep in contemplation.

Bruce ignores the food and sits in the lounge chair nearest the now-empty drinks trolley, yawning. He sinks so low in the cushions you wonder if he'll be able to get up again.

'Has anyone seen Jasmine?' you ask.

Bruce tugs at his soiled scarf. 'Probably examining the bestseller lists for husband number four,' he says as she appears in the doorway.

The door frame is low – as in all houses of the convict era – and the impressive nest of Jasmine's hair only just fits through. 'Now, honey, don't waste your breath. You can't provoke my husband any more. I know you two were rivals, but I had no idea you could be so plain nasty.'

Jasmine seems a little recovered from when you last saw her. You watch as she realises that the last seat in the room is next to Paige. She audibly sighs, limps slowly over and lowers herself into the sofa, wincing as she does.

'I could take a look at your ankle if you like,' Hudson says to Jasmine. 'Does it need strapping?'

You notice Paige tuck her head; is she hurt by Hudson's consideration toward Jasmine? She stands and offers to top up mugs with the percolator from the kitchen stove.

'I love the stuff myself,' you say, 'but you seem to drink coffee all day long.'

'It's a writer thing,' he says. 'Our ruddy readers seem to drink tea, but writers run on coffee.'

Hudson nods in agreement. 'Black bean magic juice,' he says. 'It's the alchemy of writers. We turn coffee into books.'

'Make mine a double, my dear,' says Bruce, handing her his mug. She rolls her eyes as she pours.

You again notice the faded red ink on the back of her left hand, almost washed away in last night's shower but still vaguely visible.

'Thank you all for coming. I know this is a difficult subject,' you say, as they all settle in, 'but I need to ask you all about an item in the library.'

Jasmine turns to you. 'Listen,' she says, 'Bruce may have been right about what he said earlier…'

'Miracles,' mutters Hudson sardonically.

'Quiet you,' says Bruce, his jowls wobbling over his scarf reminding you of a whining bloodhound.

Jasmine clears her throat. '…may have been right when he suggested your investigation is unwarranted as my husband probably had a heart attack.' Her voice is low, her South Carolina drawl in full effect. 'He was supposed to see a specialist earlier in the year, but he put it off.' She pulls a hankie from her sleeve to dab dramatically at a dry eye.

You decide to play along. 'Grief is hard to bear in any circumstances, let alone so far from home.'

She dabs her eye again, and her lower lip trembles. Did she take acting lessons at school? If so they weren't very good. You're less and less convinced. You continue: 'My question is simple. It concerns a chair.'

'Pardon?' says Paige.

'The antique chair Shao was sitting in last night, with a woven rattan seat and back and lacquered black bamboo legs.'

'Sure,' says Bruce. 'The chair.'

Hudson shrugs.

'What about it?' Paige asks.

'What condition was it in when each of you last saw it?'

Bruce makes a strange noise into his mug.

'Bruce?'

'Well, ah, it was on the floor, as I told you earlier.'

'Did you knock it over?'

'I don't think so, but perhaps?'

'Hudson, was it upright when you last saw it?'

He nods, his face blushing slightly pink.

'Paige?'

'Yes, but can you explain why you're asking about this?'

'In a moment. Jasmine?'

'That stupid chair was standing on all four of its legs when I was last in that room.'

Gotcha. You'd suspected Jasmine's limp and the broken chair leg were connected. Her emotional response, and the way she spat the word 'stupid', indicated you were right. 'Is that how you hurt your foot? Kicking the chair?'

She freezes for a moment. 'Ahhhh…'

That was a yes.

'And insects,' you follow up.

'What now?'

Once a suspect becomes agitated you like to throw random questions into the mix to keep them off balance. 'The last time you were in the library, did you notice any insects?'

Jasmine shakes her head, which seems genuine enough.

Out of the corner of your eye you notice Hudson fidgeting with his bootlaces.

'Why are you asking about insects?' Paige says. 'I thought you wanted to know about the chair.' She sighs. 'How can this be the way the weekend is turning out? We should be at the festival now, celebrating books.'

'Too right,' says Bruce, as if anxious to buck himself up. 'I have a life and a veritable truckload of fans who must be devastated not to see me.' He looks at his watch. 'Mann and I should have been in front of a room full of them right now, discussing how technology is a disaster for crime writers. There are no secrets anymore, we're all being watched all the time. Except here – we're back in the 1800s, here.'

'I was looking forward to that panel,' says Hudson looking interested for the first time. He is eager to make a point. 'Tech is second nature for me. It's so useful for authors. But you do have to be careful about your search history.'

Bruce raises an eyebrow.

As he continues, you notice something on the carpet by Hudson's feet – it is a round ball of spiky plant matter about the size of a marble. You lean forward, pick it up and roll it between your fingers. Prickles sink into your skin. Ow!

Hudson addresses you. 'Buzzies,' he says. 'I'm surprised there are any in this fancy garden.'

You notice they cover the laces of Hudson's shoes.

'They look like some form of alien life,' says Paige pulling a cushion onto her lap and hugging it, as though it were a small child.

The conversation is completely off track.

'Jasmine,' you say firmly, 'I know this is difficult, but when you were arguing in the library with Shao, why did you get so angry you kicked the chair?'

Her face is pinched, lips sealed.

'What were you and Mann screaming at each other about last night?' Bruce asks.

Jasmine sighs. 'You may as well know.'

Paige, sitting beside her, stiffens.

'I've never hidden the fact I fell for him because I loved Carl Kuphem.'

Bruce and Hudson nod slightly; Jasmine has apparently told this story before.

'Well, yesterday I discovered that Kuphem is going to die in *High Time*.' If looks could kill, the daggers Jasmine stared at Paige would put the ostensible editor six feet under.

'What?' says Bruce, genuinely surprised. 'He killed off Kuphem? That would have made his fans furious.' Bruce chuckles, suddenly more cheerful. He hauls himself forward in his chair with newfound energy, cuts himself a large slice of cake and bites into it. 'Anyone else?'

'I'll have another,' says Hudson. He passes his plate to Bruce.

Jasmine's fingers drum on the arm of the sofa and her lips are pressed together in a thin, hard line.

'How is Kuphem killed off?' asks Bruce, spilling crumbs on the carpet as he attempts to serve cake to Hudson.

'That's what's so offensive,' Jasmine says, continuing to stare at Paige who shrinks into her seat. 'My clever, handsome Kuphem isn't killed doing something courageous, or murdered by his arch-rival – he's killed by his washing machine.'

The character of Carl Kuphem was famous for jury-rigging household appliances to keep them running for years beyond their natural lives. He delighted in holding doors, shelves and even engines together with magnets, plastic ties and gaffer tape. For several books now, his washing machine has had no lid: it was damaged beyond repair when an infamous alpaca baron broke into his house, enraged by something Kuphem did to one of his fine, woollen sweaters.

'His tie gets caught in the darned spin cycle,' Jasmine exclaims. 'His ending is a ridiculous domestic mishap, it doesn't seem right.'

The depth of offense she takes at such an ignoble ending for her fictional hero is palpable. You believe she was in love with Kuphem at least as much as she was in love with Shao, strange as that sounds. But was it a love she would kill for?

'Why would Mann kill off his main character like that?' says Bruce to himself.

'Killing off his series,' Hudson interjects, 'would be like retiring. Why would anyone who'd written a series that successful want to stop writing?'

'Seems like the act of an unstable person,' Jasmine says glancing at Paige, her voice cold enough to freeze a person's soul.

'Did it make you angry enough to kick the chair Shao was sitting in, Jasmine?'

'No, it was…'

All eyes on her, the room still and silent, you can see a slight tremor in Jasmine's hands. She clasps them together to stop them from shaking.

'It was what?'

She laughs. 'What does it matter now? Yes, alright – my lying husband, bless his heart, sat there ignoring me and it made me so mad that I kicked his darn chair. So what? Yes, I hurt my foot. He was still upright and alive in the chair when I left to throw up.' Here, she growls with… annoyance? 'Do with that what you will, Honey.'

'Thank you,' you say, genuinely. Jasmine Quill has just confirmed a number of details that mean you now know the right direction to take your investigation.

Jasmine hadn't been limping after she left the library at 9.10 pm last night, meaning she definitely went back a second time, and during that visit kicked Shao's chair. What else had she done then?

Whatever she'd done, that was the point in her night when she became ill, not during her first visit to the library.

She also doesn't know what you were referring to when you asked her about insects, so she hadn't seen the jack jumper ants on the desk during either visit, which also helps piece together the timeline.

As you tune back into the conversation in the room – a discussion between Hudson and Paige on the place of artificial intelligence in the creation of modern fiction – you wonder why Jasmine stressed that Shao was still alive when she last saw him. Sign of a guilty conscience perhaps?

Jasmine pushes herself up out of the sofa and limps from the room, clutching her stomach once again.

Bruce has made his way behind the bar in the corner. He unsuccessfully tries to quietly sort through the empty bottles in the hope of discovering a drop or two to feed his habit.

Outside, the frog chorus grows louder as sheets of driving rain obscure the view of the mountains in the distance.

Yo, ho, ho and a bottle of rum.

Where to next?

Choose from options 1, 2 or 3.

1. Read on to Chapter 11, *Poisoned Pen* by Marion Stoneman, to find out more about Paige's pen.

2. If you need to know more about Jasmine's night, skip to Chapter 14, *The Jig's Up* by Jack Cainery.

3. Do you think you've solved the mystery of Shao's death? Go to page 213 to find a hidden chapter with the answer.

CHAPTER ELEVEN

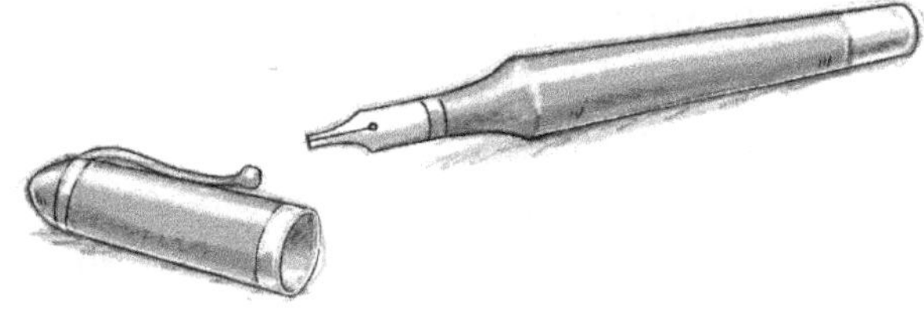

Poisoned Pen

Marion Stoneman

In which you question Shao T. Mann's editor, Paige Hybrough, regarding the red 'Marilyn' Mont Blanc pen in the library.

THAT FOUNTAIN PEN IS PUZZLING YOU. A DEEP BRIGHT RED MONT BLANC, expensive and feminine; it's hardly the sort of pen that would have appealed to Shao T. Mann. And you are curious about the way it was placed on the desk amid the dead ants, plastic bag almost empty of gummy bears, vintage book and mutilated novel. You've decided it warrants closer examination, this time with more items from the forensics case you brought to show the festival audience this weekend.

You sigh and nip into your room, put on a heavy coat, grab the case and stride back to the library door. Checking that no one is watching, you turn the key, slip from the relative warmth of the corridor into the still-icy room, and lock the door from inside.

First you don a pair of latex gloves and switch on a torch for more light. You make your way to the desk – keeping your distance from the body of Shao T. Mann – then slowly and methodically shine the torch on the items on the desk, examining everything closely with your magnifying glass. You realise you're in the groove, all your movements second nature as though you're back on the Force. Everything is automatic, a product of training, experience and mind-muscle memory. Assume nothing. Touch nothing. Observe everything.

You begin with the two books. One, a copy of Shao's latest novel, has traces of dirt and leaves between the pages. When you lift the cover using tweezers from your kit you can see more dirt lodged in the inner compartment, which looks like it was hastily cut with a serrated-edge knife. A steak knife from the kitchen?

You then turn your attention to the second book. As you now know, its green cloth cover is impregnated with arsenic, and the scratched edges of the pages coated in the same deadly substance.

Next, the pen. It's not the pen you saw Shao using last night. He'd held a blue Parker biro for signing books in one hand, and a screwdriver for tinkering with his typewriter in the other. You scan the patterned carpet beneath his body and the avalanche of yellow books surrounding him. There, peeking from beneath one of the books, is the tip of the biro. You slowly lift the pages to find the biro is intact. Since you expected it to be at the scene, and there's no visible trace of blue ink on Shao, you think it is appropriate to note it but move on.

Where's the screwdriver? There! A glint of silver metal on the opposite side of the desk. Again, you carefully lift a book to see it lying there, no traces of blood. With no signs of a puncture wound on the body it seems reasonable to conclude it is unlikely to be a weapon in this scene.

Now to the pen in question, the special edition Marilyn Monroe fountain pen. Its barrel is the same shade of red as the star's lipstick, elegantly tapered. The nib and band are silver, with 'Marilyn' engraved on the nib. It's a timeless piece for classic Paige Hybrough, and expensive enough that a girl with working-class origins would never leave it behind intentionally.

You peer at the pen through your magnifying glass. Under the torchlight you can see small flecks of pale green on the nib, and all the way up the beautiful red barrel and cap. The green matches the page-edges of the old book. You examine the plastic bag – it also has flakes of green on the outside, but curiously not the inside.

Your brain is in overdrive. You check the dead ants. Yes, tiny chips of green there too.

How to put all these pieces together?

Had Shao pilfered the vintage book during his argument with Hudson and brought it here from the museum? Why? Had he used gloves to carry it here to avoid touching the arsenic himself? And could this be responsible for the death of the ants?

A small amount of arsenic would be enough to kill an ant, even a jack jumper. How much was needed to kill a person?

You wish you could remember the details of a session on poisoning from your training, but it was so long ago. You recall that arsenic was a popular murder weapon in the nineteenth century until the development of the Marsh test, at which point its use declined to almost zero. Nowadays arsenic testing is predominantly carried out on drinking water, especially in regions where mining or fracking is common. You check the poisons test kit in your Pelican case. Bingo, arsenic test sachets.

Multiple samples from the book, pen, bag and desk all test positive, with the outside surface and edges of the book's pages seemingly coated in arsenic.

Would handling the book be enough to kill someone? Touching that pen might be enough to create some discomfort – burning, tingling, blistering of the skin perhaps? And if ingested, or even transferred to the mouth unwittingly, it might make the victim decidedly sick.

You switch on your blue light and shine it on the pen barrel. Now it's clear – there are spaces in the green dust the size of fingers. By the angle of the spaces, someone touched the pen – picked it up rather than used it to write – after it was coated with the green arsenic flecks. That person must have some signs of arsenic poisoning, on their fingers at the very least.

You swivel and crouch next to Shao's body. No signs of vomiting or diarrhoea, thankfully. You shine the torch on his hands: no signs of rash or blistering on any of his fingers, but you notice a few faint flecks of pale green staining his right cuff and – you lift the collar of his jacket with tweezers – a small galaxy of flecks on the inside of his jacket breast and on the section of his shirt over his heart. They stand out starkly against his white suit, and under the magnifying glass look exactly like the particles on the pen and desk. Did he tuck the book inside his jacket, using his cuff to pick it up?

Looking at him now, do the symptoms of arsenic poisoning tally with what you can observe? There is clearly no direct contact with arsenic on his hands. Could he have suffered dizziness, or a headache? Possibly, but there's nothing to move forward with there. Nausea, stomach cramps? No visible signs. And how quickly could this kill someone? It doesn't add up. You decide you have to track the trail of the pen further.

It has to be Paige's pen on Shao's desk. 'His desk', you think with a huff. The library was supposed to be a shared space for all the guests, but it took Shao no time at all to claim it as his own and force everyone else to surrender the space. Such an ego. It seems obvious he would assume he could take Paige's pen and anything else that took his fancy from her elegant brown leather handbag.

You decide to talk to Paige again. You leave the library, locking it behind you, then walk down the hallway and knock gently on her door. You call her name but there's no reply.

You push on the door and it swings open. Peering around you see no sign of her, although you do notice her bed is neatly made and the room is tidy. Also, there are books arranged in piles around the small writing desk, and a closed laptop in the middle. An assortment of small, zipped travelling bags are arranged in size order on the dresser, and next to them is her stylish brown leather handbag. Not one thing out of place. This woman is so organised it makes you slightly nervous.

Perhaps she has gone outside for some fresh air? You pull the door to, leaving her room as it was. You march down the hallway once more and open the front door, searching the shoe rack on the verandah for a particular set of gumboots. Paige's black and cream pair is missing, and in their place is a pair of sensible, black, low-heeled shoes, neatly placed together.

You slip on your pair of worn but well-cared-for plain black leather boots – they scream 'plod' detective – and take the stairs down to the lawn. It's so waterlogged it's like sinking into a soggy sponge. Everything off the ground is dripping.

You step off the boggy lawn onto the narrow path and head into the garden. The path is edged with early daffodils bent towards the ground, heads heavy with moisture. Below the formal garden you emerge onto what was, until yesterday, the grassy riverbank dotted with native plants. It's now the boundary between you and chaos.

The Huon River, a slow-moving sheet of darkened glass before the storm, is now a churning torrent. Twigs and branches bob along the foaming brown surface. Near the opposite bank it looks like a whole tree is tumbling in the current; and near the tree a crate of some sort – only one corner visible above the water's surface – spins and bounces its way downstream.

Then you notice a small boat out there in the chaos, headed your way from further upstream. Surely no one is stupid enough to risk a boat trip in this current? Could one of your four suspects be trying to escape? The boat spins slowly and as it passes by you can see it is unoccupied. It was probably ripped from its mooring somewhere.

You spot more movement at the water's edge behind a soggy native rosemary bush. Something that looks remarkably like a clump of spiky seaweed is deliberately moving against the current. You look closely and, as it undulates, a long, thin protuberance extends above the surface. You're so intrigued that you don't hear Paige approaching from behind.

'Oh my goodness,' she says in your ear, making you jump, 'is that an echidna? I didn't ever imagine them swimming.'

It is an echidna. Again it extends its long pointed snout up into the air, using it like a snorkel to breathe.

'It must have been washed downstream by the flood, poor thing,' you say. You consider wading into the shallows towards it, but stop yourself when you realise it's too far out and the current is dangerously strong.

You retreat, looking around for a long stick to try to scoop it towards the shallows. 'Surely we should try to save it?'

Paige chuckles. 'How do you suppose you'll pick it up? Look at those spines.'

'It would be an awkward rescue,' you agree.

The echidna swims nonchalantly past you both and makes it to shore near a clump of reeds. It clambers out of the water dripping, shakes itself off, then waddles towards the bushes.

'It didn't need rescuing after all,' says Paige. 'Plucky little creature. It's a cousin of the platypus, you know,' she continues, 'so I guess swimming is in its DNA.'

Spines, you think, and that reminds you of a pen nib and the reason you were looking for Paige. Echidnas aside, you decide to take this opportunity to ask her about the 'Marilyn'.

'Paige, when Shao made notes, what type of pen did he use?'

'Hmmm?' She is moving slowly towards the echidna to get a closer look. The echidna, unbothered by either of you, has now begun digging in the garden bed.

'Does…did Shao have a particular pen he liked to use?'

'What?' Paige stops and turns towards you. 'Whatever's closest, usually.'

'Did he borrow your Mont Blanc last night? Or did you leave it with him in the library?'

Paige pauses. 'No.'

You decide to press her. 'Where is your pen now?'

'In my room in my handbag, where it always is.'

'If I told you it's on the desk in the library, what would you say?'

Paige frowns. 'I'd say I have no idea how it got there. I may misplace notebooks occasionally, but not my pen. If it was on the desk when I went to leave the library last night I would have picked it up'

And yet, the pen was there on the library desk along with her missing bag of gummies. 'Did you go to the library again later?'

She shakes her head.

'Did you have the pen with you in the library last night?'

'Well, yes, in my handbag. But like I said, I'm sure it wasn't on the desk when I left, so I assume it's still in there.'

'Could Shao have possibly taken it out of your bag without you knowing?'

'Possibly. He asked me to get him a cup of tea at one point because he was unwell. I suppose he could have taken it then…' She looks flustered. 'I'm sure it's in my handbag in my room. Can we go and check?'

'In a minute. But first, you said he was unwell. What exactly was wrong with him?'

'He said he was feeling a bit off. Stomach, I assume. He did look a little pasty, but he had been drinking an awful lot and it often gave him a bit of reflux. Tea usually settled his stomach.' She looks out at the swollen river again and you follow her gaze. Even you find the confining floodwaters distracting, almost mesmerising.

You consider what Paige said. Was Shao's discomfort from the booze, or could it have been the beginning of stomach cramps and vomiting from arsenic poisoning? Or something entirely different? It's all so inconclusive.

'What did you see on Shao's desk when you returned with the tea?'

She thinks for a moment.

'His typewriter, and piles of the new novel he was signing for festival patrons.'

'Anything else?'

'There was an old book on the desk, vintage like the ones in the museum yesterday. Green cover, I think. Stood out against the bright yellow of the new ones.'

'But not your pen?'

She shakes her head.

'I didn't notice it when I left, just grabbed my handbag and the cup and saucer and walked out.' She pauses and looks you squarely in the eye. 'I heard Bruce arguing with Shao a while later when I went to take a shower, so any ideas you might have about me killing Shao when I was in the library are moot.'

That isn't your focus right now, but it is interesting to you that she is thinking along those lines.

If Shao already had the vintage green book on the desk when Paige visited him in the library, but it wasn't there when you saw Shao at 8.30 pm, you need to know if either Jasmine or Hudson saw it before Paige arrived. You make a mental note to follow up on that.

It also occurs to you that while Shao might have rifled through her handbag with Paige out of the room, equally Paige might be lying about any number of things. Was she the one who put the book on the desk?

'May I see your hands?'

She looks taken aback. 'Why?' Then holds them out. 'My hands are fine.'

There are no signs of rashes or blistering, so it doesn't look like she touched the book or the pen. Not with her bare hands at least.

'Let's go have a look in your handbag, shall we?' You gesture for her to accompany you and begin up the sodden path back to the verandah.

Paige invites you in, but before you enter you pop back to your room for your forensics case. Paige frowns at you. 'Is that really necessary?'

Before she can object, you open the forensic kit, whip on a pair of latex gloves and pick up her handbag from the dresser. 'We can't be too cautious.'

Paige reaches for the bag, but before she can grab it you hold out your hand to stop her.

'Careful with that, it's an original. What do you expect to find in there anyway?' she says, clearly annoyed.

'Please don't touch it – for your own safety.'

She huffs, but drops her hands to her sides.

You place the handbag on the bed, open the clasp, and pull the sides as wide as you can. You see a wallet, keys, and a mid-sized notebook in the main compartment.

'Where do you keep the pen?'

'In the left zippered pocket, here,' she points, 'on the same side as the clasp.'

You open the zipper carefully. Inside, you can see a packet of spare red ink cartridges – the screw-in type, with Mont Blanc printed on the packet – but no pen. Paige looks puzzled. You take a cotton bud from your case and swipe it around the pen compartment. You examine it closely under your magnifying glass. Nothing aside from a few specks of dried red ink. Paige peers at it as well, then looks at you quizzically.

You repeat the process on the main compartment of the handbag, around the keys and wallet. Again, nothing aside from dust and a fleck of glitter. You find a second pocket on the opposite side of the bag.

'What do you keep in here?' you ask her.

'Oh, sticky notes, highlighter pens, my gummy bears.' She falls silent.

You take another cotton bud out of your Pelican case, then unzip the compartment. Inside are sticky notes, highlighters and a few paperclips, but no pen or plastic bag of gummy bears.

You swab the compartment and examine the result. This time the cotton bud has a definite film of pale green flecks, the same as you found on the pen and scattered across the desk.

'What's that?' she asks. You're not sure if she's puzzled or panicked.

'Nothing to worry about,' you say, keeping your face as neutral as you can, 'but I think I'd better hold on to this bag until the police arrive.'

'You what?' she says, aghast. 'You can't do that. I need things out of that bag.'

'I'm afraid that would be unwise.' You try to sound reassuring.

'But I didn't do anything wrong.' She's raising her voice now, and her eyes are hard. 'Are you trying to say something from my bag hurt Shao?'

Your mind is buzzing. So far you can say that neither Paige nor Shao show any signs or symptoms of arsenic poisoning. But Paige's pen, covered in arsenic, is on the desk; and a compartment in her handbag has the same traces.

'Despite everything, you can't think that I would hurt him,' she says with a catch in her throat. She stifles a sob; you offer a consoling pat on her back. You can sympathise to some extent, though how someone who seems so rational and in control could love a narcissist like Shao is beyond you.

Your thoughts return to the matter at hand. Could someone have deliberately coated the pen in arsenic, then placed into the wrong compartment in Paige's handbag using the plastic bag that had been full of gummy bears? And then pulled it back out? Who would have done that? Shao? Paige herself, and she is lying? Or someone else who is showing signs of what might be arsenic poisoning.

Had more than one person handled the pen, other than Paige?

You had been edging toward the idea that Shao had harmed himself, deliberately or accidentally. But the use of arsenic at the scene and contaminating the handbag suggests a deliberate attempt to harm someone – kill, even. Was Shao the intended victim, or Paige? Or is the bizarre tableau in the library due to two crime scenes layered one atop the other?

This case, which you began investigating with such confidence, has become more complex than the intricate pattern on the oriental carpet beneath Shao T. Mann's body. There are even more questions to answer and clues to follow now…

Where to next?

Choose from options 1, 2 or 3.

1. Read on to Chapter 12, *Tasmania's Deadliest Creature* by E.V. Scott, to find out more about the dead ants.
2. If you need to know more about the vintage book, jump back to Chapter 9, *Green with Envy* by E.K. Cutting.
3. Do you think you've solved the mystery of Shao's death? Go to page 213 to find a hidden chapter with the answer.

CHAPTER TWELVE

Tasmania's Deadliest Creature

E.V. Scott

In which you question Hudson van Daemon, up-and-coming Tasmanian crime writer, regarding the deceased ants you found on the desk of the library.

YOU CLOSE THE DOOR TO YOUR COOL WHITE BEDROOM BEHIND YOU AND begin pacing your room again. You've retired to a quiet space to review where you are in your investigation. You create a circuit around the wrought iron bed and Huon pine armoire, letting your thoughts drift freely as you walk.

This method of thinking allows your mind to throw up interesting connections. Your thoughts churn, running through the lists in your notebook of each person's possible reasons for harming Shao and the means by which they could have attacked him. The faces of your suspects revolve on the carousel of your thoughts.

You pat your pocket, double checking you still have the key to the library. If one of these people is responsible for Shao's death, they will be nervous as hell right now. They may consider tampering with the evidence. In your experience, the old adage about a criminal returning to the scene of their crime often holds true. You might be thinking cynically, but cynicism is a by-product of the job, or rather, was a by-product of the job.

As you pace, images and faces float to the top of your mind then disappear again. Two items in the library keep appearing. The dead ants and the vintage book with the green-edged pages.

You catch a glimpse of yourself in a mirror above the ornamental fireplace. The face staring back at you is careworn. With dark rings under your eyes and a mop of untidy hair you may not look like a crack detective, but you still feel like one.

You gaze at a vintage Tasmanian travel poster on the wall, showing a black swan swimming serenely on the Huon River. The backdrop shows the verdant green of the valley.

The colour brings you back to the emerald book which, in turn, draws your mind to the ants. They lay scattered across the top of the desk, their legs splayed out as if they had been trying to make a run for it.

When examining the scene in the library this morning you had used the tip of your biro to lift one of their heads, seeking any clue as to how they died. Then, when checking the scene again you'd found tiny green flakes on their little legs – the same green flakes that were scattered across the surface of the desk. Those flakes had tested positive for arsenic, and you were certain they came from the emerald-green book.

Given what you've observed, can you say with certainty that the ants died from arsenic poisoning? Even if they did, does that explain what they were doing in the library in the first place? Or if they were involved in Shao's death?

You need to know more about the ants. You recall the shelves and shelves of books on Tasmanian flora and fauna in the sitting room.

You walk to the empty kitchen and pour yourself another coffee. It's rich and fragrant, and hopefully the extra caffeine will fire up the old brain.

Next door, you find a book on Tasmanian insects, its bright spine standing out from the rest. You slide the book from the shelf, noting that the content is intended for young readers. As you flick through the pages you come across a section on ants.

There they are, the ants in the library: they are called 'jack jumpers'.

These ants are much larger than ordinary ants. Their mandibles and legs are yellow, as if signalling their dangerous nature with built-in crime scene tape. You wish humans came colour-coded. It would make your job much easier.

You return to your room with your coffee and the book and decide to read it at a small table outside. You open the French doors leading out to the verandah and step through, greeted by the cawing ravens still perched in the monkey puzzle trees.

The invigorating freshness of the Tasmanian air embraces you. You take in a great breath, filling your lungs. There is nothing quite like the air of the Huon Valley, scented with eucalypt and edged with cold, to remind you that the next stop south of here is Antarctica.

You sit and read more on the ants. They are extremely aggressive and their sting is painful, causing anything from hives and abdominal pain to anaphylaxis. The Guinness World Records certifies jack jumpers as the world's most dangerous ant. Interesting.

The book has a small section on the habits of jack jumpers, but not enough to answer your questions.

Is it possible they came into the house looking for shelter from the flood? Or, as you suspected, were they brought inside by someone who wanted to hurt Shao?

You need more information to be able to understand how they fit into the picture.

As you sip your coffee, you catch a flash of red out of the corner of your eye. Down in the garden, a figure steps out from behind a white waratah bush. It's Hudson, with an armful of logs for the sitting room fire. There is no mistaking that shirt; it really does match the pattern of your childhood picnic blanket.

Just the person you need to speak to. Of your four suspects, Hudson is the most likely to know how to find and transplant the dangerous jack jumpers. You could appeal to his wildlife expertise to find out more about the ants and his possible involvement in their transport to the library.

He hasn't noticed you. You withdraw into your room, closing the French doors behind you.

You finish the rest of your coffee in one gulp and decide to head to the sitting room to question him.

Bruce is pacing the kitchen when you pass through, still searching, you assume, for any remaining alcohol. Each time you see him he appears more bedraggled than before. He's standing in front of an open cupboard, scraping a hand over his face, reminding you for a moment of Edvard Munch's famous painting, *The Scream*.

As expected, Hudson is kneeling in front of the sitting room fireplace.

'When you've finished with the fire, could I ask you about ants?'

He looks up at you. Was his expression a touch nervous?

Hudson continues stacking wood in the grate and agitates the coals beneath them to encourage flames to lick the new logs.

'What did the Pink Panther say when he stepped on an ant nest?' he says, still looking down.

Ah, the French Inspector Clouseau movies. Classic. 'I don't know, what did he say?'

'Dead ant, dead ant, dead ant dead ant dead ant dead ant dead aaant.'

Hudson sings the words to the tune of the Pink Panther movie theme tune. You groan at the terrible pun, hoping to keep your interaction with the young writer light. 'Good one,' you say.

He finishes stoking the fire and sits back in an armchair, one foot across the opposite knee, his bare shins gleaming in the blazing firelight. He begins picking at burrs in the shoelaces of his boots.

'I was hoping you could tell me about jack jumper ants,' you say.

'Ahhh.'

'Of everyone here, you're the most knowledgeable about the bush and the creatures in it.'

He smiles, unable to ignore the compliment.

Silence can be a powerful tool in interrogation. You let it stretch for a moment longer than necessary. Feeling uncomfortable about manipulating a younger person, you lean back and stare into the fire.

Hudson shifts in his seat, rearranging his limbs and resumes his picking, this time on the shoelaces of his other boot.

'Jack jumpers are well known for their aggression,' he says, filling the silence. 'They're found all over the Huon Valley.'

You nod. 'I imagine that they're quite difficult to pick up?'

Hudson uncrosses his legs. 'You'd have to know what you're doing to avoid being stung.'

'Stung? I thought ants bite.'

'Jack jumpers bite and sting. Their mandible can pack a punch but it's the stinger in their abdomen that delivers the poison.' Hudson leans forward in his chair, his arms resting along his thighs. He's engaged, happy to be your expert.

'There's something called the Schmidt Pain Index,' he says. 'Jack jumpers rate at level two of four.'

'I've never heard of it.'

'Dr Justin Schmidt developed it. He says level two feels as painful as having a hole in your oven mitt when you're pulling cookies out of the oven,' says Hudson.

You wince. 'Ouch.'

'Exactly,' says Hudson.

'You know that they can kill?'

He frowns. 'Only if you're allergic to their venom, which is rare.'

You'd read that three percent of the population was allergic. It was twice as common as an allergy to bee sting. 'Don't they hold the record as the deadliest creature in Tasmania?'

His brow furrows deeply. 'Yes.'

'Do you think there could be a nest close by?'

Hudson freezes for a split second, appearing to consider your question, before shrugging. 'Probably. But jack jumpers are known for ranging widely.'

'Likely to be some next to the manor?'

'Sure. Given all this rain, it's possible they could have come up to the house seeking dry ground.'

'All the way inside the manor and into the library?'

That frozen look again.

'Would a handful of ants, who like to hunt alone, get together to find a dry spot in the library?' you say.

He plucks vigorously at a patch of burrs on a new section of shoelace.

'Seems odd,' you continue. 'Why only these guys and not the whole nest?'

'Food in the library?'

'Was there, do you think?'

'Bound to be something,' he says.

Apart from the gummy bear in a plastic bag, there was nothing on that desk for ants to eat. And from the looks of it, they hadn't made it into the bag.

You read that jack jumpers are solitary hunters. Which means they didn't travel to the desktop as a group – they were either attracted by the same thing or were carried. You're certain it was the latter.

'I think someone moved them into the library in some kind of container,' you say.

You're thinking about the mutilated copy of *High Time* on the desk near the ants. The cut-out section would make the perfect Trojan horse for a tiny swarm of insects. 'When you were in the library yesterday, did you see the copies of the new Kuphem novel?'

He's picking at a particularly difficult burr. 'Of course, there were piles of them.'

'Did you see one with a hole cut out of the middle? A compartment?'

His hands are still.

You lean forward. 'Given your understanding of jack jumpers, do you think it's plausible that someone collected them from the garden and placed them inside a book, then left them on the desk for Shao to find?'

Hudson tenses, then tries to smile. 'Maybe an obsessive fan? Jasmine told me they'd turn up wherever Shao went. One of them might have sent him a box of jack jumper ants.'

It is a ridiculous suggestion, Hudson is grasping at straws. Why would he do that if he wasn't trying to throw you off the scent?

You recall the way the ants were arranged on the desk, dying so close to each other. 'I can't imagine that jack jumper ants are easy to kill,' you say.

'No,' he says as he looks towards the door.

You sit back again. You don't want to push him too hard. Not yet.

'I'm curious to hear your thoughts on how the ants died.'

'Shao killed them by hitting them with a book?'

'No, they hadn't been squashed. They appeared to be perfectly intact, just expired. Not only is it strange that they were in the library in the first place, it's puzzling as to how they all died close to a book with a compartment cut out of it.' You fold your hands over one another, place them on your lap and settle in to wait for Hudson's answer.

'I can't think of a reason off the top of my head,' he says. He's in such a hurry to get his words out that he trips over them, but this answer, at least seems genuine.

'What could explain all of them dying at the same time?'

Hudson frowns again. 'Typically, pyrethrum-based ant killer dust,' he says.

'Daisy juice dust? That kills jack jumpers?' you say as your mind ticks at a million miles an hour.

It was hardly likely that there was a convenient pile of pyrethrum-based ant killer lying about on Shao's desk. No, if there was poison on the desk – and you're certain there was – it was not intended for the ants.

You need to think, to concentrate. And you'd like to end this uncomfortable conversation. After getting along so well with Hudson earlier in the day – at least, you thought you were – the tension between you now over the question of the ants is unpleasant. You need to regroup in the silence of your room.

'Thank you,' you say, 'that's been most helpful.' You slap your hands down on the arms of the chair and push yourself to standing.

Hudson stands too. He swallows hard, his nerves on show. 'Do you think Shao died of an ant bite?'

As much as you might want to, you can't make this easy for him. 'We won't know anything for certain until after his autopsy.'

He moves to walk in front of you to the door outside and stumbles, suddenly awkward.

You open the door and Hudson steps out of the room.

'Thanks again,' you say before you shut the door behind him.

Now you're certain you know how the ants arrived on the desk: courtesy of Hudson's taxi service. At some point last night he took a copy of *High Time*, cut a compartment out of it to create a makeshift container, collected some jack jumpers from the garden, then left the book on the desk.

Your next thought makes you feel queasy. You were growing to like the young Tasmanian, but if he took the jack jumpers to the library he did so knowing there was a possibility – however rare – that they could kill Shao.

You now have the strongest combination of motive and means for killing Shao T. Mann that you've uncovered so far, but you're not happy about it. If the up-and-coming writer was so insulted by Shao last night that he attempted to murder him, had he succeeded? And if he had, what does that say for your instincts where other people are concerned? Has retirement dulled your edge?

Where to next?

Choose from options 1, 2 or 3.

1. Read on to Chapter 13, *Too Many Books* by Carys King, to find out more about the boxes of books in the library.
2. If you need to know more about Hudson's night, skip to Chapter 15, *Dashed Hopes* by Sarah Barrie.
3. Do you think you've solved the mystery of Shao's death? Go to page 213 to find a hidden chapter with the answer.

CHAPTER THIRTEEN

Too Many Books

Carys King

In which you question Shao T. Mann's rival, Bruce Tossington-Smythe, regarding the boxes of yellow books in the library.

HERE YOU ARE, TRAPPED IN A HISTORIC CONVICT-BUILT MANOR AND GARDENS in the wilds of southern Tasmania, under the same roof as four potential suspects and possibly even a murderer. But you're frustrated by how circular your enquiries are this morning. Despite Shao T. Mann displaying a clear wound to the head, signs of possible poisoning, and there being umpteen clues in the library as to how he could have died, you're no closer to piecing together what happened last night.

You've been jotting down questions in your notepad since you first discovered his body. Quite a few relate to the boxes of books you saw stacked around Shao at 8.30 pm last night – boxes that have tumbled and strewn their contents around the internationally famous deceased author on the floor.

Last night the boxes had been stacked four high: some opened and empty, some filled with newly signed copies, and towers of books all around awaiting signatures. As a budding writer, you can only imagine how fulfilling your first book signing as a published author must be.

With an internal nudge, you remind yourself of the task at hand. Had one or more of the boxes fallen on Shao? Hit his head? Crushed him?

Or had someone picked up a box and thrown it at him? Or brought it down on top of his skull?

If anyone pushed the boxes over and caused a fatal injury, or used them as a weapon, Bruce is the most likely suspect as he was the last person to visit Shao. He already admitted he thinks the boxes were still upright when he entered the room. Figuring out what he truly recollects throughout the alcohol blur of last night, and what he imagines he remembers, is tricky. His burgeoning hangover is also making him testy, which is both annoying to put up with and helpful to you as it makes him less able to maintain a lie.

With rain pelting yet again onto the bullnose verandah outside, making a distracting stroll in the garden an unattractive proposition, you find three of your suspects ensconced in various chaises and sofas in the blue sitting room.

One of them, you suspect Paige, has lit a row of tealight candles along the dark wood mantel above the fireplace. They are flickering, almost burnt out already, but add a pleasant hint of lavender to the room's atmosphere.

Bruce is attempting to read an old novel, the title of which you can't make out in the shadow cast by a fringed reading lamp. It presumably comes from one of the many antique bookcases with lead-patterned glass doors that line the walls of the sitting room. He appears to be nodding off more than focusing on the page.

You have to wonder about him and his capacity for injuring others. Bruce's almost universal disrespect for everyone, including himself, is annoying to say the least. His need to be the centre of attention, in control of the situation, and a victim, all at once, is maddening. You've come across narcissists like him before, though usually in the bodies of sixty-year-old men whose families have put them in charge of multi-million dollar corporations or branches of government. It's never pretty. At least this one's focus is on uninterrupted drinking time, as opposed to uninterrupted exploitation of workers.

He might be harmless. He certainly portrays himself as such. But you can't shake the thought that some people are like Jekyll and Hyde when drunk. You know from bitter experience in past cases when you were on the Force, that it's possible for someone to be so inebriated they kill, forget it immediately, and are as shocked as everyone else to see CCTV footage of their crime. The potential for self-delusion can never be dismissed.

He begins to snore, ignored by Jasmine who sits at a sidetable, sipping tea, staring into the flickering flames of the fire. Given that she doesn't seem to like anyone else in the mansion, you're not sure why she's here. Perhaps she is an extrovert and simply seeks company, no matter whose it might be. Perhaps she feels the need to monitor the conversations held between the others this morning, in an attempt to discover what happened last night, or possibly to cover it up. Years of police work taught you to never assume a motive, good or bad, but instead to ask questions.

'Biscuit anyone?' Hudson's head appears in the doorway to the kitchen, waking Bruce. 'I found a stash tucked away in the back of the pantry. They have the festival logo on the box, so I assume it's fine for us to eat them.'

Paige is standing in front of the French doors to the verandah. She turns to Hudson with a slight smile. 'Well, we certainly wouldn't want any biscuit stealers around here, given the circumstances.'

It's a strange attempt at humour, which doesn't seem to land – one of those jokes that would only work for an in-crowd, perhaps.

'Were you responsible for the candles?' you ask her.

'I may not be religious,' she says, taking a biscuit from the tray that Hudson offers, 'and Shao may not have always been the best of men–'

Here you, Bruce, Hudson and Jasmine all cough or clear your throats.

'–but I always light a candle when someone passes. It feels right.'

The room is warm and quiet for a few seconds. Then…

'I still think *Foul Play Underground* is in with a chance to win the Devil,' says Bruce.

Jasmine makes a little sound, perhaps a groan. 'After all this time, my dear man, I don't think it's going to you. It will be my husband.'

You wonder again why Jasmine isn't shouting from the rooftops about Shao and Paige's secret arrangement. Is she buying herself some time, working out how to spin this publicly? There won't be any more Kuphem books, but as his widow Jasmine must stand to earn a fortune in posthumous sales, even if they are split with Paige. Actually, have you given that angle sufficient deliberation?

Jasmine and Bruce continue sparring as you realise you haven't examined what Paige's move to end the Kuphem series meant for Shao. Once he realised what Jasmine was saying to him last night – that Kuphem died in *High Time* – he must have understood in an instant what Paige had done.

Paige, having known Shao for thirty years, had decided to end her involvement without a word to him. If he had lived, would he have sought some kind of retaliation against her? You can't imagine the unpleasant man you met in the library last night letting Paige escape without some kind of retribution.

As astute as she is, surely the same thing had occurred to Paige. She lived in a world of make-believe murder and real-life duplicity – if she didn't care what actions Shao might have taken against her after discovering her killing of Kuphem, was that because she intended to get rid of Shao too? She doesn't seem vengeful or vindictive, but you can rarely tell true character through the mask of appearances in such a brief interaction.

'And why wouldn't my book win?' Bruce is saying as your attention returns to the room. 'It's been nominated for several awards this year.'

'Which your publisher or agent schmoozed you into, no doubt,' Hudson says. 'Let's be honest, you can wheedle your way onto a shortlist if even one judge can be swayed, but your work is too rough, vulgar even, to win over a whole judging panel.'

'That's not fair,' Bruce's shouts, his anger ratcheted up several notches in a split second, startling everyone in the room.

Bruce's obsession with the awards might be a stronger motive for violence than you first thought. For Bruce, the Kuphem books seem to symbolise the success he craves and expects, but that somehow has only flowed to Shao T. Mann.

'For god's sake, grow up!' To your surprise, Paige responds with fury, flinging an accusatory finger toward Bruce, pinning him to the back of the navy sofa. 'I'm so sick of your whinging. If you want to win awards write better bloody books.'

'I'm only one person. Mann always had you,' Bruce's frustration also seems to reach boiling point. 'You were an amazing writer in uni, I never understood why you chose to put your eggs in his basket and edit his work without acknowledgement. Why him?'

'She did more than that,' says Jasmine, her throat sounding a tad raw.

Was she about to reveal to Bruce and Hudson that Paige was the real author of the Kuphem series? That could force a few more truths into the open.

Bruce flicks a dismissive hand in Jasmine's direction. 'Who cares about that? We all slept with each other at uni, who could keep track? I'm talking about writing.'

Jasmine gasps, then glares with incredulity at Paige, who avoids her eyes. Hudson, you note, is frowning.

'That's right,' Hudson says. 'The three of you were at uni together weren't you.'

'We were a great trio,' Bruce says, switching gears again, now in some kind of fond reminiscent state, 'until–'

Paige sighs. 'Until, like the male idiots you were, you and Shao decided one had to be superior to the other – get the higher grades, win the awards.'

'And the girl,' he murmurs.

Paige sniffs, refusing to acknowledge his comment. She moves to toy with the wick of one of the flickering tealights as it turns from bright yellow flame to a snaking column of smoke. When she speaks again, her voice has returned to its normal calm tone. 'You were both blinded by your competitive urges, making losers of all three of us.'

His jaw slightly ajar, eyes wide, Bruce looks exactly like a man about to face some long-avoided truths. 'What are you saying?' he asks her.

'In the past year I've had reason to re-evaluate my life. I may have made mistakes,' she closes her eyes and swallows; you assume she is trying hard not to look at Hudson, 'but I think collectively, back then, we made many more.'

Bruce is looking at Paige as you imagine a hiker does when they realise they are in the path of an avalanche.

'If the two of you had focussed on working together rather than treating everything like a boxing match, the three of us had the potential to create some amazing work together, to have actually been the best of friends, not entangled in this ridiculous decades-long nastiness and enmity you both insisted on.'

'I don't understand,' he says, plucking at the fringe of his scarf.

'I'm saying, I wish we'd made different choices.'

Bruce appears to be rocked by Paige's candour. He looks directly at her. 'You were the best of the three of us. I always thought you'd done yourself a disservice editing for Mann rather than writing your own books.'

Paige sighs again. 'You may be right.'

Bruce looks chagrined. 'The things I said about Kuphem. It was never really about the books. It was–'

'I know.' Paige says, moving to sit next to her former friend, folding her limbs in neatly to tuck herself beside him on the chaise.

'Look, old man,' Hudson says, picking up the barely touched plate of biscuits, 'I'm not sure why you're so fixated on awards you haven't won, but I have to say, perhaps stop caring about them?'

Bruce bristles. 'No-one asked you.'

'If you had won,' Hudson continues, 'you'd know that whoever wins is told well before the ceremony. They make sure you're going to be there, if they can.'

Paige nods. 'That's true.'

'Was Mann told he was winning The Devil tomorrow?' Bruce asks Jasmine.

The Devil was awarded by the Huon Valley Crime Writers Festival for the twistiest, most cunning crime, mystery, thriller or cross-genre novel of the year – one with a solution hidden in plain sight. In your heart of hearts it is an award you hope to win one day, though perhaps once you've got a couple of novels under your belt.

Jasmine shakes her head. 'He didn't say anything, and we all know he loved to gloat.'

You note, again, how quickly she has accepted her husband's death. No denial, no anger, no bargaining. As one well-acquainted with the cycle of grief, her reaction is rare and odd given the suddenness of his departure.

Bruce looks askance at Paige.

'Not as far as I know,' she says.

You, too, had assumed last year's Kuphem novel would win the award for Shao yet again. It was one of the best in the series.

'But there were only four books shortlisted,' says Bruce, 'and one was…'

No one wants to say it, but you already know what they are thinking. The last of the four shortlisted books is the subject of a plagiarism scandal that broke last week. Even if the allegations are false, there is no way it could be awarded the prize now. You can see their minds whirring as they put it together – if the award isn't going to Kuphem, or Bruce's offering, or the scandalised story, that means…

'Oh Hudson,' Paige's voice catches. 'Congratulations.'

'No,' says Bruce, thumping the arm of his seat. 'Bloody hell.'

'New world order, old man,' Hudson says, without a trace of rancour. 'You may move through the world expecting it to part for you, but some of us understand the importance of flowing with it.'

'What irritating drivel,' Bruce spits.

Bruce's obsession is a lesson for you – chasing awards can kill your enjoyment of writing. Do accolades really matter if you feel the joy of creation? But none of this is why you came looking for the suspect quartet.

'Keep in mind that I'm trying to piece together what happened to,' you point at each of them as you speak, 'your husband; your partner; your rival; and your erstwhile inspiration; in the library last night. I must ask each of you about the boxes of books in there.'

'The signing copies?' Paige says.

You nod. 'Some have been opened, some signed, but mostly they were still stacked in boxes around the edges of the desk. At least, they were when I left the library around 8.40 or so. Were they still stacked up when each of you were in there last night?'

'Yes,' says Jasmine, putting the fingers of one hand to her mouth as if to suppress another wave of nausea and lurches for the door.

'Interesting woman,' says Paige.

It seems like a loaded comment. The crusty old Sydneysider beside her shrugs, his errant Collingwood scarf emphasising the movement of his shoulders. 'Just another of Mann's women. I haven't bothered to take much notice of them since–'

'Since?'

'University,' he says gruffly.

Paige claps her hands together. 'Right. All the sadness, angst and memory lane-tripping aside, we have something to celebrate.' She smiles at Hudson. 'Let's go see if we can find something to mark your latest success.'

He smiles back. 'That's really sweet of you.'

'My pleasure.'

'We'll even see if we can find an overlooked bottle of liqueur,' she says with a mischievous look in her eye.

Bruce groans theatrically.

'First though,' you say to Paige and Hudson, 'where were the boxes of books when you were in the library last night?'

Hudson shrugs. 'On the desk, as they were yesterday afternoon.'

'Same,' says Paige, smiling more broadly at the young man beside her.

Bruce straightens in his chair as they head into the kitchen.

'How much do you think each box would weigh?' you ask him.

He seems to be drifting off again, more relaxed than you've seen him all morning. 'Around ten kilos.'

'If a stack of them fell on someone, could that hurt them do you think?'

'Anything with weight can do damage.'

That's true. You've seen crush injuries caused by all sorts of things over the years.

'I'm thinking specifically of the books, though'

Bruce's voice takes on a conspiratorial tone. 'There is a story going around the publishing world about a bloke, a bookseller in Hong Kong, killed by a pile of books falling on top of him.'

'Really?'

Another tealight flickers to death on the mantel, catching your eye. 'You're the only one who hasn't answered my question,' you remind him.

'Where were the books when I last saw them in the library?' he repeats to himself, gruffly. 'All over the floor. But I know what you're getting at. I didn't hit Mann with one of those bloody boxes.'

'Then how–'

'Look, detective,' His sarcastic tone is back, 'I didn't get the girl, and I didn't get an award, and I don't have to answer your damned questions, but I do want a bloody drink.'

'I doubt there's a cupboard in the house that you haven't already tried,' you say as he stands to go on what you assume will be another futile search.

Where to next?

Choose from options 1, 2 or 3.

1. Read on to Chapter 14, *The Jig's Up* by Jack Cainery, to find out what happened between Jasmine and Shao in the library at 9 pm.
2. If you need to know more about Bruce's night, skip to Chapter 17, *Hazy Recollection* by Jo Dixon.
3. Do you think you've solved the mystery of Shao's death? Go to page 213 to find a hidden chapter with the answer.

CHAPTER FOURTEEN

The Jig's Up

Jack Cainery

In which you question Shao T. Mann's wife, Jasmine Quill, on her movements at 9 pm last night.

THE STORM HAS PASSED, AT LEAST FOR NOW. YOU FIND JASMINE ON THE bullnose verandah outside the warm sitting room, seated on one of the benches with dark sunglasses across her eyes and a scarf around her head. The expensive, colourful scarf clashes with her drab black dress; perhaps a sign of a deeply ill woman who no longer cares.

She can't have been out here long. Steam curls from a gold-edged teacup on the wrought iron table in front of her. She is absently scratching the fingers of one hand into the palm of the other, her dangling jewellery swaying. Scritch, scritch.

'May I join you?' you ask.

She turns her head, removes her sunglasses, then waves at the cushioned metal seat beside her.

The staccato call of kookaburras floats across the valley, laughing in celebration of a break in the weather.

'They're quite impolite, cackling at me like that,' she says. 'I can't blame them, but I thought they'd be more collegiate.'

She's in a talkative mood. Perfect. 'And why would they be laughing at you?'

'They're transplants like me; native to mainland Australia, but not Tasmania. Did you know that?'

'I didn't.'

'And,' she continues, 'they're snickering at me because of how oblivious I've been to what was happening around me, like a colour-blind raccoon.'

She pulls a lace-edged handkerchief from the sleeve of her dress and dabs at an eye. You follow her gaze out to the garden. A small creek is flowing across the sea-green lawn now, meandering in undulations down the slope before rejoining the river. It looks to you as though the flood is rising. White splodges are pasted to a tree trunk, pages of Carl Kuphem novels Jasmine flung off the verandah earlier, while others are lodged beneath a bush nearer the house.

Jasmine stands and shuffles to the railing. She's still for a while, peering into the mist silently. You realise why – she's waiting for an audience. You move to stand beside her.

'Golden pea bush,' she says as soon as you join her, nodding towards a yellow-flowered plant in the garden. 'I collect plants for our villa in Tuscany, you know, including that one. Yellow flowers from all over the world in neat little rows. Creating that garden felt like taming sunshine.'

'Taming sunshine,' you repeat. 'I like that,'

She sighs. 'It was easier than taming my husband.'

'Is that how you saw your marriage to him? An attempt to tame him?'

'In my heart he was a creator of worlds; a god who could bring characters to life with a few keystrokes. If he loved me, that meant I was loved by a god.'

She giggles. It is jarring.

She continues. 'My mother would judge that sentence scandalous, not to mention blasphemous.'

'To think of writers as gods?'

'Good ones.' She scratches at her palm again, then picks up her cup from the table and takes a sip. The gold edging mirrors the crushed golden sandstone lining the garden paths. 'For me the key to great crime fiction is a convincing protagonist, someone you can get inside the mind of as a reader.'

'No easy feat,' you say, now cognisant of how difficult it is to write any novel, let alone a good one.

She dabs at a dry eye again. 'Who wouldn't want to possess someone who can do that?'

That's a strange choice of word. 'Possess?'

'Possess, partner with. Same thing.'

'Not really.'

Jasmine sips her tea and ignores you.

'And could you possess him? Would he let you?' you ask to keep her talking.

She gives a most unladylike snort. 'As is now evident, no.' She turns and places her cup on the table with a wince, clamping a hand to her belly. She sits again and you join her. You suspect her discomfort is increasing though she's trying to hide it. 'I feel silly to have missed so many clues that he lied about writing the Carl Kuphem novels.'

'Such as?'

'Making up calls, supposedly his publisher badgering him for the latest manuscript, even though I never heard a phone ring. Empty whisky decanters when he said he'd pulled an all-nighter to finish a book.' She scratches absently at her palm again. It looks decidedly raw. 'And he repeatedly told me he wouldn't discuss the details of his books because he didn't want to jinx them, but now I see that was obviously deflection. I've been such a fool.'

She stops to look you squarely in the face. 'Then again, I guess there were the endless public appearances, the book signings, the festivals. Not many people could keep up the pretence through all that.' She plucks at the handkerchief with trembling fingers. 'Most people would have been fooled, even someone like you, ex-detective.'

The kookaburras – mischief makers that they are – let fly with their mocking laughter again. Jasmine winces.

'It's possible,' you say, hoping to soothe her injured pride enough to keep her talking.

'When he told me we were coming here for a festival I convinced him to take a few days off, so we could explore this little island at the bottom of the world together. I booked a hideaway for two and we drove to the Lymington peninsula as soon as we landed.' She sighs. 'He was the best version of himself; refined, respectable, gentlemanly.' She turns her gaze towards you. You notice her eyes are suddenly shining. 'We went for walks, looked for birds.' She trails off, takes a deep breath.

'At night, we sat on a rock overlooking the river. A rock! It was the first time we'd sat on anything but velvet in years. But it was wonderful, gazing out at the lights on the boats making stripes on the water. He held my hand and told me about the desperation he'd felt trying to deliver this latest manuscript…'

She takes a sip from her cup.

'…how he'd fought the siren song of sleep and the liquor cabinet, for months, and forced himself to grind it out. He opened up, showed me something of himself I hadn't seen before, or so I thought. And then–'

'Then?'

'As we packed up the cottage to come here I found his proof copy of *High Time*, this book that had caused him such angst. When we pulled up here yesterday afternoon, he said we'd arrived just in time.'

'In time for what?'

'I assumed a meeting with Paige, his trusty editor.' She made an air quote sign. 'I pulled out the book and read it. It was the worst few hours of my life.'

You wonder how to guide her toward revealing more of what happened when she confronted Shao last night. 'I can't imagine how it must have felt,' you say.

'At first I was puzzled,' Jasmine said, warming to the subject. 'There was no reasonable explanation for killing off Carl, his bread and butter. I couldn't believe it, wondered what on earth he was doing shooting himself in the foot like that. He'd worked so hard to create one of the world's best fictional heroes – or so I thought – and here he was dismissing his creation with such a trivial death.

'I had to talk to him about it. But first there were festival obligations; the meet and greet, the tour, the dinner. Then he said he was going to the library to sign books for the festival. I followed him, but you beat me to it.' Here she raises a quizzical eyebrow.

You choose your words carefully. 'I went to speak with him about his writing, about my writing, to seek his advice,' you say. Seeing that she has no reaction, you continue, 'But he wasn't interested in discussing it at all.'

'No regard for anyone else's dreams. Sounds about right.' Jasmine shrugs one shoulder, dismissing any disappointment you may have felt about her husband's behaviour. 'Once I realised he was alone again I went to demand an explanation for what he was doing to Carl.'

'I left him sometime after 8.30 pm…' You let it hang.

She takes a sip of her tea. 'I suppose I went in at about 9 pm, or thereabouts. I felt as though my heart was going to burst. I needed an explanation about why he'd done what he'd done.'

You nod, knowing the broad strokes of that meeting already, but are keen for more detail.

'He was taken aback when I asked him why he'd killed Carl. Shocked. Incredulous,' she pauses. 'Then he became angry. Spat Paige's name in the middle of a string of expletives, said she was trying to destroy him.'

Should you show her some sympathy? You tsk sadly.

'That's when I realised he had no prior warning about Kuphem's end. I saw straight through him. It was as though,' she pauses, 'there were bells in my ears, deafening me. I barely heard what he said, I guess it was shock. I knew suddenly that my life – our entire marriage – was based on a lie. He was no godly writer conjuring wonderful mysteries; he was a trickster and a liar, no more substantial than a boo hag from the swamp.'

You assume this is some kind of creature of mythology from the American Deep South, but now is not the time for a follow-up question.

She pauses, head still bent over her cup. You're not sure whether she's in pain or falling asleep. You give her a moment. Her eyes flicker and she swallows hard, her free hand pressing her stomach.

'He was a total fraud,' she continues. 'And me, I was a complete sucker. All his whining over lost sleep at that damned typewriter, all fake.'

The hand holding her cup seems to shake. You watch it closely as she places it, rattling, in its saucer.

Time to press her a little. 'Do you remember exactly what he said, Jasmine?'

She shakes her head. 'No. But something definitely snapped inside him, he lost all composure.'

You note a quiver in her voice. 'It could be important, help me to piece together what his thoughts were?'

'He said something about how he couldn't believe Paige would betray him, as though he had cornered the market in duplicity.' Jasmine's flash of anger makes her face glow pink, the first colour in her complexion you've seen today.

'Can you recall anything else?'

'Yes, only I couldn't make sense of it. He said something about one country bumpkin being much the same as another, and since the boy was on his way anyway, he'd do.'

'Did you understand the reference?'

'Not then. But thinking about it, Hudson? Maybe?' Jasmine shakes her head again making her jewellery flash in the soft sunlight. 'Then he looked straight at me and said maybe he didn't write Carl Kuphem, but he'd read enough to know how to deal with a problem.'

'And then?'

'I feel that, ah, it might be best if I don't recount exactly what I said to him then.'

'It must have been hard,' you say, showing a little more sympathy.

She looks away. 'Couples have secrets,' she says. 'But this?'

'Would this be about the time of the raised voices the others heard?'

Jasmine blushes. 'Yes.'

You don't need to know the expletives Jasmine may have yelled at her husband. You don't even need to know if her show of embarrassment is genuine. You do need to know what Shao said, and what Jasmine decided to do next. 'Do you know what problem your husband was referring to?'

'Paige, I assumed.' Jasmine snorts, then tugs at the knot of the scarf beneath her chin. 'On that, at least, we agreed.'

'Did he say anything else?'

She frowns. 'He looked at the covers of *High Time* stacked all around him, and said, *High time indeed*. If she wants to take the high ground, so be it.'

Now it's your turn to frown. *High Ground* was another title in the Kuphem series. 'Did he mean the book in the High series?'

'Detective Kuphem series,' Jasmine corrects you automatically, then tsks at herself.

And a penny drops. Paige had hidden a tiny clue to the books' real author from the beginning – a 'high' in every title for the 'hy' in her surname.

After thirty instalments you weren't certain you remembered which crime featured in *High Ground*, but you think it had something to do with an invisible substance absorbed through the skin. Your mind goes to the green vintage book and Mont Blanc pen on the desk in the library. Did they have anything to do with how Shao had died?

While there weren't any obvious signs on Shao's body to indicate he was poisoned that way, you'd need a toxicology report to rule it out.

You've run all the tests you can with the tricks in your forensics case; perhaps if you re-examine some of the results something will twig?

In the meantime, you note that Jasmine has avoided telling you exactly what she thought after she discovered Shao's betrayal. The time to push her has come.

'Help me go over this.'

With closed eyes she waves a hand. You take it to mean agreement.

'You entered the library at around 9 pm?'

'Yes, Sugar.'

Ah, she's switching on the charm again. 'You confronted Shao about Kuphem's death, realised he'd lied to you about being the author of the series; he realised Paige was ending their ruse, and then?'

'What do you mean, and then?

'Did anything else happen before you left?'

'No.'

You don't believe her. 'Do you happen to remember what was on the desk?'

Was that a sly twitch in the corner of one eye? 'That darn typewriter, of course.'

'Yes.'

'Piles of the new book.'

'Were there any other books?'

'Ahhh…'

'One of the vintage books from the museum?'

Eyes still closed she frowns, then nods, her jewels flashing again – the sun has briefly emerged from the clouds. 'Yes, there was one on the desk. He'd taken it from museum, I'd say. He was always free with other people's possessions.'

'Anything else?'

'Like what?'

'What about the bamboo chair he was sitting in? Was it intact?'

'Yes.' Her face is particularly still. 'I mean no, I mean I told you before.'

Yes, she had, but you like to ask the same question multiple times to see if there is a shift in a suspects' answers. And Jasmine's are swinging like a pendulum. 'Did you see any insects?'

She opens her eyes and looks at you quizzically. 'No. Why do you keep asking that?'

This is a more genuine response than her answer relating to the chair. Jasmine is limping today because she kicked the chair Shao was sitting in last night. Why did she try to hide that earlier this morning?

'Anything else on the desk?'

She sips her now cold tea. A distraction? 'There could have been, it's not as though I have a photographic memory.'

'And you left around ten past, as Hudson came in?'

'Yes.'

'And what were you thinking when you left?'

Her eyes blaze. 'All that time I'd worshipped his mind but it wasn't him at all, it was her.' She swallows. 'I couldn't make any sense of it – who have I idolised all these years? Lord, it's so confusing.'

'What did you decide to do about it?'

Her eyes flash a warning, but she remains silent. You try a different tack.

'Since Carl Kuphem was being killed off, and the man you married turned out to be someone else entirely, did you intend to stay with him?'

She snorts. Her derision speaks volumes.

'And it didn't cross your mind to lash out? To seek revenge?' You watch her closely for reactions. 'To hurt him?'

She starts to snicker but it quickly becomes a hoarse cough. Her throat really is raw from being sick all night.

You decide to appeal to her intellect. 'You're well read and have multiple degrees. If this were a novel, what would you – as a crime fiction fan, as a woman of learning – think happened?'

'I'd be drawn to the most obvious suspect: the person my husband had already upset to the point she was prepared to end their successful deception of thirty years, a con they'd perpetrated on the whole world,' she sighs, 'and me.'

'And what do you think that person might have done?'

'She was with him in the library – left her pen on his desk – and you said he had a blow to his head. Perhaps that someone, in his life for so long,' she says, arching her eyebrows, 'pulled the ball and chain off the shelf above him so that it fell on his head. It's the most obvious means, and explains the gash on his forehead.'

'Why would she do that?'

She sighs. 'I know how cruel he could be.'

So do you.

'He may have hurt her feelings so badly that she decided to hit him with something. Pain, jealously, the desire to control someone, can do strange things to the mind.'

You nod non-committedly. Yes, it can, but Paige isn't the one who uses the word 'possess' when it comes to Shao T. Mann. Does Jasmine keep pushing this idea of Paige as a killer because she is an astute woman, or a murderous one trying to cover her tracks?

You are quite aware – as is Jasmine – that Paige had decided to end her entanglement with Shao when writing *High Time* months ago, on the day she killed off the star of their detective series. The end of Kuphem is not a motive for Paige to kill Shao now. However, if she felt driven to protect her son, Jasmine's scenario might make sense, albeit not for the reason she is suggesting.

Except, you still haven't got the truth from Jasmine Quill. Time to try again. 'You left the library at around ten past nine and Hudson entered. Did you go back to see your husband again later?'

Jasmine laughs with such bitterness and hurt it has form and edges. 'I didn't speak with him again, and it will be one of the greatest regrets of my life that our last words were words of anger and recrimination.'

That could be the truth, even though she hasn't answered your question at all.

'Did Shao apologise to you? For any of it?'

She rounds on you now, her eyes narrowed. 'No.' For just a moment every trace of her genteel mask is gone, revealing the fury beneath. Then the lace-edged handkerchief rises and she dabs at her still-dry eyes once more. 'I could do with more tea,' she says. 'You?'

'Not right now, thanks.'

As she stands, gathering her sunglasses and cup, her eyes widen in distress. 'Excuse me,' she says and quickly limps towards her room, presumably to the private bathroom within.

You sit back in the cold iron chair to think over all she said. Jasmine may have left her husband intact in the library at 9.10 pm, as Hudson entered, but your overall impression is that she isn't unhappy about his demise. The question is, did she do anything to contribute to his death? A third husband dead in mysterious circumstances certainly seems suspicious.

Why is Jasmine so fixed on pushing the idea of Paige as a killer? And why did she suggest Paige had used the ball and chain to do it? What has actually caused her rapid illness?

Most importantly, why is she misleading you about not having returned to the library for a second time last night? Shao T. Mann's widow has just confirmed she was lying about that, at the very least. You need to know what transpired between Shao and Hudson hot on the heels of the older man's confrontation with his wife before you speak to Jasmine again.

Kookaburra laughter echoes across the river once more as you leave the verandah of the homestead and go in search of the strapping young Tasmanian writer.

Where to next?

Choose from options 1, 2 or 3.

1. Read on to Chapter 15, *Dashed Hopes* by Sarah Barrie, to find out what happened between Hudson and Shao in the library at 9.10 pm.
2. If you need to know more about Jasmine's night, skip to Chapter 19, *Dazed and Confused* by Alison Alexander.
3. Do you think you've solved the mystery of Shao's death? Go to page 213 to find a hidden chapter with the answer.

CHAPTER FIFTEEN

Dashed Hopes

Sarah Barrie

In which you question Hudson van Daemon, up-and-coming Tasmanian crime writer, on his movements at 9.10 pm last night.

YOU DECIDE TO TALK TO HUDSON AGAIN ABOUT HIS MOVEMENTS LAST NIGHT. The young man who likes to dress as though he doesn't know what season it is needs to fill in the blanks against his name in your notebook. But you have to find him first.

He doesn't appear to be anywhere in the house, so you step out the front door into the shadow cast by the verandah. There are still plenty of heavy grey clouds lurking, but the sun has snuck through and its effect on the soaked surrounds is dazzling. You find yourself squinting and reaching for your sunglasses.

You see and hear nothing other than rustling plants dancing in gusts of wind, and the occasional patter of droplets shaken from leaves and branches. You consider waiting inside for Hudson to return. You aren't particularly keen on slogging through the waterlogged, windblown garden, but you really do want to speak to him. Hoping your well-worn work boots are still reasonably waterproof, you set off to locate him.

Your boots squelch on the sodden path as you make your way through snaking displays of brightly coloured rhododendrons and azaleas, cut leaf maples and deep pink magnolias, all nestled under a canopy of ancient gums and pine trees. This section of garden is sheltered from the worst of the wind, but also from the sun, so the ground is inch-deep in mud. You silently hope there are no leeches waiting to latch onto you. You soon reach a pond flashing with sparkling, myriad-coloured koi. You hear the faintest hint of conversation and slow your steps.

There are two voices. You catch a glimpse of Hudson's distinctive red shirt through some swaying young conifers that frame a pathway towards a sunnier, open stretch of garden. You move quietly now, rolling your foot heel-to-toe to silence the squelching, curious to know who is with Hudson and what they are discussing out here away from the rest of the guests. You might not be welcome, so you barely breathe as you sneak up as close as you safely dare.

'It's an Olearia phlogopappa,' Hudson tells his companion.

'It's impressive that you know the botanical names for so many plants.' You immediately recognise Paige from her voice.

'If you're going to include botany in your writing you need to know the botanical names to be taken seriously,' Hudson muses. 'Olearia phlogopappa is this plant's correct, botanical name, but it's commonly known as the white daisy bush, which most people find easier to remember.'

'Yes, much easier,' she says. 'It must be a hardy shrub. I noticed an entire hillside dotted with it on the way in. The sheep seemed to be leaving it alone.'

You risk one more step toward them, so that they come into view, and hear a crackle as Hudson crushes a few leaves between his fingers and holds them to Paige's nose. 'That strong, musky scent is made by the essential oils in the leaves,' he tells her. 'Sheep don't enjoy the flavour.'

Paige runs her hand lightly over the top of the plant. 'The profusion of white daisy flowers against this greyish green foliage is simply stunning. I wonder if it could be hedged.'

'You know, I've never seen that. Perhaps.' Then after a short silence, he asks a little edgily, 'Ah…can I talk to you about something?'

This might be the reason they have separated themselves from the other guests.

'Of course,' says Paige, her voice warm but also a little tense.

'Shao's proposal that I write for him made me furious.'

Is Hudson about to reveal something? In an attempt to move even closer, your boot slips in the sludge and one knee slams into the muddy ground before you can steady yourself. Ouch! You freeze in place, hoping they haven't heard you, while bone-numbingly cold water soaks into your pant leg. Thankfully there is so much white noise from the windswept garden that their conversation continues.

'And rightfully so,' says Paige. 'You're an accomplished author and a walking nature encyclopaedia. You had every right to object.'

The strained expression leaves Hudson's face as his chest puffs from the praise. 'I've spent thousands of hours on this island doing conservation work, hiking and researching fabulous locations for my novels. Anything at all you want to know about the Tasmanian wilderness, I'm your man.'

'I suppose that's how you are able to describe the settings in your books so vividly,' Paige says. 'Have you chosen one for your next story yet?'

'Yes, I have. In fact, it's just a few minutes back up the river on the Egg Islands near Franklin. Did you notice them when you came in? There's so much history in that area, and a nice, secluded patch of forest for the murderer in my story to hide dead bodies where they likely won't be disturbed.'

'Dead bodies? I'll...take a look when we finally get out of here.'

'I'm sorry.' Hudson's tone is filled with regret. 'I shouldn't have brought up dead bodies at a time like this. That was thoughtless of me, even though he was, I mean–'

'It's okay Hudson. Thank you for considering my feelings.' You hear profound sadness in her voice. 'Shao was the person I spent the most time with over the past thirty years, so this weekend has obviously been a shock. But as you saw yesterday, he wasn't the best of men.'

'Last night,' Hudson says after a moment, 'he told me something, about you.'

'Yes?'

'He said you wouldn't be around anymore. I'm sorry if you didn't know he was going to fire you. Not that it makes any difference now, but did you know?'

'I'd already tendered my resignation, so to speak, so yes, I knew.'

You hear the conflict in her voice and wonder if she's going to reveal why.

'What are you going to do next?' he asks.

'Actually, I've decided to help new writers through those first few difficult years of their careers.'

Of course, you already know she's decided to help one young writer in particular.

'That'd be marvellous, for anyone who could afford it.'

'Oh, I think there could be a special discount for someone who knows their native daisy bushes as well as you do.'

Why is there a lump in your throat? You shake your head, maintaining focus on the investigation and ignoring the cramp threatening to develop in your calf. You can't afford to move and give yourself away.

'Perhaps when all this is sorted out we can talk?' Hudson says.

'Definitely,' says Paige.

You hear the catch in her voice and wonder if Hudson does too. The sky dulls as a heavy cloud covers the sun and a sudden blast of icy wind carries with it a hint of more rain. You start to shiver.

'It's freezing out here,' Paige says.

Suddenly, the pair starts moving in your direction. You know you're about to be discovered, so you stand and, stiff from crouching, do your best to meander casually a few steps in their direction before stopping in apparent surprise. 'Oh, hello,' you greet them.

'We've been admiring the gardens,' Paige says. 'Hudson has a fabulous knowledge of all things flora and fauna, did you know that? There's a lovely daisy bush he's identified for me,' she continues without giving you a chance to speak, 'but it's starting to drizzle so we're heading back in. Would you care to join us?'

Hudson's gaze locks on your muddy knee before moving to the

scuffed area you left in the mud where you'd been hiding. His expression darkens. A shot of anxiety twists in your stomach. He knows what I was up to, you think to yourself, but with little choice, you press on anyway. 'Actually, I'm hoping to have a quick word with Hudson.'

'Once we're inside,' Hudson says, moving briskly away up the path toward the homestead. 'I need to dry off,' he calls over his shoulder, his tone as cold as the wind, 'and it looks like you do too.'

You return to your room, rattled at being discovered and potentially losing the trust you had been building with one of your suspects. If Hudson is guilty, have you lost your chance to dig a confession out of him? You need to resolve this, fast.

You change into a dry set of clothes and tidy yourself up before heading to the sitting room. Paige is already seated on the sofa nearest the fireplace, the small fire still crackling. On the coffee table there is a steaming percolator, three cups, and a china plate laden with rounds of shortbread and gingersnap biscuits.

'Hello again,' she greets you. 'I'm sure Hudson won't be long.'

'Sounds like you two had a good chat?'

She beams. 'Yes, thank you.'

You share a smile but your analytical mind is racing. You can't begin to fathom the conflicting emotions she must be feeling today, yet her exterior calm has barely wavered. You silently take note of that in the context of your investigation.

'How about a biscuit?' She offers you the plate of shortbreads and more dentally challenging varieties.

'I won't, but thank you.'

'Well, I'll have another. Shao was a pilfering demon when it came to anything sweet: I never got to have any around him.' She bites into a cream-filled biscuit with apparent delight.

'So you might work with Hudson in the future? As his editor?' you ask.

'I hope so,' she says as Hudson appears in the doorway. 'Ah, speak of the devil. Milk and two sugars, correct?'

'Thanks.' He sits on the sofa next to Paige and props one ankle over the opposite knee. 'You were talking about me?'

'General chitchat,' says Paige.

Hudson raises an eyebrow at you, his face otherwise a calm mask. 'So, what would you like to know? Oh, thanks,' he adds when Paige slides a mug and the plate of biscuits in his direction.

You flip open your notebook and glance at your H.V.D. page. 'You said earlier that you went into the library at about ten past nine, at Shao's invitation?'

He nods. 'It was supposed to be at nine, but when I got there the door was shut. I could hear him inside arguing with Jasmine.' He pauses to sip from his cup. 'I waited in the corridor for a while, not sure whether to interrupt. Eventually I thought I'd better go in because Jasmine was sounding more and more upset, so I knocked on the door. That's when she burst out.'

'Did you notice if she was limping at that stage?'

Hudson's brow furrows. 'No, come to think of it.'

'So you went in? Where was Shao?'

Hudson picks up a shortbread, lets it hover in mid-air. 'At his desk, red-faced and looking furious. I offered to come back later but he waved me into a seat off to the side. It was awkward to begin with, but then we started talking books and everything settled down.'

You glance at your notebook again. 'But you said that the conversation turned?'

He waves the biscuit up and down. 'Before yesterday, Shao was one of my heroes. I lived for the Carl Kuphem books.'

Paige groans, then turns it into a small cough.

'I assumed he would have my best interests at heart.' Hudson's expression turns bitter. 'Instead, he insulted me and all but ordered me to write his books for him.' He bites the shortbread with a little snarl.

'And you said?'

Hudson's eyes flash with fury as he swallows. 'As I told you, and as I told him, I refused.'

'And how did Shao take that?' Paige asks.

Hudson laughs humourlessly. 'He told me I was an idiot to turn down such an amazing opportunity. That I should be thrilled. That coming from this backwater corner of the world I couldn't make it without his help.'

Paige squeezes his arm. 'Of course you can.'

'And then?'

'We argued for a bit.'

'About what exactly? The more detail you can give me the better.'

'Well, I was f…,' he glances at Paige, 'bloody furious at that point so I shouted at him, called him a stinking big-islander, said he had no right to come here and tell me or anyone else what to do.'

Despite the tense turn of the conversation, Paige chortles then shakes her head. 'Sorry, it's just that term big-islander. It was a shock the first time someone called me that, having grown up here.'

You nod in understanding. A Tasmanian epithet for those from continental Australia, 'big-islander' had been thrown at you more than once. Some locals use 'mainlander', but big-islander could be very rude indeed, especially since big rhymes with pig.

'My whole life I've been told what I am and what I'm not,' Hudson says. 'My family's only been here two generations – I'm the third – so we're not fully accepted as locals. People here say writing is for sissies, but then turn around and tell you not to leave the island.' Hudson appears to be struggling with his emotions and Paige puts a comforting hand on his arm again. 'And everyone who's not from here tells me I'm not good enough for the outside world either. Then along comes my hero, the reason I began to write, and he puts me down too. I'd had it.'

You feel as though you understand Hudson more fully now: an innate writing talent hoping to win international success, yet simultaneously shunned and discouraged by both his own community and those he wants to join. Add in his former hero Shao T. Mann's insulting but also threatening offer and you can understand his furious response.

'Surely your parents didn't discourage you?' Paige asks.

'No, but the kids at school and their parents did. And even a few of the teachers. They said it was pie-in-the-sky.'

Paige sighs. 'It's one of the reasons I'm glad I left to go to uni in Sydney – to escape that pressure, especially as a girl.'

Hudson's eyes widen. 'I didn't think of that. School here must have been so much worse for you.'

She smiles and breathes out heavily through her nose. 'I don't think I could ever explain how hard it was.'

Hudson seems calmer, more centred. 'Now I feel a bit silly about how I reacted when Shao made that offer. I could have just said no and walked out.'

'But…' you prompt.

'But I was mad, so I yelled at him. Quite a bit. Then he seemed frustrated, said he needed a break to think and walked out.'

'For how long?'

'Just a minute or two. But he started in with the manipulation again as soon as he got back. It was so insulting. I reminded him I was an award-winning writer and I didn't need his guidance to write good books, and definitely not books he put his name on.' Animated by the recollection, Hudson snatches another biscuit and snaps it violently in half.

'How did he respond?'

'He made out I was an idiot. He said there were thousands of authors who'd jump at the chance, so I suggested he should go find one because as far as I was concerned, he could stuff his offer up,' he glances at Paige again, 'um, where the sun doesn't shine, and that he'd be lucky if I didn't tell everyone what a fraud he was. And that was that. That's all I can tell you, I'm afraid.'

You glance at your notebook again. 'Just a few more questions. While you were there, arguing with Shao, what did you see?'

'What do you mean?' he asks. He seems confused by the new line of questioning.

'Would you mind describing everything you remember seeing on the desk and around it?'

'Huh? I don't know. Piles and boxes of *High Time* everywhere. That wonderful old Olivetti typewriter. Why?'

'Did anything in the library look different to when we were all in there for the tour?'

'Like what?'

'Did you notice where the convict ball and chain sat?'

Hudson's brow furrows and he slowly shakes his head. 'Still on the shelf where you put it back at the end of the tour, I think, but I couldn't swear to it.'

'If it had fallen, what would it have hit?'

He shrugs. 'The typewriter? Shao?'

Ah. That was quite telling. 'And the vintage book with green-edged pages from the museum?'

'I don't remember seeing that.'

You glance at Paige, then back to Hudson. 'Did you see a red fountain pen?'

'I don't think so.'

'What about a plastic bag? It may have looked empty.'

Hudson shakes his head. 'I don't know. Honestly, why would I remember details like that?' He shifts in his seat looking like he's just about at the end of his rope.

'We're almost done,' you tell him. 'Just a couple of final questions. Did you take anything into the library with you?'

'No.'

'Did you touch anything while you were in there?'

'I don't think I did.'

'Did you take anything with you when you left?'

'Er ... What?'

'Did you take anything when you left?' you repeat, noting Hudson's sudden discomfort. You wait until you have his eyes back on yours. Decades of experience have made you expert at detecting lies through the eyes. 'A copy of *High Time,* perhaps?'

His eyes flick quickly away from yours. You can tell his mind is racing, searching desperately for a plausible answer that isn't a lie.

Your attention is broken by a snicker as Bruce moves into the sitting room to pick up a biscuit.

'I'm sorry,' he says, falling onto the sofa beside you with a wicked chuckle, 'but I overheard the last bit of that, and I can't imagine Hudson bothering to nick an autographed copy of the new release.' He laughs. 'Maybe now you all understand what I've been dealing with all these years.'

You ignore the distraction. 'Well?' you press, your gaze back on Hudson.

'I really don't remember.' Hudson replaces his mug on the coffee table, and you wonder if it hit the surface a little harder than necessary. Then he pushes to his feet and flashes a weak smile around the group. 'I think I'll take a quick walk. I need to clear my head.'

Well, that had been an interesting, if somewhat disappointing, chat. You settle in a chair on the wrap around verandah outside your bedroom once more, notebook and pen in hand. You pause to watch a flock of noisy black cockatoos fly overhead, chased away by ravens, then begin updating your observations on the complex, likeable and possibly very guilty Hudson van Daemon.

Where to next?

Choose from options 1, 2 or 3.

1. Read on to Chapter 16, *Tea Leaves* by Maggie Veness, to ask Paige what happened at 9.20 pm.
2. If you need to know more about Hudson's night, skip to Chapter 20, *A Dark and Stormy Night* by Craig Cormick.
3. Do you think you've solved the mystery of Shao's death? Go to page 213 to find a hidden chapter with the answer.

CHAPTER SIXTEEN

Tea Leaves

Maggie Veness

In which you question Shao T. Mann's editor, Paige Hybrough, on her movements at 9.20 pm last night.

YOU TAKE A SEAT AT THE LONG KITCHEN TABLE, THE RICH HUON PINE boards almost glowing against the black-and-white chequerboard floor. You place an old-fashioned first-aid box that you found under the laundry tub in front of you. It's not the most obvious of places to store it, but you're used to the unusual.

Moments ago, when everyone else was safely in the sitting room, you'd scoured the kitchen cupboards, pantry and laundry for anything Paige might have used as a poison in the cup of tea she offered Shao in the library last night. As a teenage wannabe cop, the movie *Arsenic and Old Lace* had taught you the process of elimination: always investigate the obvious before you rule it out. You'd found nothing.

The once white plastic case of the first-aid kit has yellowed. It has a faded red cross on the lid. Releasing the snap-lock, you search the contents. Again, nothing you can imagine being used to harm another person, unless they tourniqued or bandaged a body part too tightly. But there is a ten-sheet of paracetamol with six tablets remaining, which you figure Paige will appreciate.

The kitchen is almost eerily quiet. You take the opportunity to pull out your notepad and pen and review your thought process so far.

You have a lot of question marks against Paige's name. On meeting her yesterday your first impression was that of a well-spoken, well-groomed, smartly dressed woman. Wearing a pale yellow trouser suit over a white silk blouse, she could have passed as a high-profile business executive.

During that first meeting she had been quite withdrawn – though became more relaxed as the evening went on – and was then almost happy this morning as she worked alongside you and Hudson to get the isolated homestead up and running. Did her mood change fit her circumstances? It seemed incongruous that she was so positive given her partner of thirty years lay dead just a few rooms away, but you knew the reason was Hudson.

What have you learned about Paige's relationship with Shao?

First: he owed his success to her.

Second: although she had loved him for thirty-odd years, he had not returned her love and she had finally committed to moving on by killing off Carl Kuphem.

Third: he was an awful human being, by which you mean it's a mystery as to how and why she maintained their arrangement for so long.

As you ponder this, Paige wanders into the kitchen, headed for the stove.

'Look what I found,' you say, indicating the sheet of paracetamol on the table.

'Thank you.' She snatches it off the table, removes a glass from the cupboard and half-fills it with water from the sink. She then takes a seat opposite you and downs three tablets, grimacing as she swallows them then shudders slightly.

'I'm glad to have a break from the others,' she says. 'The way Jasmine is sniffling, for goodness' sake. Not an actual tear in sight. She and her loud American drawl and big, silly hair – all show, that woman.'

Everyone grieves in their own way, you remind yourself. Paige is dry-eyed in sharp contrast to Jasmine, but that doesn't mean she's guilty of anything. Not necessarily, anyway.

On the wall opposite you hang several photos of this grand old homestead – dating back to the early 1900s, you think – and a portrait of the original owners. The master wears braces and a bushy beard, his wife a full-length dress cinched in at the waist. It is a touch surreal to be interviewing suspects in a possible homicide in their home over a century later.

You proceed cautiously. 'People react to shock in many different ways. I've seen people go mute for hours, and others laugh hysterically. Some collapse to the ground kicking and wailing. Yet others sprint away in random directions, their fight-or-flight response taking over, perhaps trying to escape the terrible news.'

'I suppose you've seen it all. How long were you a detective?'

'Decades. Perhaps too long. I joined the Force straight out of school, worked my way up, developed a special interest in forensics and eventually made detective. How about you, Paige? For Kuphem to have sold so well from the very first one, where do you think your talent came from?'

'Maybe it was a childhood spent with my head in a book?'

'You certainly have the knack for it. You built Shao into one of the most famous modern Australian authors. When news of his passing gets out his fans will be devastated.'

'They would have been devastated anyway,' Paige says.

'Because of the plot of *High Time*?' you ask. 'That was a huge decision you made.'

Paige sighs. 'Even before I decided to kill off Kuphem, it was all coming to an end anyway.'

'What was?'

'Shao's and my relationship, the book series. I'd seen it coming for a few years. Our fights were longer and more bitter; my enthusiasm for working on the series was all but gone. He resented relying on me, I think, and I resented him for many things.'

She lets out a small whoop. 'I resented him. There, I've said it.' She laughs as tears well at the corners of her eyes. She wipes them away with her sleeve. The back of her hand is still covered with red ink, the writing so smudged and faded that it's illegible.

'Paige,' you say gently, 'what happened last night?'

Her chin quivers, tears threatening to spill.

Bruce stumbles into the kitchen, head down. He fumbles in the pantry, swearing under his breath, then grabs a can of soft drink from the fridge before returning to the sitting room without acknowledging either of you.

Paige has recollected herself during the brief Bruce interlude. Her pinched expression from moments ago has softened.

You plunge straight in. 'You said earlier that Shao would steal things from you?'

Placing her elbows on the table, Paige leans her chin on her interlocked fingers and clenches her jaw. 'We went to an expensive restaurant last year. He left with the pepper mill from the table in his pocket. At a recent book signing I watched him hide a lovely gold pen belonging to a fan under a pile of papers, then take it with him when he left. And there are many rare old books in his personal library that I doubt he paid for.'

'Did he do the same with bank accounts?'

She shakes her head. 'Not that I know of. It was always sleight-of-hand. He was surrounded by wealth, always had access to money, but took things.'

'What else?'

She purses her mouth sadly. 'A pocket diary. Nail scissors. A chocolate bar from my handbag – he had a really sweet tooth.'

'Did you ever confront him about it?'

'Yes, but he'd always deny it, even with the chocolate still in his mouth.'

You notice that her knuckles have turned white. She has also begun to loudly tap a shoe on the floor. Paige Hybrough is furious, sitting on decades of accumulated anger. How you wish you were back in police headquarters videoing this – body language is just as important as words. Did it come to the surface last night and result in her harming Shao physically?

You're interrupted again when the heavy front door bangs shut. You both look over to the window and see the top of Hudson's head as he walks by.

'He has a great future in the industry,' she says, her voice soft and warm once more, 'so long as he continues to write.'

You both watch his back as he walks away across the lawn. 'Do you think he might stop?'

Paige grows serious. 'The career of a budding author is fragile. They start out enthusiastic, but perhaps their second or third novel doesn't sell well and they're dropped by their publisher. A writer with fabulous potential can believe they aren't good enough and give up, when it was actually down to poor marketing. With the right guidance and support they can weather the ups and downs and continue on.'

'And you would like to be that support for him?'

'Yes,' she says emphatically. 'I definitely would.'

'Forgive me,' you say, 'but with your talent and expertise couldn't you make your own way? Aren't you just substituting service to one man for service to another? Why not claim your rightful place as the author of one of the most successful series in history?'

'It was never about that for me. I love to write, I don't need the accolades.' She shrugs. 'Besides, it wouldn't be the same. Hudson showed me a fresh carpet of miniature purple orchids around the back of the mansion earlier.'

'I don't follow?'

'In thirty years Shao never once showed me flowers.' She takes a deep breath. 'What I said earlier – that my and Shao's relationship was ending – I didn't mean that lightly. I expected that this weekend might be the last time we ever spoke.'

'That seems extreme.'

'Shao…he…' She sighs. 'If you weren't serving a purpose to him he would cut you off, walk away and never speak to you again. I knew that was possible once he realised I'd killed off Kuphem.'

Paige Hybrough had, in a sense, expected Shao T. Mann to die this weekend, or at least for her to figuratively be dead to him. Was that why she seemed pensive when you first met last night? Was she already grieving the impending loss of the central figure in her life, even though he was a toxic narcissist?

'You must have had a stressful year,' you say sympathetically.

She harrumphs. 'I've had a lot of headaches.'

You give her a few moments, then lean in toward her a little. 'Sorry to ask this again, but what exactly did you see when you went to the library last night? You said Shao was re-entering the room himself?'

Her eyes flick upward, a sign she's scanning her memory. 'I was walking down the hallway and glimpsed Shao entering the library. Hudson was already in there – I heard their voices once Shao went in.'

'Then?'

'I paused outside the library, heard Shao try to trap Hudson into writing his books and then,' she speaks as though in a trance, 'there was this screaming white noise in my head. I wasn't taking much in when Hudson passed me on his way out.'

'What was Shao doing when you entered? Where was he in the room?'

'Sitting at the desk, back to me. He was putting something down, maybe? I'm not sure what.'

'You had your handbag with you?'

'Yes.'

'Anything else?'

'No.'

'And then?'

'I told him I heard what he said to Hudson – that he wanted to make him his new ghostwriter – and I told him it wasn't going to happen,' she swallows, 'that I would stop it from happening.'

If Hudson had accepted Shao's offer it would have thwarted her plans to be Hudson's mentor before she even had a chance to suggest it to him.

'How did Shao respond?'

She frowns. 'He was remote – cold, even. He said it was clear to him that I had decided to end our arrangement, and he was moving on. It was no longer my business what he did, and he'd thank me to leave him alone.'

'That seems, aah, much calmer than you'd expect, given the circumstances.'

You know Shao had only discovered Paige's betrayal a few minutes earlier – or had he? Had he known for some time and been playing his own game? Was his surprise at Jasmine's revelation that Kuphem was being killed off genuine?

'After that all he said was that he didn't feel well, and asked me to make him a cup of tea.'

A thought strikes you, sharp as a razor blade. 'If your relationship was ending, why did you make it for him?'

'My heart was pounding against my ribs, my ears were ringing. I needed to calm down. My hands were shaking so much in the kitchen that it took three tries to get a spoonful of sugar into the cup.'

'But you were calmer when you returned to the library?'

'I thought so, but I saw red again as soon as I walked in,' she says. 'I told him his offer to Hudson was cruel. But he just…'

You can see how hurt she was, that despite her plan to leave Shao she had still hoped he might treat her with a shred of decency.

'How long did you spend alone with Shao in the library?'

'Not long. Perhaps ten minutes, minus the time it took to make his tea – so four or five in total? Less?'

Experience tells you that a minute, thirty seconds even, is more than enough where foul play is concerned.

A scenario is forming in your mind that might explain some of the incongruous items in the library, though it is somewhat convoluted. 'Indulge me?'

She looks at you with a mixture of interest and frustration. 'All right.'

'You had your handbag with you when you went into the library?'

'Yes, as I said.'

'Did you take it with you when you went to the kitchen?'

'We've been over this, no.'

'Please,' you say, holding out both hands, 'this is my process. There is a reason behind my repetition.'

'Oh,' she smiles faintly. 'That I understand. No, I didn't take the handbag with me to the kitchen.'

'And to your knowledge,' you continue, 'the handbag you left in the library contained your red pen and your plastic bag of gummy bears, in their usual compartments.'

'Yes.'

'No ants, I suppose?'

'What?'

'Never mind. And you assumed your pen and bears were still in the handbag when you left the library to return to your room.'

She nods. 'Of course.'

'Then you?'

'Took the cup and saucer back to the kitchen, and my handbag to my room. Why?'

Not only was Paige in the kitchen on her own for about five minutes sometime between 9.20 pm and 9.30 pm last night, but Shao T. Mann was in the library on his own for those same few minutes. Alone, with Paige's handbag.

Could Shao have requested the tea in order to get Paige out of the room so he could do something? Steal the gummies from her handbag, perhaps? No… It all kept coming back to that pen. What if he wasn't after the gummies but the pen?

He sent her out to make him a cuppa, to buy time to pilfer her pen, took the gummies because he happened to see them… No, that wasn't quite right either.

What about this? He took the plastic bag – which happened to have gummies in it – and used it to protect his fingers from arsenic as he rubbed the pen on the poisonous page-edges of the vintage book he stole from the museum. Then he returned the pen to the handbag, but into the wrong compartment, and hid the bag of gummies from sight.

Then Paige returned, he drank his tea in silence, she left, he threw the plastic bag on the desk as Bruce came in and… No, that still didn't add up.

If Shao put Paige's pen back in her handbag, how did it end up on the desk in the library sometime between 9.30 pm and 10 pm? If you could narrow down when, perhaps that would tell you who had placed it there, though a suspicion has formed in your mind.

And where were the bears? Paige said they weren't sweet, so unlikely to please Shao's tastebuds.

'This is too much,' Paige says, breaking your concentration. She scrapes her wooden chair backwards on the black and white tiles. 'I need a break.'

'Please tell me one more thing?'

'Sure.'

'Exactly where was Shao when you left the library?'

She closes her eyes in concentration. 'Sitting at the desk, sulking or whatever it was he was doing, ignoring me.'

'Did he say anything when you picked up your handbag and the cup and saucer to leave?'

'Nothing.' And with that, Paige stands and disappears through the doorway to the sitting room.

You groan inwardly. You can feel the solution to this puzzle almost in your grasp. It is simple, you sense it, but it slips away every time you try to complete the picture.

You know Paige Hybrough had decided almost a year ago to end her working and personal relationship with her…employer? Former lover? Both.

And you know the matter had come to a head last night in the library, but wasn't resolved, nor even properly discussed.

And according to Bruce, Shao was still moving, still being his rude, obstinate self long after Paige last saw him.

So how did Paige's decision months ago to end her involvement with Shao lead to his death last night?

Logically, you know it should be a factor, but is it even related? Or did Shao die of natural causes as Bruce keeps suggesting, and the bizarre scene in the library this morning was nothing but a fluke?

You groan again. This is turning into a frustratingly complex case.

Where to next?

Choose from options 1, 2 or 3.

1. Read on to Chapter 17, *Hazy Recollection* by Jo Dixon, to find out what happened between Bruce and Shao in the library at 9.30 pm.
2. If you want to know more about the gummy bear in the plastic bag, jump back to Chapter 7, *Bear Attack* by Karen Brooks.
3. Do you think you've solved the mystery of Shao's death? Go to page 213 to find a hidden chapter with the answer.

CHAPTER SEVENTEEN

Hazy Recollection

Jo Dixon

In which you question Shao T. Mann's rival, Bruce Tossington-Smythe, on his movements at 9.30 pm last night.

YOU STAND ALONE IN THE MIDDLE OF THE FOYER ONCE MORE, WONDERING where the other guests have taken themselves. It is showering again and the drumming on the roof muffles any noise within the building. Last night these rooms were glowing with free-flowing wine and verbal jousting. Today, there is silence, the house heavy with sadness, recrimination and regret.

The guests have scurried away into corners, or are hiding in their rooms, but you have more questions for Bruce. You need to pin down when particular items entered the library last night. You saw the ball and chain above the library desk yourself when you went in to speak, briefly and uncomfortably, with Shao. It was already there, along with Shao's Olivetti typewriter and piles of boxes of books to sign. When, though, did the pen, mutilated book and ants join the typewriter on the desk? And when and how did the books and ball and chain end up on the floor along with Shao?

Bruce seems pivotal in putting the chain of events together – a man plagued by the failure to reach his own expectations, who ensures others suffer for it. His constant picking at Shao, who bit right back, seems to have been the bane of a number of lives for many years.

Had Shao pushed Bruce too far last night? And had Bruce retaliated, killing him in the process? More than ever, you need to confirm a timeline for Bruce's movements after last night's meal.

To find Bruce you head to the sitting room first. The row of tealights has expired and the fire is low. Despite the tall windows, the room is dim and quiet. It is only as you're about to leave that you notice someone is there. Tucked into one of the large armchairs, a guest is staring out the window. They are silent and still and appear not to have noticed your arrival.

'Hello,' you say, as you walk further into the room.

Paige Hybrough turns her head toward you. 'Oh, it's you.'

She appears as immaculate as she did last night, her flustered moments earlier in the day now smoothed over. Her eyes meet yours, though, and you notice a deep crease between her brows.

'I'm looking for Bruce; do you know where he's gone?'

She doesn't immediately reply, her gaze shifting back to the view out the window. 'Did you know the world's tallest blue gum is in the Huon Valley?'

It's an interesting fact but not at all helpful. 'No, I didn't know that.'

'I thought I'd go and see this wondrous ancient tree. But I now know it's not an easy venture. Needless to say, I did not come prepared for hiking deep into the bush. Perhaps on another trip…' Her voice trails off into silence.

She seems distracted, a little disorientated. You think you would be too if so many foundations of your life had shifted in such a short time.

You pause for a moment, then ask again. 'Do you know where Bruce might be?'

Her intelligent eyes consider you for a bit, that crease deepening further. Then she gives a small nod. 'Yes, but please don't press him too hard. Like Shao, he may not be the best of men, but he usually means well.' She raises a hand and points vaguely out of the sitting room. 'He went in search of something to settle his stomach. He's always hungry when he's hungover.' She smiles a wan smile. 'Some things never change.'

You check next door, in the high-ceilinged dining room. The fire Hudson lit some hours ago has died down and the chandeliers are dark, but the room is warm from the radiator, and soft light enters the room in fingers through the sash windows.

No one is sitting at the long table. There is, however, a perfectly laid setting for one. The placemat, cutlery and napkin are positioned at the head of the table at the far end. The door through to the kitchen is ajar and food preparation noises echo through the opening. The clink of glass and the clatter of plates is followed by the sound of something solid hitting the floor. Then a grunt and chuckle.

You stand quietly under the door lintel and watch as Bruce tries to rescue a side of baked ham from the floor. 'I'm not too sure wiping that with the tea towel is ideal,' you say.

'Bloody hell, you scared me,' he says, putting the greasy cloth to his chest, wiping it against his scarf. The black-and-white stripes are now splotched and stained with various morsels of food.

He uses the tea towel to pat the meat where it is now sitting on the bench. 'What are you doing sneaking around? And don't look at me like that. I'm helping myself to a bit of protein. The events of the morning have been devastating. The shock has left me peckish. I need to replenish.' He neatly folds the tea towel and re-hangs it on the rail, but leaves the ham where it is.

You make a note to only eat bread and cheese at lunch, and to discard the towel at the first opportunity, and certainly before anyone uses it to dry the dishes. Slightly raised eyebrows is your only response.

Bruce picks up a plate laden with heavy slices of pale meat, and some dabs of what looks like hot English mustard, and moves past you to take his seat at the table. The tragic demise of his rival has not diminished his appetite. You follow and sit to one side. You angle your chair so you are facing him, to watch his face while you talk. Often people say more with their expressions than they do with words.

'What?' he asks between bites. 'If you want some, you'll have to cut it yourself.'

'Thanks, but I'm fine.' There is a tall sash window directly behind him, and you can see the rain has eased to a drizzle. The view through to the gardens and the bush beyond is mesmerising, the blue gums standing tall but wreathed in soft mist. Unfortunately, you can't think about nature right now. You return your focus to the writer. 'I want to clarify something you said earlier, about last night.'

He pauses, his fork in mid-air. 'What about it?' he says before taking the bite.

You keep your voice neutral. 'You said earlier that you went to the library to speak to Shao around half past nine.'

Shrewd eyes consider you for a second before Bruce returns to his plate. He deftly cuts another chunk of ham, adds a knife-end of mustard, and lifts it to his mouth. 'I did, yes.'

'And you wanted to see him about?'

Bruce shovels two more mouthfuls between his teeth, before he sets down the fork. He picks up the napkin he'd laid out earlier and wipes his face and fingers. 'I already told you, I wanted to see Mann – my old friend and constant rival – to smooth things over. I wanted us to be on somewhat friendlier terms before we presented ourselves to the astute members of the festival audience. There's no need for us to go at each other directly in a public forum. We are both professionals.' He pauses and pats his lips again with his napkin. 'I guess I should rephrase that. We were both professionals.'

None of this accords with what you know of Bruce and his behaviour, or what you discussed with him earlier. Bruce is a changeable man, irritable and aggressive at times, who sought conflict to help promote his books. He's rewriting history as he goes, you realise, casting himself as some kind of long-suffering hero as he tinkers with his memories of last night. It is easy to see why his five spouses called it quits – how do you deal with someone who refuses to acknowledge the reality of their actions?

He yawns, his shoulders rising and falling as he sighs deeply. He puts the napkin on the table and adjusts his scarf. 'I am going to miss him, you know,' he says. 'I've been angry with him for so long. But I did have hope that one day we might lay down the animosity and be less combative. Now, we'll never have that chance.'

His sentiment might seem genuine to some, but you've been closely observing Mr Tossington-Smythe for almost eighteen hours now and can recognise his theatrics for what they are.

Then he continues. 'What is perhaps hardest to bear is one day I really wanted to hear him acknowledge the value of my work.' And there it is. 'Now that will never happen.' He meets your gaze, then picks up a glass of water and takes several slow sips.

'Tell me, was Shao receptive to this idea? Was he prepared to accept a ceasefire?'

Bruce closes his eyes for a moment. He swills the water around in his mouth and swallows. 'No. He was not. He was not receptive at all.'

You wait until Bruce opens his eyes and resumes eating. 'He disagreed with your suggestion?' you ask, prompting him to continue talking.

Bruce finishes his 'snack'. Smacking his lips, he leans back in his chair. He takes his time, as though structuring his response before speaking. 'He didn't disagree as such, he barely acknowledged me.' Bitterness hangs off every word. 'You know what, Detective? The great Shao T. Mann enjoyed being rude to me. He delighted in throwing out insults and disparaging my accomplishments. You saw that, didn't you? At dinner?'

Bruce glares in your direction and you give a small nod. From your point of view, they both did.

'I wanted to be the better man. Divorce number five changes you.' He guffaws at his own dismal joke. 'I had decided to play humble, see if I could get things back on an even keel with him. I suggested it was not in his best interests to be seen as nasty and vengeful. But he wouldn't even turn around to face me. He just sat there in silence, head resting on the palm of one hand, elbow on the table, practically ignored me.'

'I imagine that would have been infuriating.'

'It certainly was.' He laces his fingers together and rests them over his stomach. 'I did get a little angry.'

'You raised your voice?' you suggest.

He drops his chin to his chest, jowls spilling over the collar of his shirt, then raises a hand in a gesture of acknowledgement. 'Yes. I may have shouted. I'm not proud of myself. I want you to understand that I'm not usually a man of aggression.' He peers up at you without lifting his head and lowers his hand again. 'But honestly, that man was utterly selfish and self-centred. The most he deigned to do was grunt at me, as though I was not even worthy of speech. Grunted like a pig. He couldn't even bother answering me with words. So, yes, I raised my voice. I wanted more than a grunt of acknowledgement.'

Had Bruce become angry enough in his inebriated state to physically lash out? Or had Shao still been alive, unharmed, when Bruce returned to his room?

'What time was this?'

'I've already told you. My heart pill alarm went off at nine twenty-five, as it always does. I took it, then went to the library.' He reaches for his drink and drains the last drop. Holding the empty glass high he says, 'It's easy to get caught up in what I'm doing, and those pills are all-important.'

You refrain from pointing out that sobriety would also be beneficial to his health. 'When you entered the library, where was Shao?'

'As I've told you repeatedly, sitting at the desk. He must've pushed it closer to the wall so he could plug his stupid electric typewriter into a socket. He was hard-up against one of the bookshelves.'

This description tallies with what you observed last night and this morning. 'Did you notice anything out of the ordinary while you were talking to him?'

Bruce lets out a short bark of laughter. 'Out of the ordinary?' He chuckles without humour. 'No. Not at all. The desk was crowded with piles of his own books. Towers of them, which, let me tell you, was perfectly normal. He liked to wallow in his own glory, all those paperbacks with their glossy, expensive covers. He lived to see his name in huge print on the front of them, and the words *bestselling author* and *a million copies sold*.' He shakes his head a little, the anger seeming to seep away.

You don't see the problem with that, per se. What writer wouldn't want to be in that position?

This morning those books were spread across the floor. Some had fallen on Shao's body, which would suggest they tumbled after Shao had collapsed, had landed on him with force after being thrown, or were deliberately placed to appear that way. But other items had remained on the desk.

'Can you recollect what else was on the desk, besides the typewriter and books?'

Bruce narrows his eyes and stares into the distance, apparently attempting to remember the scene. 'There was an old book,' he says at last. 'I remember thinking he must have nicked it from the history display in the museum. But that's all. I was focused on trying to make my point and to elicit a response.'

'Thank you, that's helpful–'

'Rubbish,' he adds, with great enthusiasm. 'There was some rubbish, a small plastic bag Mann threw on the desk when I first went in.' He looks pleased with himself now, as though delighted by his ability to recall such a small detail.

'No other writing implements?'

'Not that I saw.'

'That's helpful, thank you,' you say. 'One more thing: how long were you in the library, do you think?'

'Not long at all. I quickly realised that I was wasting my time. No amount of reasoned words – or angry ones, for that matter – were going to help. Mann just sat there in silence, head in one hand, elbow on the table, staring ahead.'

'Ten minutes?'

'Not even that. I would think it was less than five.'

'Can anyone corroborate that?'

'I should think so. The two women, Paige and Fishwife Jasmine, were loitering in the hallway. Probably eavesdropping. I'm sure they heard the whole thing. Look,' he says with a roll of his eyes, 'I know you're pursuing the idea that someone did Mann harm, and that it was most likely me. I'm telling you, he died of natural causes. Now, if you don't mind, I'm going to have more ham.'

You don't think it was natural causes, even though you haven't determined exactly how Shao died, but you leave him to his indulgences and return to the foyer.

If what Bruce said is true, Shao was still alive at around 9.35 pm, sitting in his chair, with the ball and chain still on the bookshelf and the piles of books still on the desk, and the stacked boxes still upright. You're narrowing down the exact time the plastic bag and antique book appeared on the desk, and therefore who left them there. By the same token, you're building a picture of when the red fountain pen and disturbing pile of dead ants appeared.

Time to breathe. You walk into the hallway, open the heavy front door and stand on the top step. A small swamp wallaby emerges from the mist. It stops, turns to look at you for a moment, then bounces away, unconcerned by your presence. It is quiet outside, only the sound of pattering drops falling from trees and gutters to break the silence.

You close your eyes and breathe deeply of the cool, fresh air, letting the information you've gathered swirl through your mind. You've missed this. Missed the methodical accumulation of small details, sifting through them, confirming facts. You've especially missed the satisfaction when those details start to fit together, giving you a sense of what might have taken place. That's what's happening now. Your brain is fitting pieces of the puzzle together, trying different combinations. But you still need more information.

Back to work.

Where to next?

Choose from options 1, 2 or 3.

1. Read on to Chapter 18, *Last Stand* by Narrelle M. Harris, to find out what happened at 9.40 pm.
2. If you need to revisit your first conversation with Paige, turn back to Chapter 3, *Skeleton in the Closet* by Natalie Conyer.
3. Do you think you've solved the mystery of Shao's death? Go to page 213 to find a hidden chapter with the answer.

CHAPTER EIGHTEEN

Last Stand

Narrelle M. Harris

In which you question Shao T. Mann's editor, Paige Hybrough, on her movements at 9.35 pm last night.

You are once more on the verandah outside your room, hands on the railing, thoughts whirling. This quiet space has become a place for you to stop for a moment and think.

The saturated air makes the distant horizon fuzzy. Peering across the manor's gardens and the swollen river that runs by them, you can see that the floods that have trapped everyone here may be worsening rather than retreating. Without mobile phone reception you have no way of knowing. Thank goodness the manor has its own power generator.

You are acutely aware of how alone you are here. The house, and everyone in it, is completely isolated. You are effectively on an island, floating lost in the middle of the Huon Valley.

Do you hope the flooding will recede to allow the actual, active police to arrive and take over the investigation? Or would you prefer it to continue forever? Being in charge of the scene is deeply satisfying; it's the way it used to be. Talking about crime-solving at writers festivals as you do now is enjoyable, but it lacks the stakes of actual crime-solving.

You are alert today in a way that you've missed since you retired. The sleeping tablets knock you out cold at night, but you are rarely refreshed upon waking. Discovering Shao T. Mann's body in the library, on the other hand, has sparked a fire in your belly. Everything about that scene suggests foul play, but none of the individual elements add up.

The chaos of it has stirred all your old instincts. Today you are on the hunt, surrounded by false tracks, muddied clues, and at least one liar. You consider it your duty to explain this crime scene, but also a challenge and a thrill.

Right now your mind is cluttered by everything you've seen. You need to take stock of every loose thread and organise your thoughts to find the gaps in your knowledge, identify conflicts in the evidence, and weave it all into a tapestry.

You take a deep breath, letting cool air and the scents of the gardens fill your lungs. The cider gum trees beside the verandah smell like apple cider, while a native parrot squawks merrily in their branches, beak dipping into leaking sap like a compulsive drunk. Mingled with that fragrance is the honeyed scent of the nearby wattles, along with a pleasant mintiness from a flowering bush in the beds further down the slope.

Listening with eyes closed, the patter of the drops on the plants, the lawn and the bullnose roof over the verandah creates a soothing white noise, making it easier to concentrate.

In your mind's eye, the patterns form: the people in the house move in your imagination to the ticking of a clock. They make a stately dance as last night's crucial minutes tick by. Dinner finished by 8.30 pm; your visit to the library; nine o'clock, ten past, twenty past; onward to ten o'clock and beyond. You consider where the evidence fits in the timeline, what you can deduce, what you can guess at; and all the blanks you have yet to fill.

A muffled sound behind you breaks the spell, bringing your attention back to the present. You hear voices, a disturbance coming from Paige's room.

You step back into the mansion. The old carpet in the hall deadens your footsteps and you can hear Hudson's raised voice down the hallway. He sounds annoyed, as though he's a disappointed teacher delivering a stern lecture to a failing student. The substance of his problem isn't clear, but as Paige's bedroom door opens you hear his final words. 'I can't believe you would defend him. How could you?'

He freezes when he sees you in the hallway. The distress in his eyes changes to alarm. He quickly closes the door and hurries past you down the corridor towards the common rooms on the other side of the foyer.

You knock on Paige's door, and when she makes no sound you open it. You don't even pretend it's to check that she's okay. Rather, you're hoping to catch her in a vulnerable moment, to reveal a piece of missing information that could help complete your investigation.

Paige is sitting on her bed, her face a study in misery. She looks away towards waterdrops spattering against the windowpane.

You enter without a word and let your gaze roam. The house's decorations of driftwood and vases of native plants are the same in every bedroom. So are the old-fashioned pictures of flowers, seascapes and local animals. The prints in Paige's room are a Tasmanian Tiger, a still life of some red apples and, over the fireplace, a landscape of some Huon Valley waterfalls tumbling into a sea of tree ferns.

She still hasn't acknowledged you.

'Why is Hudson upset with you?'

Paige gives a short, bitter laugh. 'My integrity, or as he put it, lack thereof.'

Which of her lifelong secrets has he discovered? 'Did you tell him about your past?'

She shakes her head. 'He came to talk about what Shao said to him last night, and to ask me what I knew.'

Your eyes drift along the mantel above the room's fireplace. An open book about Tasmanian wildlife rests on a table next to it, along with a box of tissues. Paige's glasses sit across the fold of the book, one lens warping the entry about the platypus.

'How did that become a conversation about your integrity?'

'At first Hudson said he felt sorry for me, that he thought Shao was dumping me as his editor without warning.' She swallows. 'But then he wondered if Shao had used a series of young, easily fooled ghostwriters all along, and I had helped him cover it up.'

'Oh,' you say. 'How did you reply?'

'I said that as far as I knew he had only ever done that to one person, but that it wasn't what he thought, that Shao wasn't all bad.' She gulps the air. 'But he didn't let me finish my explanation. I didn't tell him that I was referring to myself. He became angry and left before I could.'

Paige takes a fresh tissue from the box and dabs her red eyes.

You turn your head to give her a moment to collect herself. You notice the door of the room's wardrobe is ajar and Paige's dressing gown hangs inside. On a shelf, a small canvas bag of toiletries is open: a hairbrush, pot of cleansing cream, foundation to match Paige's skin and a lipstick are lined up in order of descending size. A pair of low-heeled black shoes sit beside the wardrobe, and a metal rubbish bin next to them is full of used tissues, some blotted with what looks like mascara.

You notice Paige has only stockings on her feet. The way she is sitting on the bed looking out the window makes her appear both young and fragile.

'Writing is a solitary business but it shouldn't be lonely as well,' she says bleakly into the silence.

'Lonely?'

'Everyone thinks writing a book is just one person and their laptop, but it's not like that at all,' says Paige.

Clearly she expects you to listen to the explanations Hudson refused. In your policing experience, witnesses want to explain and justify themselves. The emerging writer in you also tells you to be quiet, to listen to what might be wisdom from the creator of your favourite crime fiction series. 'It's hard to position more than one person at a keyboard,' you say drily, encouraging her to continue.

'Getting the book down the first time – out of your mind and onto the page – is intense,' she says.

You know this from firsthand experience, how all-encompassing it was for you to write the manuscript that currently sits inside your satchel.

'You're very much alone when you do it,' she says. 'But after that, you need other people. You need feedback, and for someone to help you see where things don't work. It's wonderful when you can brainstorm ideas, or at least have someone listen while you explain the problems you're having with the plot or a character's motivation.' She laughs ruefully. 'Half the time you talk yourself all the way to a solution without the other person saying a word. But it's so helpful that they listen.'

Her laughter fades. 'To begin with, I had that with Shao. For the first few books in the Kuphem series he would at least talk the plot through with me.'

Paige wipes at her eyes again. 'It was meant to be a partnership. We were supposed to work together to make each story better. I need that collaboration, to discuss issues in the manuscript and how to fix them,' she says, frustrated. 'But when Shao stopped caring, I didn't have anyone to work with to find those solutions.'

She's looking outside again. You think she has exhausted her subject, but then she continues. 'When I no longer had that sounding board, I took up walking to help me clarify things. When I worked on drafts I went for long walks to clear my head so that I could see the sticking points from a fresh perspective.'

You recall standing on the verandah a short while ago, emptying your mind to the sounds of nature so that you could re-arrange the evidence. That was your way of gaining a fresh perspective since you don't have your old colleagues to talk through the case with you.

'I'd walk in nature,' she continues, 'and talk to the birds, the trees, the air. Usually, I could talk my way to the solution.'

'Hudson was telling me earlier that he does something quite similar,' you say.

She smiles at the reassuring message in your voice. No matter what Paige or Hudson did last night, you privately hope they can create some kind of relationship in the future. You old softy, you.

'But you didn't come here to talk about the virtues of collaborative editing,' she says wearily, 'nor about how Hudson has lost respect for me.'

You hear a faint sound out in the hall. Paige straightens and listens, so you know you didn't imagine it. You open her door but find no one in the corridor, and every door you can see is closed: Hudson's room to the right, Bruce's room opposite, your own next to it, and the bathroom beyond. Perhaps someone was passing through to one of the common rooms at the other end of the homestead?

You'd rather nobody eavesdropped on your investigation. Secretive listening is part of your own repertoire, but being overheard is not ideal.

'Let's talk in the museum,' you suggest.

'Why not here?'

'I'm hoping for a fresh perspective.'

Paige stares at you. You think she will say no, but then she rises from the bed. She slips her feet into her low-heeled shoes, picks up her glasses and pushes her hair behind her ears. 'All right.'

With their air of hoarding, prissy handwritten tags and general lack of broader context, you never quite know what to make of local museums. A museum tucked away in a historic homestead threatens to be overly focused on its former inhabitants, and you can only fake so much interest in silverware, chamber pots and vintage combs.

Thankfully, as you saw during the tour last night, the display cases here feature fewer stuffed, moth-eaten native animals and discoloured petticoats, and more antique firearms. Some colourful pages from an outrageous diary is a little too much to hope for though, sadly.

Greeting you as you re-enter the rich, red-walled room is a mannequin dressed as a colonial-era policeman standing beside a case bearing the tools of his trade: a thick pair of outdated Darby handcuffs sits beside a Colt Navy revolver in its green-lined box, a pitted wooden baton and the museum's ball and chain set, like the one in the library. They are items with a sorry, brutal past, and speak not only of Tasmania's history as a penal colony, but also the cruel treatment of this land's First Peoples.

You've brought Paige here to distract her from her current mood, and to pry for more details of her night. You gently lean against the side of a cabinet full of crockery and silverware with what you hope is an air of cool command. 'I'm still piecing together everyone's movements last night, and wanted to go over what you did after leaving Shao in the library.'

Paige looks pensive, then says, 'Around half past nine I walked back down the corridor to my room. As I said earlier, I collected my toiletries, pyjamas and dressing gown and headed for the bathroom.'

You note that she answers without hesitation. 'Did anyone see you?'

'Jasmine was in the hall when I left my room. We both heard Bruce in the library yelling at Shao. Then Bruce stormed out – well, staggered out, really – stumbled back to his room and slammed the door.'

You didn't hear any of that yourself as you were already deeply asleep. You might write to the makers of your sleeping tablets about their effectiveness, though whether to praise it or complain about it you aren't yet sure.

'And Bruce saw both you and Jasmine on his way out of the library?' you continue.

'We were right there, but what he saw I can't tell you. He wasn't exactly sober.'

'And then?'

'I went into the bathroom and locked the door.'

'You didn't go back into the library to confront Shao again?'

'No,' she says with a hint of sadness, 'and now I'll always remember the sight of his back turned to me when I brought him his tea – refusing to speak to me – as the last time we saw each other.'

'You weren't curious about his argument with Bruce?'

'Shao and Bruce have been arguing for thirty years, it was unlikely to be about anything new.'

'What did you do next?'

'Had my shower.'

'Did anyone see you go into the bathroom?'

'As I said a moment ago, Jasmine.'

'How do you know?'

'Because she gave me the dirtiest look possible before I shut the door. I had a hot shower, changed into my pyjamas, went back to my room and to bed. And before you ask, I don't know if anyone saw me do that. I wanted the day to be over and to start afresh this morning. You'll have to take my word for that.'

You're unlikely to do that under any circumstances. Interrogating everyone and everything from a starting point of doubt is the only way to find the truth.

None of what Paige said this time contradicts anything you've heard earlier. But it still doesn't help fill in any gaps in your timeline, particularly regarding the movement of Paige's pen in and out of the library.

'Did you take your handbag with you to the bathroom?' you ask.

'No, why would I?'

None of the bedroom doors have locks.

You and Paige turn to leave the museum when Hudson appears, knocking on the open door to let you know he is there. He appears much calmer, and possibly a little embarrassed. He looks past you to Paige.

'I want to apologise,' he says. 'I was a bit harsh.'

Paige blinks rapidly, the way people do when they're trying not to cry. 'That's all right.'

'I thought we might talk some more?' Paige doesn't respond. 'No more unfounded accusations?' he says.

She smiles at him. 'That would be lovely.'

You stand aside to let her pass and, as you turn, you spy a stuffed potoroo – one of the taxidermied exhibits you were hoping to avoid in this little country museum. Its glassy eyes somehow stare straight through you to the case of colonial police equipment. It fills you with gloom and sorrow for the sins of the past, and for innocent dead things.

You return to your own room for some privacy while you review your notes once more.

Both Bruce and Jasmine saw Paige enter the bathroom at around 9.35 pm. Check. So they both knew her room was unoccupied. Did one of them go in there and steal from her handbag while she was showering? You aren't certain of Hudson's whereabouts at the time, so he, too, could perhaps have done the same.

Bruce had just exited the library; and he returned again later, as did Hudson. Only you and the two women, Paige and Jasmine, said they hadn't seen Shao twice in the library last night, though Paige had left him briefly to fetch his tea.

But only one person is showing symptoms consistent with arsenic poisoning this morning.

You increasingly suspect Jasmine entered Paige's room while the latter was in the shower and stole her pen, then saw Shao again and…what? If that's what happened, it seems she had no idea the pen was poisoned, so she couldn't have been planning to use it to harm Shao. And why go to the trouble of stealing the pen only to take it to the library and leave it on the desk, then lie about it?

Of course, none of this rules Paige either in or out of last night's malfeasance. You suspect she is the most intelligent person currently under this roof, and she could be outplaying you like a chess grandmaster. But the more evidence you gather, the harder it is to piece together a scenario where Paige Hybrough deliberately harmed or killed Shao T. Mann.

Where to next?

Choose from options 1, 2 or 3.

1. Read on to Chapter 19, *Dazed and Confused* by Alison Alexander, to learn what happened in the library at 9.40 pm.
2. If you need to revisit your first conversation with Jasmine, turn back to Chapter 2, *Third Time's the Charm* by Livia Day.
3. Do you think you've solved the mystery of Shao's death? Go to page 213 to find a hidden chapter with the answer.

CHAPTER NINETEEN

Dazed and Confused

Alison Alexander

In which you question Shao T. Mann's wife, Jasmine Quill, on her movements at 9.40 pm last night.

JASMINE QUILL, A.K.A. MRS SHAO T. MANN: AMERICAN SOCIALITE WITH A villa in Tuscany; loud, forceful, fiercely intelligent. Falls in love with fictional characters, marries at the drop of a hat and believes in karma. Oh, and one tough cookie beneath that ridiculous southern belle act.

Her attraction to Shao was based on her infatuation with the main character of the international best-selling Carl Kuphem series, with Shao as the ostensible author. Last night Jasmine discovered Shao had made a fool of her by lying about who he was, specifically his authorship of the series; their marriage was a charade and he was using her only for her money.

Not a happy evening for Ms Quill.

With two dead husbands in her wake – and a third as of last night – your instincts, logic and the balance of probability suggest Jasmine decided to murder her husband and planned to escape suspicion by shifting the blame to Paige Hybrough. You feel like getting out the handcuffs right now.

The question is: can you prove it?

With last night's glamour long since faded, the remnants of her heavy makeup and rain-would-slide-off-it hairdo now a crumbling ruin, you find Jasmine slumped in a chair in front of the sitting room fire, cup of tea beside her.

'Not you again.'

Her genteel facade continues to slide as hour upon hour of illness chips away at what you imagine was years of childhood training in etiquette. Perhaps sympathy will encourage her to engage with you.

You try to sound genuine. 'Sorry to bother you. You must be feeling terrible.'

She perks up slightly, sits forward and raises her cup to take a sip. 'I'm thinking of suing the festival for food poisoning.'

'When the flooding recedes, you should definitely get a check up in case it's more serious,' you say. 'I wonder if it also caused the rash on your palm?'

Jasmine glances at her right hand and her face sours. 'I must have brushed it against something in the garden yesterday. Everything in this godforsaken country is trying to kill you – the weather, the wildlife, the hedges…' Her expression shifts; it appears to you that she's remembered she should be sad, '…and then there's my poor husband.'

'You don't remember when you first felt the itch?' you ask, careful to keep your voice neutral.

Jasmine shrugs and then winces at the movement.

'I have a few more questions for you, if that's okay?'

'No, it is not. I've already told you everything.' She takes a deep breath, powering up. 'Do you know how rude this is, constantly pestering me? I'm a grieving widow for goodness' sake, have some respect.'

The words spilling from her mouth sound as though they were scripted for a daytime soap opera. You don't feel anything genuine behind them. 'I'm trying to explain what happened to your husband,' you say in the gentlest tone you can muster. 'If there was foul play involved, you don't want that person to get away with it, do you?'

She slumps back into her chair again.

'I need you to be truthful, please Jasmine. When you went back to the library last night, did you fight with Shao again?'

Jasmine's face twitches. 'I don't remember.'

And now you know what her face looks like when she tells you a direct lie. 'Hudson says he saw you leaving the library for a second time at about ten to ten, and you were limping and in a rush. What happened between you and Shao?'

She twitches again. It is the slightest movement in her right cheek, a micro-expression where she looks down and to the right, signalling as loudly as though she were shouting that she is calculating another lie. 'I wanted to apologise for our argument and wish him a good night.'

'You apologised?'

'Yes, and then I left. I was only in there a few moments.'

That statement contained at least one lie. 'How did Shao respond to your apology?'

For a split second, her face twists in a sneer. It appears Jasmine is so worn out from endless hours of being ill that she isn't able to properly control her facial expressions any longer. 'He said nothing.'

She leans forward and grabs a gingersnap biscuit from the coffee table, breaks it in half, then puts both halves back on the plate. 'He had no right,' she mutters.

'No right?'

'To give me the silent treatment. I'd done nothing wrong.' She's picks up a half of the biscuit and grinds it to crumbs between her fingers. 'I am not a woman you treat that way.'

'On the desk in the library, was there a book with the centre cut out?' you ask, changing topics slightly, hoping to keep her off balance, keep her thoughts moving.

'What? I don't know. There were books for signing, that stupid typewriter, some rubbish and that traitor's precious red pen.' She huffs. 'You are so slow. Paige never forgets her pen, so if it was there, that means something happened between them and she ran away.'

'What is it that you think I've missed?'

'Oh, only that Paige killed my husband.' She fixes you with a triumphant glare, as though she has revealed to you – dunderhead you – what you should have seen all along.

'Have you considered it might be a red herring planted to suggest she did?'

She coughs, then dabs her handkerchief to her face. You feel as though you're watching choreography, a series of practiced distractions.

'After Paige came out of the library,' she says in a rush, 'after she saw him, she went straight to the shower. Maybe she was washing away blood, or something else incriminating.'

That didn't make any sense to you given the crime scene, but it did confirm again that Jasmine was in the corridor around 9.35 pm last night.

'Why were you in the hallway at the time?'

She looks confused. Are her internal stories beginning to clash?

'Bruce was there, shouting. I came out of my room to see what he was fussing about and saw Paige going into the bathroom.'

'How do you know Paige had a shower?'

'I heard the water running, obviously.'

'But you were sure it was Paige, not one of the others.'

'Yes, I saw the door to her bedroom open.'

And there it is. 'Did you go in?'

Twitch. Jasmine is preparing another lie. 'I beg your pardon?'

'You said Paige's door was open. Did you go in?'

She stares at you, presumably calculating what to say if someone witnessed her enter Paige's bedroom. 'I returned a comb, yes.'

A lie. 'What kind of comb?' you ask.

'I don't know.' She's exasperated now, obviously used to talking her way out of consequences and not being called on her deceit. 'Just a comb.'

'What colour?'

She stares at you; you stare right back.

Fury begins to colour her face, her lips thin, a crease between her eyebrows grows. 'Don't you know who I am? I can have you fired for this kind of impertinence.'

You are close now – once they start threatening you, you know you are close to the truth. 'Fired from what? I'm retired, remember.'

She waves her good hand in dismissal. 'Look, we were married. Paige was his employee. Essentially, she worked for me, so I can do what I want where she's concerned.'

You give her your sternest look. 'None of that is true, and you know it. Beside which, common courtesy dictates you don't enter other people's rooms unless invited. You have manners, you know that.'

She murmurs something under her breath, then scratches her palm, becoming agitated.

'What was that?'

'Listen to me, you imbecile.' Her voice is low, certain, and controlled. 'Your rules don't apply to me. I've played your little game this morning, but now I'm bored of it. I'm wealthier than you can imagine – I buy and sell people like you before breakfast – and there's not a darned thing you can do about it. Now, stop your ridiculous questions and go do something useful, like row a boat to civilisation and call me a helicopter.' She clamps a hand over her mouth as she dry retches.

And now you recognise her. Jasmine Quill personifies lack of gratitude and a complete absence of self-reflection. She has no empathy, nor any sympathy for others. People serve her purposes or they're nothing to her.

You laugh, a truly tickled pink belly laugh. 'Does that ridiculous spiel work where you come from?'

She appears shocked that you aren't cowed. Her eyes widen, her jaw slackens, illness momentarily overwhelmed. She has revealed her true personality and there is no pulling the mask back on now.

Time to end the courtesy – it isn't as though you have anything to lose. Your voice hardens. 'Jasmine, when you returned to the library and Shao wouldn't engage, what did you do?'

'I said goodnight to my husband and left,' she says. Her expression says she doesn't expect you to believe a word of what she's saying.

'I don't believe you. I know you kicked his chair because he was ignoring you. What else did you do?'

'Nothing.'

'Come on Jasmine, I'm not a fool, I know there's more you aren't saying.'

'I don't have to put up with this kind of treatment,' she says, turning to stare out the window.

'Hudson saw you limping from the library toward your bedroom. He said he was concerned because you looked so ill.'

She can't resist. 'I've never felt this sick in my life. It's not just the nausea, it's the cramps, and my hands are tingling and my breath smells so bad. I chewed a mint earlier and afterwards I could still smell garlic.'

She's describing the symptoms of arsenic poisoning as if she's reading from a textbook. She definitely touched the poisoned pen, and she's genuine in her confusion about what has made her sick. If she didn't poison the pen but was poisoned by it, who was it intended for? Paige?

'You took the pen from Paige's handbag while she was in the shower, then put it on the desk in front of Shao, didn't you?'

'No.'

'And, I suspect that you nudged the ball and chain – while he was ignoring you or passed out or asleep – to be more directly over his head in the hope that it would fall and kill him, didn't you?'

She inhales a large breath through her mouth and makes a display of holding it. Goodness, when had she stopped emotionally developing? Age five?

Jasmine and Shao had been a perfect match for each other, narcissists living shallow lives swanning around literary circles—him taking credit for Paige's work, and her infatuated with the story-world, mistakenly believing Shao created it. No wonder Jasmine imploded last night; all the foundations of her castles in the air crumbled to dust in a few short minutes. A woman betrayed was usually someone you felt sympathy for, but in this instance you felt it couldn't have happened to a more deserving person.

'Jasmine?'

She turns her head further from you, then stands and hobbles out.

You are certain the instant she has access to outside communication she will make arrangements to be whisked away out of the country. She has the means and the motive.

You pull out your notepad, sit back and flip to your J.Q . page.

Discovered last night that her husband had betrayed her. Tick.

Lacks empathy for others. Tick.

Believes she is special, above the law. Tick.

Has two dead husbands, now three. Tick.

That's a lot of ticks pointing towards Jasmine killing her husband, which was your theory when you sat down to talk with her just now. In earlier conversations she repeatedly brought up the Mont Blanc pen and the ball and chain. You are now confident she moved the ball and chain closer to Shao's head both times she visited the library. But somewhere in past five minutes, she unintentionally raised a doubt in your mind as to whether she had been able to follow through with dislodging it.

There's one more detail you need to nail down before finalising your investigation of Jasmine Quill.

Where to next?

Choose from options 1, 2 or 3.

1. Read on to Chapter 20, *A Dark and Stormy Night* by Craig Cormick, to find out what happened between Hudson and Shao in the library at 9.50 pm.
2. Jump to Chapter 21, *The Domino Effect* by Alan Carter, if you want to find out what happened between Bruce and Shao in the library at 10 pm.
3. Do you think you've solved the mystery of Shao's death? Go to page 213 to find a hidden chapter with the answer.

CHAPTER TWENTY

A Dark and Stormy Night

Craig Cormick

In which you question Hudson van Daemon, up-and-coming Tasmanian crime writer, on his movements at 9.50 pm last night.

YOU ARE PERPLEXED. THE CASE IS PROVING TO BE MORE INTRICATE THAN YOU envisioned, even given the bizarre crime scene. All four of your suspects have strong motives for harming Shao, and after five minutes alone with him last night you can empathise.

You review your notes on Hudson again. Against your better judgement you've grown to like the complicated young writer, naturalist, and dad-joke connoisseur. He had a powerful motive to lash out at Shao, an obvious means, and a clear opportunity to attempt to harm the old charlatan, but you need to be certain.

Searching for Hudson, you meander through the various rooms of the sandstone mansion, soaking up the ambience of the building. You find him in the kitchen sitting at the table across from Paige.

'Greetings,' you say from the kitchen doorway. They both turn their heads to you, then the kettle's shrill whistle fills the room. 'Good timing for a cuppa.'

Hudson goes to the stove and removes the kettle from the hot plate, causing its chirp to recede as the water cools off boiling point. He pokes around among the mugs and sugar, placing the necessary items on a tray, then makes a fuss of checking the fire in the belly of the old wood-fired oven.

You've seen displacement activity before, and this is it. 'There's something I want to ask you about, Hudson, if you've got a moment?'

You indicate you'd like to speak to him outside. He glances at Paige then follows you through the sitting room to the verandah overlooking the lawn and the heaving flow of the Huon River.

'There's something invigorating about the bush after rain,' you say.

Hudson gives you a small smile, then reaches out to pluck some leaves from a nearby eucalyptus hedge. He crushes them in his fingers and sniffs them. You've seen him do this before.

He holds the crumpled leaves out for you to smell. 'Peppermint gum,' he says. 'If you keep it clipped as a low hedge it will live for a hundred years. My home has so many peppermint gums on the block I can smell them from down the road.'

You inhale vigorously. 'Refreshing,' you say. 'Why do you smack the leaves between your palms first, then crush them?'

'To release more of the essential oils.'

You notice movement on the ground near Hudson's feet, a small length of dark colour against the yellow flagstones. You stoop for a closer look. You recognise the oversized ant and it's bright yellow markings from its picture. 'Isn't that a jack jumper?'

'Yes,' he says, 'and heed the name.'

'Jack?'

'Jumper. They can leap quite a distance to bite or sting you. And they don't have any fear whatsoever.'

'Ah ha, thanks for the reminder,' you say, standing up. It seems the right time to ask your questions. 'How do you think a bunch of these ants could have gotten into the study last night? Probably at around ten to ten?'

Hudson half groans. 'I can't take this anymore,' he says, then looks around, presumably to see if Paige or the others are within earshot.

'What can't you take?'

'Nothing is the way it's supposed to be and I can't stand it.'

Hudson is wearing his emotions on his sleeve, but you're not sure how to help, or even whether you should. You are investigating a potential murder, after all.

'This was meant to be a weekend of triumph for me. I was supposed to receive the Devil in the Detail Award today.' He begins drumming on the balustrade with his fingers. 'But then the flood came and Shao's death, and now everything seems murky.' He shakes his head. 'Last night I was seriously considering giving up writing altogether and like you said, that is okay. I mean, Shao was my idol, but he turned out to be a massive fake. And now he's dead and you think I killed him.' His voice is getting louder. 'Maybe I did, I don't know, I certainly didn't mean to.'

That is a stunning admission. Does Hudson realise what he just said?

The tempo of his drumming fingers on the railing increases. 'But now there's this amazing editor who will work with me, so I shouldn't give up.' He thumps the balustrade with a fist. 'I don't know what to do but I can't take any more of this uncertainty.'

Neither of you speaks for quite some time as Hudson breathes deeply and tries to recover his composure. A chorus of frogs, joyous in the abundant wetness, fills the silence between you. You notice at least four different calls combining to create an amphibian symphony.

You touch his shoulder lightly to make it clear you aren't leaving but also won't push him to speak. You both stare out at the river and the bushy ranges beyond.

Hudson clears his throat. 'You know what? I'd rather tell the truth and face the music than end up like Shao, pretending to be someone I'm not.'

You nod. 'That's a solid decision. Tell a big enough lie and you'll be running from it the rest of your life.'

'What do you want to know?'

You fix him with a steady look. 'What gave you the idea to use the ants in the way you did?'

Hudson startles as though zapped by the Olivetti typewriter. He smiles ruefully. 'Of course – detective.'

'Guilty as charged.'

'Okay. Well, when Shao tried to convince me to sacrifice my career for his money, to sell out my talent to prop up his fame, I went into shock. My head started buzzing and my vision got a bit blurry. I felt betrayed, but also deeply foolish that I'd misjudged him so severely.

The feeling was the same combination of shock and emotional pain I felt as kid when I was bitten by a bunch of jack jumpers.'

'Ow, that must have been painful.'

'I'll never forget it. My parents and I were in our veggie garden and I was really happy. I don't remember why, it just felt like a great day. Suddenly, I felt agonising pain on my leg and I screamed. Jack jumpers had crawled up my trousers, then for some reason bit and stung me all at once on the back of the calf, knee and thigh.'

'That sounds awful,' you say, wincing.

'It's still one of the worst things that's ever happened to me. Mum pulled my trousers down to see what was wrong and there I was, butt naked from the waist down, screaming in pain to get them off me. Just then this girl I really liked, Jennifer Brown, rode by on her bike and saw me in this state and laughed. It was the worst day of my life up to that point.'

You squeeze his shoulder. 'I'm sorry,' is all you can manage.

'That's how I felt last night when I realised what an awful person Shao was.'

'So you wanted to hurt him?'

'I was in shock, then that turned to anger and then I wanted him to feel the same pain I felt.'

Lashing out in retaliation was one of the most common types of violence you'd had to deal with during your years on the Force.

'Did you expect the ants to kill him?' you ask gently.

He shakes his head. 'I know they can kill people who are allergic to them, but I didn't think about that, it was about inflicting pain. But is that any better?' He looks at you with pleading eyes. 'How do I know if he died from the ants – if I killed him?' He starts tapping on the railing.

'What happened next? You decided to use jack jumpers to hurt Shao and then?'

Hudson takes a deep breath. 'I let him finish his pitch, feeling more and more angry. I told him there was no way I would do what he wanted. I think he was surprised, because then he excused himself and walked out. In that moment, the idea of causing him pain with the ants came to me.'

'What did you do?'

He takes another deep breath, slower, calming himself. 'I thought of putting some inside one of the books he was going to sign. That way it would be hard to trace where they came from, or so I thought.'

'So you expected him to be bitten or stung on the hands?'

Hudson nods. You knew from examining Shao's body that there were no signs of stings or bites on his hands, nor anywhere you could see his skin.

'How did you set it up?'

'While he was out of the room, I tucked one of the *High Time* books inside my shirt, and as soon as I left the library I went to the kitchen, grabbed some scissors and went to my bedroom to cut a hole in the book pages deep enough to hold some ants.'

'Did you get that idea from anywhere in particular?'

He shrugs. 'Childhood stories about secret compartments, I guess.'

'How did you collect the ants?'

'It was raining buckets at that point, but I knew where to look for them. I grabbed a jar and a serving spoon from the kitchen and went out into the garden. I found a spot under the shelter of some eucalypts with lots of ant holes, then dug them out one by one with the spoon. I transferred them from the jar to the book in my room.'

'How long did all that take?'

'Maybe half an hour? The clock in the library said it was 9.50 pm when I went back in with the ants.'

'Half an hour is a long time to stay that angry,' you say. 'I'm surprised you didn't cool off.'

The balcony tapping begins again. 'I suppose so.'

'What was going through your mind? Something more than Shao's insults?'

Hudson grits his teeth. 'It wasn't just the old man, it was the others too.'

'Who do you mean?'

'I don't know if it's just an Australian thing like they say – tall poppy syndrome – but it seems the harder you work and the more success you have, the more people come out of the woodwork to drag you down.'

'And you are successful.'

He gives you the hint of a smile. You can see that he knows you're flattering him for your own ends, but he can't resist the compliment.

'It's a massive ball of Catch-22s, though,' he says. 'The more you sell, the higher you climb, the more people tell you you'll fall, hope you'll fall, try to pull you down. They criticise your writing for being too commercial and too literary at the same time. You're too available to your readers and not available enough. Your books are too realistic and unrealistic all at once.' He snorts. 'I've even had people tell me straight to my face that I don't deserve any success, that I haven't earned it.'

'That's a lot of pressure,' you say.

He begins rolling up the sleeves of his shirt. 'It's constant. And all those voices, all that negativity, that's all I could hear when Shao spoke. I knew he was playing on my fears, making me feel small to convince me to do his bidding, but I still became furious and…'

He looks sheepish again. 'It was like the voices of all my detractors were playing on repeat in my head. So yeah, I was still steaming half an hour later.'

You nod. Over the years you'd seen people under that kind of social pressure snap, lash out, hurt others, break things. 'This may or may not help, Hudson, but in my observation the people who try to drag you down usually have sad lives. They criticise others in order to feel better about themselves, but it's never the solution.'

'They're just jealous?'

His tone makes you realise he's heard that platitude too many times before to take any comfort from it.

You shake your head. 'Not jealous, exactly. It's deep emotional insecurity. If you are at peace with yourself, happy and fulfilled, you're not interested in running others down – it would actually make you feel sad to do it. Whereas these people make themselves feel a little better temporarily by making you feel worse, like emotional vampirism. It's hard to understand if you aren't that way, but they are trying to fill a hole inside themselves.'

It's a while since you've spent this much time philosophising, but the young writer seems to need it, maybe even appreciate it. You remind yourself to refocus on your questions.

'Can you to tell me what happened at ten to ten when you returned to the library?'

'Sure.' Hudson's tone is flat. He seems to be mostly through the emotional echoes of the previous evening.

'I headed toward the library door from my room, but as I reached it the door was flung open and Jasmine came limping out, really fast, one hand clamped over her mouth. She ignored me, or maybe didn't even notice me, and headed for the Hartz Suite. I waited until she was inside then went into the library myself.'

'Where was Shao, exactly?'

'At the desk, head down, farting in his sleep. My heart was beating so hard I thought I might have a heart attack. But there he was, passed out, having tried to derail my career less than an hour before.' Hudson clenches his fists. 'He didn't care about what he'd done at all.'

'And then?'

'I went over to the table, put the book down, opened the cover so the ants could come out and hopefully bite him while he was asleep. I wanted to hurt him, that's all. I didn't mean to kill him.'

And yet, you think, Shao is dead. 'What did you do after that?'

'Slept really badly,' he says, 'all those thumps and bumps from Bruce's room. When I got up to go to the bathroom I realised the power was out, so I started work on the generator and forgot about Shao until breakfast.'

'You forgot?'

'I never heard anything from the library, so I figured he was okay – that the ants ignored him, or he woke up from his stupor and went to bed or something. It was only in the morning when Jasmine said he didn't come to bed that I started to worry. Then you came in and said he was dead. That's when I first thought oh god, was he allergic to the ants? Then I figured if I didn't say anything no-one would know what I did. But, well, you obviously figured it out and… What's going to happen to me?'

'I can't say for certain of course, but if you're as honest with the police as you have been with me that's your best chance at leniency.' Something is troubling you about Hudson's confession. 'Also, I'd suggest you not say anything to the others until we know how Shao died.'

He draws breath to object.

'I don't mean lie, I mean…' What do you mean? 'Just wait until I have the full story.'

Something is bothering you about the way the ants were clustered together, as though they barely made it out of the book before expiring. It's plausible they walked through the arsenic dust on the desk surface and were poisoned to death immediately. You couldn't swear to it without more involved forensics, but you suspect the ants died before they had a chance to sting or bite Shao.

But what does that mean for your investigation? And the question marks in your notebook? And for Hudson?

You turn to head back inside, beckoning for Hudson to follow you, leaving the frogs to sing to their hearts' noisy content in the amphibian paradise of the flood.

Where to next?

Choose from options 1, 2 or 3.

1. Read on to Chapter 21, *The Domino Effect* by Alan Carter, to find out what happened between Bruce and Shao in the library at 10 pm.
2. If you need to revisit your first conversation with Hudson, turn back to Chapter 5, *An Impatient Youth* by Elaine Kelso, or
3. Do you think you've solved the mystery of Shao's death? Go to page 213 to find a hidden chapter with the answer.

CHAPTER TWENTY-ONE

The Domino Effect

Alan Carter

In which you question Shao T. Mann's rival, Bruce Tossington-Smythe, on his movements at 10 pm last night.

YOU WONDER WHAT POSSESSED YOU TO GET INVOLVED IN THIS. WHAT MADE you think you had the answers; that you weren't washed up? True, there's little choice in the matter, you're it unless the police sail through the floodwaters and take this investigation out of your hands. But admit it – it's been a while since you were the centre of attention, and you can't help enjoying that shiver of excitement at being back in the game, even if the goal is shrouded in grey mist like the distant cone of Hartz Peak.

Is this what writer's block feels like? The blank page, the blank mind, the ultimate white-out? Everybody is hiding something, you're sure of it. The truth remains out there somewhere. What possessed you to attempt to solve this? You know full well: you're a truth-seeker and you won't give up until you've unearthed it. Isn't that why they made you take early retirement?

You stroll out onto the verandah connecting your room with Paige's, and gaze out into the distance. Green trees and rolling hills are rendered vivid by the wetness. There is a shimmering lake all around, where yesterday there was none. You notice a flicker of movement in the curtains of Paige's room. Your presence on the verandah has been acknowledged.

Paige Hybrough, the smart, loyal editor, who for years helped bring clarity and form to Shao's literary efforts, or so it seemed. You're still surprised she turned out to be the true author of all those acclaimed international bestsellers – the unsung heroine. You know yourself what it's like to be an unsung hero, how brutal it feels.

Perceptive, precise, put-upon Paige. In bed, she claims, by the time Shao would have met his untimely end. But she did hear Bruce shouting angrily at Shao near the likely moment of his demise.

Angry displays feature repeatedly in this tableau, and anger can be a great motivator. Earlier in the evening the young writer Hudson overheard Jasmine Quill shouting at her soon-to-be-dead husband. Then later, around 9.30 pm, three people heard Bruce going off at Shao for several minutes; and again at 10 pm. Shao T. Mann infuriated those close to him, and you now understand the many reasons why.

Bruce Tossington-Smythe, the needy and unappreciated literary rival who believes himself to be the better writer despite his poorer book sales and lack of awards. Endlessly divorced, drunk, demanding – the downward-spiralling author from central casting. Or is that simply an excellent cover story for a cold, calculating killer? What was the last bout of shouting truly about and did it end in a violent act by Bruce?

He's there, slumped in a chair in the sitting room again, yawning, still oozing last night's whisky fumes and staring balefully at the empty drinks cabinet next to the ornate fireplace. His expensive jacket and shirt are rumpled, the Magpies footy scarf soiled with food and coffee from this morning. With grey stubble to boot, the man is channelling seedy.

'Can you help me with a few more questions, Bruce?'

'There's got to be something to drink in this Godforsaken place.'

Several hours into the hangover now, Bruce is suffering. 'I reckon I can probably rustle up another coffee,' you offer.

He looks at you like he just found you on the bottom of his shoe. 'I need a drink, not more bloody caffeine.'

You sit down upwind of his stomach-turning hangover breath. 'Look, you have to realise that if there's any blame to be apportioned over Shao's death, people will happily point the finger at you as the last person to see him in the library last night. You need to sober up and start accounting for yourself. Sometime in the next while my ex-colleagues are going to come barging in here wanting to know whodunit, and some of them aren't too choosy about niceties like evidence and proof. Finding a rude, obstinate, obfuscating soak at the scene will make their lives so much easier.'

'Now hang on a minute–'

'I'm explaining the lay of the land.'

Something stirs in him. A memory? An instinct for self-preservation? Perhaps an avenue of escape. Or the simple realisation that his goose may be cooked if he doesn't co-operate. To cook one's goose: a charming phrase straight out of the manor murder mysteries of the Golden Age, but certainly applicable here. You're tiring of this game of charades, half-truths and evasions, this wretched *Cluedo*. You're no Poirot or Marple, not even Clouseau. You want to get this done and show everyone you know how to do the job.

'You were apparently the final person to see Shao last night – around 10 pm you had a second clash filled with shouting, crashing and banging. There are three witnesses, so no denying it. On top of that, you're a man whose public stoushes with the deceased, record of arrests, failing career, and failing personal life make a fine recipe for murder. That is why you'll be the prime suspect in a possible homicide.'

'It's not true, though,' Bruce says weakly.

'Then what happened in there exactly?'

You don't know how much he could possibly remember, but it's worth asking again, pushing, prodding, in case a synapse or two fires. By 10 pm last night Bruce had drunk at least three, possibly four, bottles of wine, and a hip flask of Lark whisky. Most people would have been in a coma, but he'd been stumbling around the homestead seeking something from Shao.

'Nothing. Nothing happened at all, besides what I've told you already,' he says.

'I don't believe you.'

'I need you to. You must.' He shakes his head. 'I need–'

'You need to step up, Bruce. Shao's dead, he can't outshine you anymore, can't patronise you, can't belittle you. The feud is over. The story belongs to you now, so tell me what really happened – in your own words.'

He takes a deep, shuddering breath. 'I wanted to try and apologise. I knew I shouldn't have acted like I did earlier. Too much to drink, you know?'

Bruce wants approval from you, or at least sympathy; endorsement that the actions of a drunk are understandable, forgivable. He's asking too much – you've seen just how far that can be taken – and you're not having any of it. 'Go on.'

'Mann always had this way of making you feel invisible, like you're nothing. He was an expert at pressing people's buttons.'

Was he ever. 'You were angry. You'd had enough.'

'Yes. No. Yes and no.' Head in hands, a portrait of pathos. 'I really did try to apologise. You have to believe me.'

'I don't have to do anything. You have to convince me.'

'He wouldn't even acknowledge my presence, just sat there in front of that stupid bloody typewriter of his, with a wall of his books around him to keep us lesser mortals at bay.'

His hatred of the inanimate object was still disturbing. 'Why are you so angry about the typewriter?'

He frowns, looks at his hand, spreads his fingers. 'I already told you. I got a shock from it.'

He was right. He had already told you. And you believed that part of his story. The Olivetti had shocked you too. But getting suspects to repeat their answers often gave you more information.

'I'd only slammed my fist on his desk to stir the bastard up, but the bloody machine gave me an electric shock.' Bruce falls silent.

He hadn't mentioned hitting the desk before. 'You got a shock,' you say, by way of a prompt.

'I startled. I jumped a little and accidentally bumped the desk with my hip. Then there was a lot of crashing and I looked around and Mann was on the floor.'

'What?'

'It was like that *Mousetrap* game, you know?'

'How do you mean?'

'A chain reaction. A domino effect. Ball rolls down a slide, knocks something over; that knocks something else, and all of a sudden,' he clicks his fingers, 'the trap comes down and the mouse is toast.'

Mousetrap, you're thinking, like the famous murder mystery play set in an isolated country mansion. You can't make this stuff up. Or perhaps you can. There's a brief screeching cacophony out the window as a flock of white cockatoos fly past. It stirs you from the fog of the moment.

'Maybe when I knocked the desk it caused the ball and chain on the bookshelf to fall, then the piles of books, and then they hit Mann and he went with it, decided to sleep it off on the floor of the library.' He looks at you with a shrug. 'Like we haven't all done that at some point.'

'Did you check him to see if he was okay? The fall would have woken him up, yes?'

'No.'

'No you didn't check him? Or no he didn't come to?'

'He just lay there.'

'A man is lying on the floor unconscious, perhaps even dead. And you didn't check on him?'

'I remember now. He burped.'

'Burped?'

'A long slow burp. Disgusting, really. But it made me think he was probably okay. He would get like that during our drinking bouts at uni, absolutely paralytic. I gave him my damned apology and left him to it.'

Shao and Bruce had drunk like fish last night. Was Shao sufficiently inebriated to pass out in the manner Bruce described? Another point of inquiry for the pathology checklist.

Falling antiques, avalanches of books, collapsing chairs, burping bodies. And hadn't Hudson also mentioned Shao farting? It all seems slapstick and hard to believe.

And yet from *Forensics for Dummies* you know that dead bodies can fart and burp with the best of them. Shao could have died up to half an hour before he received his last visitor at 10 pm. According to all the information you can gather, the last time he was definitely alive and moving of his own free will was when Bruce went to the library at 9.30 pm. He put something on his desk, turned his back on his rival, and did little more than grunt as Bruce berated him.

Tossington-Smythe had put it down to Shao's customary rudeness. Maybe those grunts were akin to death rattles. That puts the spotlight back onto put-upon Paige, his previous visitor. Hell, it leaves the door open on all four of them; none are off the hook yet as far as you're concerned.

'Then what?'

He shrugs. 'I went back to my room, shut my door, shut the world out and slept it off.'

There are still three items in that library you need to account for. You'll hit him with another barrage of questions, see what you can scrape from his addled memory.

'When you went back at 10 pm, was there anything new on the desk?'

He looks at you with unfocused eyes. 'What?'

'You told me that at 9.30 you saw the typewriter, the ball and chain and the signing books, as well as a vintage book and a plastic bag. Think, Bruce – was there anything else on that desk when you returned?'

He huffs, and a wave of rotting breath washes over you. 'What does it matter?'

'It could help point my colleagues in a direction other than you.'

He straightens in his chair. 'Ants. There were large ants.'

'Yes, and?'

'A book, one of his books, the new one. It had been cut up, or into, or something.'

'Yes, and?'

He swallows. 'No. She would never do anything wrong – I keep telling you, it was natural causes.'

And with that Bruce Tossington-Smythe tells you that he noticed Paige's red Mont Blanc fountain pen appeared on the desk between his two visits at 9.30 pm and 10 pm. And that he wants to protect her from the fallout for anything she may or may not have done.

There's a desperate look in his eye, the baleful glare of a suffering alcoholic.

You sigh. 'Have you tried the laundry cupboard for cleaning spirits?'

Bruce pushes himself reluctantly to his feet and stumbles towards the kitchen. You hear him searching the laundry cupboards, then the pantry for the umpteenth time, a chorus of clattering and swearing.

You study your surroundings while you wait for him. The furniture: old, plush, comfortable and lived-in. Mostly paintings on the walls, a few old wooden bookshelves scattered in. There is a still life on the wall behind where Bruce was sitting: Tasmanian native violets in a ceramic vase beside a bowl of Huon Valley apples – the purple of the flowers, reds and greens of the fruit, contrasts with the creamy-grey background. Everything is tasteful and subdued.

Outside, you see splashes of blue as the clouds break apart. Thin pale shafts of sunlight peep through here and there.

The floodwaters will recede soon enough and the A-team will arrive to take over. They will look you up and down and measure your worth. They will ask you how retirement is going, and some may even be genuinely interested. They will take note of your observations and what you have learned from your enquiries. They may, or may not, allow them to count for something. All in good time.

'A-ha!'

Bruce returns and takes his seat. He sloshes a slug of what appears to be twenty-year-old Chinese cooking sherry into a tumbler. You can't imagine under any circumstances it could taste good, but Bruce begins to relax, and a relaxed drunk is a talkative drunk. For now, Bruce Tossington-Smythe is back in the mood to talk.

'I've wished Mann dead countless times,' he says, in what you've come to recognise as his reminiscing voice. 'You'd never believe that we were once the best of friends.'

'And now your wish has come true,' you say.

Bruce savours his drink. 'Yes, I suppose so.'

'You don't seem so sure.'

A wistful smile. 'At university I was the double-barrelled rich boy but, for all my wealth and privilege, socially awkward and an involuntary loner.'

The drink must be warming his heart, or numbing his soul, for him to offer such apparent honesty. 'Mann had a spark about him, you saw it immediately. But it also marked him as an outlier.'

'In what way?'

'A kind of bulletproof self-assuredness; a belief that the world would revolve around him whether it wanted to or not. Believe me, there was no shortage of arrogant young blokes who had a declared sense of entitlement about them at that university.' A sip of the salty amber fluid. 'But Mann's was focused, intense. He seemed not to need anybody or anything, but I knew that's exactly what he craved. He wanted everybody to love, perhaps worship, him. But he'd be damned if he ever admitted it.'

'You must have been a perceptive young man.'

He glares at you, searching for any hint of mockery, sarcasm, or scepticism in your words, but you've hidden them well.

'So, you found each other?'

'Yes. Creative Writing, one-oh-one.'

'You recognised each other's talents.'

'After a while, yes.' Over the rim of his tumbler he gives you the measure of his gaze, but even from here you notice his eyes are cloudy and unfocused. He's play-acting at being an accomplished storyteller. 'But not in so many words.'

'And what was his opinion of you?'

'He never offered one, but it became evident as the months unfolded.'

'How so?'

He dredges up a brief wintry smile. 'Don't they say imitation is the sincerest form of flattery?'

'Plagiarism?'

'Not word for word, more in form and rhythm. Vocabulary. Style. The vibe, if you like.' A shake of the head. 'As we all wrote pieces for the class, he adopted a mix of my style and that of the woman who became his editor, Paige. By gods, back then she sure could write. And by the end of that first semester our tutor was marking me down for aping Mann, not the other way around.'

'That must have rankled.'

He downs the drink in an angry gulp. 'Like the theft of my very soul.'

'And yet you became friends, for a while at least.'

'We were useful to each other. I had the talent he wanted and he offered me something I'd rarely experienced: friendship. If it suited him, he could make you feel like you were the centre of his universe, as if we'd been mates forever. It wasn't until later that I realised he could turn it on and off like a tap.'

'And all the time he was stealing your ideas?'

'Not exactly. I learned to keep story ideas and plotlines to myself. But it was like he crept under my skin and inhabited me. He appropriated how I thought, how I used language, how I saw the world, my power to describe. As my craft developed over those months and years at university it almost immediately became his, as if he somehow absorbed everything I did.'

There are tears in Bruce's eyes. The tears of a veteran alcoholic, or real tears recounting old hurts that haven't healed? Having read his books, and those with Shao's name on them, you know the latter were of a significantly higher quality, thanks to Paige. The two sets of books hadn't struck you as being particularly similar in tone or style.

He frowns. 'We got drunk together, chased girls together, everything. And all the while he was leeching from my writerly existence, my reason for being.'

'Until one day…'

A sniff. Lips trembling. Yes, those were real tears of pain. 'The final year, final semester. By then he'd been nominated for the Chancellor's Literature Award, had agents and publishers sniffing around him, was widely regarded as that year's Next Big Thing.'

'And you?'

'I'd just lost my mother to cancer; received my third publisher rejection in as many days; had recently broken up with my girlfriend. Had a cold, or a hangover, something, I don't know.'

'Things came to a head.'

'I needed someone to talk to, someone to listen to me. A friend.'

The thin shafts of sunlight have disappeared once again, obscured by clouds. Maybe there will be more showers after all. Rain or shine, it doesn't matter to Bruce Tossington-Smythe. He is not in this moment: he's in another over three decades ago, re-living a terrible moment that changed the course of his life, a moment that potentially led all the way to the death of his tormentor less than twenty-four hours ago.

'It was early summer, sunny, in the gardens outside the uni library, under the shade of a flowering red gum. He had a gaggle of disciples around him and was holding forth. I was in his line of vision – he could see me approaching. I offered him a smile, gestured towards the coffee shop.'

Bruce's face hardens, even the jowls seem to steel themselves. There is a sudden chill in the air, light fading fast. You nod for him to continue.

'He ignored me. Cut me dead like I wasn't there, like I had never been there. Ever.'

'What happened then?'

'I lost it. I broke through the gaggle of sycophants like parting the Red Sea. Prodded him in the chest. Got in his face.' Bruce is there now, you can see it. There's spittle forming on his lips, his eyes are ablaze. 'Fraud, parasite, leech, thief. All the words I could conjure to describe him I threw his way. His treachery, his hollowness, I told everyone he was an absolute void of a human being. You hear these days of art and books being created by artificial intelligence? That was Mann, ahead of his effin' time.'

'How did he react?'

'Like stone.' He thumbs out the window. 'Like those grey crags out there in the distance, as if those last three years had never happened. Like I'd never happened.'

'That's how you described his behaviour in the library last night. That must have pressed a few buttons for you?'

'You think I waited thirty years to kill him?' A bitter snort. 'I've had countless opportunities since then. All those festivals, sitting beside him at the book-signing desk while his queue snaked off into the distance, and I sat twiddling my thumbs pretending I had messages on my phone? Those panels where he would toss a crumb of a compliment my way and then snatch it back in the guise of a joke a few minutes later. The green room! I could have clobbered him in the green room with the candelabra.'

You know yourself that revenge doesn't always take place on a schedule. 'A dish best served cold?' you venture.

'You're a copper down to your toenails, aren't you? Black-and-white with you lot, isn't it? Why can't you be more like our fictional creations? See the grey, see the twists, see the complexity of the human condition?'

You don't appreciate being patronised but you'll let it go. Finally, we may be approaching the truth of the matter, regarding Bruce anyway. 'Enlighten me.'

'I wasn't only in the library the second time last night to apologise. I was there to thank him.'

'What for?'

'By stealing my writing style, my worldview, he forced me to adapt and find a new one. In so doing he made me realise how derivative I'd been back then. Clever, yes. Talented, yes. But not my own true self.' A giggle. 'Mann spent all that time stealing my stuff to be a derivative of a derivative.'

You aren't sure that there's any merit to Bruce's assertion. 'It didn't stop Shao from becoming hugely successful though.'

Bruce's face darkens. 'In publishing, talent is one thing,' he spits, 'marketing is another.'

'So you didn't kill Shao?'

'Give me a break, won't you?' He's tiring of the encounter, clearly has better things to do with his time like drink his life away.

Do you believe him? He certainly believes himself. But you've come across countless drunks in your time who've done vile things to other human beings and swear black and blue it couldn't have been them.

Bruce Tossington-Smythe has crafted his own narrative for the death of his long-time rival Shao T. Mann, and has written himself out of it. Does his story hold?

You think you have the shape of it now, what occurred in the library last night.

Where to next?

Choose from options 1 or 2.

1. Do you think you've solved the mystery of Shao's death? Conintue to page 213 find the hidden soltion chapter, *Murder You Wrote*, by L.J.M. Owen.
2. If you're not ready, turn back to the start of the book and begin a new path with Chapter 1, *Your Body in the Library* by Z.E. Davidson.

A HIDDEN CHAPTER

Murder You Wrote

L.J.M. Owen

In which you, a retired police detective, reveal how international bestselling author Shao T. Mann died.

Jasmine limps from the verandah into the sitting room leaving the door behind her ajar. She perches on the arm of a velvet chair by the fire, looking like a kitchen cloth left floating overnight in a sink of dirty dishwater. She warms her palms in front of the fire, then scratches at one – it's clear she feels compelled to be here while definitely resenting the invitation. You don't care in the slightest.

The heavens open once more and the downpour makes a deafening din on the verandah's corrugated iron roof. A few micro-droplets splash into the room through the gap left in the door by Shao's widow. You wander across the room and close it properly – grateful for the lowered decibels – then take a seat across from Jasmine.

You've asked your four fellow house guests to join you with the promise of revealing your conclusions regarding the death of Shao T. Mann.

Paige sits on the sofa to your left, appearing as calm and collected as ever. The impression created by her neat hair, spotless glasses and perfect posture is softened only when she glances at Hudson; otherwise she is a study in precision and control.

The young, bare-shinned naturalist sits on the sofa next to Paige, picking at the buzzies in his shoelaces. Bruce slouches in another armchair near the fire.

It is time to begin.

'When I left the library at around 8.35 pm last night,' you say, 'Shao was sitting up in his chair with piles of books stacked around him waiting to be signed, his typewriter in front of him, and the antique ball and chain on the shelf above and to the left of him where I placed it at the conclusion of our tour earlier in the afternoon.'

Bruce, who has decanted the remainder of the decades-old bottle of salty Chinese cooking wine into his silver flask, sips as you speak. Then he yawns and says, 'For god's sake, you're not Miss bloody Marple. Get on with it.'

You ignore his lack of propriety and continue. 'On re-entering the library this morning, I found Shao lying on the floor, still in his chair, surrounded by drifts of his books. A chair leg was broken, the ball and chain was by his body, and his forehead was damaged and bleeding. On the desk alongside his typewriter there was also a red Mont Blanc pen, a vintage green book, a small plastic bag with one gummy bear inside, a few dead jack jumper ants and a mutilated copy of *High Time*.'

Hudson plucks at a particularly tenacious burr.

'It was a bizarre scene,' you say, 'a twisted, tangled set of clues that have taken all morning to unravel. After speaking with each of you several times,' you tap your notebook with your forefinger, 'I believe I've pieced together which of you was responsible for the death of Shao T. Mann.'

Where to next?

You can read this hidden chapter in two ways.

You can start here and read straight through to the end to find out what each suspect did and how Shao died; or, if your investigation points to one of your four suspects as the guilty party, you can skip to their section of this chapter and read only their part.

If, in doing so, you discover that you somehow missed a clue, you can always go back to the beginning of the book and choose a different pathway through the chapters – as many times as you like – before turning to the final reveal section.

Then, of course, if you like you can read it all over again and choose a different path.

Part One – Bruce

If you think Bruce caused Shao's death last night, continue reading on page 216.

Part Two – Hudson

If you think Hudson caused Shao's death last night, turn to page 218.

Part Three – Jasmine

If you think Jasmine caused Shao's death last night, turn to page 222.

Part Four – Paige

If you think Paige caused Shao's death last night, turn to page 224.

Part Five – Final Reveal

You can skip forward to the explanation of exactly what happened to Shao last night by turning to Part Five – The Final Reveal on page 227.
But beware – once you read this section it may change what you see when you read through the book again.

Part One – BRUCE

'Come on,' Bruce says again, tugging at his soiled scarf, 'stop playing games, just tell us what you think and let us get on with our day.' He yawns again. 'I need a siesta.'

He seems to be mellowing with each sip of the awful wine.

'You and Shao were famously bitter rivals for decades,' you say.

'Don't be ridiculous,' he says. 'It was just a bit of fun. Mann knew that.'

'You've been arguing in public for as long as I can remember,' says Hudson.

'The two of you ruined one event after another with your endless bickering,' Jasmine adds.

'One does one's best,' Bruce smirks. 'Look, I didn't try to harm the old man. As Inspector Clouseau here discovered, our rivalry was good for business. I had no reason to kill Mann.'

'Yet you shook with anger when you spoke of Shao's typewriter, and when you listed the awards his books won,' you say.

'And you suspected Shao had been trolling you with fake reviews,' Paige adds quietly.

You continue. 'Add to your personal hostility the fact you've been arrested in the past for drunken brawling, drank several bottles of wine last night, were the last person to see Shao in the library, and admit to leaving him on the floor of the room–'

'It was that bloody typewriter of his,' Bruce says. 'It shocked me, I told you that.'

'Perhaps, in a fit of rage, you picked it up and hit him over the head with it?'

'No!'

'Look at it logically,' you say, prodding him again, 'you went to see him at half past nine last night intending to apologise for needling him at dinner. When he ignored you, you shouted at him and stormed out of the library, witnessed by everyone else.'

Your three other suspects nod, reminding you of a row of bobble heads on a car dashboard.

Bruce appears nonplussed.

'When you returned again at ten o'clock – having imbibed even more while stewing on all the reasons you hated Shao – he ignored you again. Drunk, enraged, and letting go of reason, you picked up either the typewriter or a box of books – maybe even attempted to pick up the ball and chain – and hit him with whichever it was so hard that the force of it snapped the leg of the chair he was in and he went tumbling to the floor, dead.'

Bruce jumps out of his chair. 'THAT DID NOT HAPPEN!' Flecks of spittle fly from the corner of his mouth.

You fall silent, letting the figure of Bruce loom over everyone in the sitting room. Paige and Jasmine both appear to have frozen; Hudson's fists are clenched as he starts to rise from the sofa.

'You're right,' you say and watch the three other writers deflate. Bruce, shocked into submission, flops back into his seat.

It's an old interrogation trick: making the suspects' cortisol levels rise and fall, rise and fall, tiring them out, unbalancing them. A destabilised suspect is a careless suspect.

'Were you the last person to see Shao in the library last night?'

Bruce glares at you and refuses to answer.

'Yes, I believe you were,' you say. 'Did you have a motive to harm Shao?'

Again, he refuses to speak.

'Yes, you had plenty – deep, personal, long-standing jealousy over his career and popularity.'

You glance at Paige who still seems oblivious to Bruce's feelings for her. 'In summation you had a motive, were the last person to see Shao in the library, and the one whose actions caused him to fall to the floor, dead.'

'No.'

'You set off a chain reaction, an unwitting game of dominoes,' you sit forward, 'but you didn't kill him.'

'Unwitting?' Bruce's jowls wobble like ripples on a pond.

It was telling that his mind gravitated to that part of your statement.

'You weren't responsible for Shao's demise, Bruce, and you didn't attempt to murder anyone,' you say.

Except, you think to yourself, by boring them to death.

Part Two – HUDSON

You shift in your chair to square up with Hudson. 'You've read the Carl Kuphem novels all your life?'

He looks like the proverbial kangaroo staring into the headlights of an oncoming logging truck. 'Yep.'

'And you loved them so much it inspired you to start writing for yourself?'

He nods.

'Irritating drivel,' Bruce mumbles.

'Shut. Up. Enough out of you,' Paige says.

Bruce looks confused and affronted.

'And you've turned out to be a strong writer,' you continue, 'almost as though you were born to it.' Here, you risk a glance at Paige, whose face flickers involuntarily.

'But meeting your literary idol didn't turn out as you'd dreamed, did it?'

Hudson sighs from deep in his belly. 'You can say that again.'

'Despite your successes – and knowing you'd won this weekend's Devil Award – you had to bite your tongue as Bruce and Shao ridiculed you over dinner. Then, when you met Shao in the library, he let fly with his own particular brand of dismissive arrogance. He assumed you'd be overjoyed to serve his interests with no regard to your own.'

'It's almost as though you knew the man, Detective,' Bruce continues his muttered commentary.

'Quiet from the peanut gallery,' you shoot back at him with a glare.

Bruce grins mockingly in response. You return to Hudson.

'Then, to add insult to injury, Shao rubbed it in, denigrating your home, your writing, and your future chances of success, all in a misguided effort to convince you to be his ghostwriter.'

'Why would I want that at my age? Why would anyone want that?'

'That is a fair question, Hudson,' Jasmine interjects, her bloodshot eyes boring into the side of Paige's head.

The alleged editor stares out the sitting room window, her face calm. Bruce and Hudson both frown, as yet unaware of Paige and Shao's decades-long arrangement.

'Shao offered you financial security,' you say, 'but not fame, nor the freedom to find your own destiny.'

'He was an arrogant arse,' says Bruce.

'But I passed Paige on the way out of the library,' Hudson says, 'and he was definitely still alive when I left.'

'The first time he was, yes. But you were deeply insulted by his words, and as Shao tried to convince you to do his bidding you formulated a plan to retaliate against his insults. He put down Tasmania, so you decided to use that against him, more specifically an animal famously found here.'

'The jack jumper ants.' Bruce must be reasonably sober at this point for his brain cells to still be firing so cooperatively.

'Indeed,' you say, 'Tasmania's deadliest creature. When Shao stepped out briefly during your argument just after nine o'clock, you took the opportunity to pilfer one of his new books–'

'You didn't need to steal one, I'd have given it to you,' says Paige to Hudson.

'–with the intention of cutting a section out of the middle to form a vault, popping as many jack jumpers as you could into it from a nest you noticed while exploring the property, and leaving it closed on Shao's desk for him to sign. Their extremely painful stings might teach him some humility. If he happened to be dangerously allergic to them, so be it.'

Hudson's cheeks bloom from pink to deep, sunburnt red. 'I didn't, didn't mean...I just didn't think it through.'

Outside, a particularly well-timed murder of ravens begin crowing.

'Oh Hudson, no.' Hudson's hidden mother, Paige, appears anguished at the thought her surrendered son might have unknowingly killed his biological father. It could be a tragedy of Shakespearean proportions, except...

The young writer's face shades a deeper hue still as he looks down and tugs at the sleeve of his flannelette shirt. 'I didn't mean to kill him.'

'There's a turn up for the books,' says Bruce.

'Are you certain of all this, detective?'

That from Jasmine, with her particular brand of deference intended as flattery. You've learnt this indicates she is either hiding something or things are going her way.

'I only did it to hurt him, to teach him a lesson, not to…' Hudson trails off sounding miserable. He makes no attempt at deception, the pressure of the situation too much for someone unused to duplicity.

You continue. 'At ten to ten or thereabouts you returned to the library only to find Jasmine leaving again.'

Hudson looks up at the older American. 'You looked like you were going to be sick, and you were limping.'

Jasmine emits a tiny groan.

'I thought maybe you'd had too much wine then stubbed your toe,' Hudson continues.

If only, you thought.

'And where was Shao?' you ask.

'Slumped over the desk,' says Hudson. 'I figured he'd drunk more after I left and then passed out, especially as he, er, passed wind.'

'So you–'

'Walked in, careful not to disturb him, put the book down, flipped open the cover and walked out again.'

'How close were the ants to Shao?'

Hudson swallowed hard. 'Very.'

'Did my husband die from an ant bite?' asks Jasmine. 'Not…'

You didn't help her by finishing her sentence – not from a ball and chain to the head.

'As a naturalist you know jack jumpers have killed many people over the years,' you say to Hudson, 'and for those allergic to their stings death can occur within fifteen minutes.'

'So quickly?' Bruce asks. He seems to be taking note for future reference.

'Oh god,' Hudson says, his hands trembling, teeth beginning to chatter. 'I knew they could kill, but the chances are pretty slim. I didn't think he'd… oh god! Am I murderer? What happens now?'

'First things first,' you say as you take a slow, deep breath. 'You took the book from the library when Shao ducked out during your conversation.

And you returned later to leave the tampered book with potentially deadly jack jumper ants on the desk…'

Paige sways, half reaches for Hudson's hand, then pulls back.

'…and that led to a number of deaths.'

'Sorry?' Jasmine says, confused.

'Capturing the ants and moving them into the library caused their imminent deaths, but not Shao's. He has no signs of ant stings or bites anywhere that I can see.'

Hudson's boots hit the floorboards hard as he half-launches himself to his feet, then slumps in his chair. 'What?'

'Even if they had stung him, and he was allergic to them, it would have been too late anyway.'

'I'm thoroughly confused,' says Bruce. Coming from a know-it-all like him, that was saying something.

'As much as you wanted to hurt him, Hudson, you couldn't.'

'Why?' three voices ask you in unison.

'Because he was already dead.'

Part Three – JASMINE

You turn to Jasmine. Her face is a mask of calm, but she has a white-knuckled grip on her cup of tea.

'Jasmine. Used to getting your own way in all things. If you can't charm you threaten, and if you can't threaten you walk away, preferably burning your bridges – and exes – behind you.'

'That's a bit harsh,' Hudson frowns.

Jasmine scoffs at you. 'You sound like my therapist.'

All pretence of her southern belle façade is now stripped away. Perhaps this is Jasmine's true self.

'Last night you discovered Shao lied to you and used you, so you decided to leave,' you say. 'But not before killing him and framing Paige for his murder.'

'Not true,' she says.

Paige stares at her, incredulous. 'Things were never friendly between us, but you framed me for murder?'

Jasmine pulls at the sleeve of her drab dress. 'Carl Kuphem is based on my husband, isn't he?'

'Carl was a perfect Shao, I suppose,' says Paige. 'But how is that relevant?'

'I knew there was a reason I didn't like that character,' Bruce mutters.

'It's relevant because I fell in love with Carl,' says Jasmine, 'then projected that love onto my husband. You could have warned me, told me what he was really like,' she hisses, her anger almost visible. 'Instead, you kept his secrets, let me believe the pretence was all real.'

Paige is clearly taken aback. 'I assumed he told you everything. I didn't think it my place to pry into your marriage.'

'I'm missing something,' says Hudson.

As interesting as this conversation is, you need to get it back on track. 'Jasmine, your plan was simple. When Shao was distracted, you pushed the ball and chain along the shelf above him so that it was above his head.'

'You really should stop talking for your own good. I have all these witnesses.' Jasmine takes in the other three house guests with a wave of her hand.

Her confidence would unnerve anyone not used to inveterate liars. You can see how she has bluffed and blustered her way through life.

You continue. 'Then, you returned to the library between 9.40 pm and 9.50 pm confident that you would find Shao dead from a blow to the head by the ball and chain. You returned to plant a clue framing Paige for his murder, but you found him still upright in the chair and the ball and chain still on the bookshelf above him.'

Jasmine is stoic as she listens to you, but her eyes narrow.

'Angry that your first attempt bore no fruit, furious that he was ignoring you, you checked to see if he was awake. He appeared, to you, to be asleep so you quietly planted your false evidence and moved the ball and chain to be right over him and teetering on the edge. Then before you left, you kicked his chair, fracturing the chair leg and hurting your own foot in the process.'

'My lawyers will have a field day with this slander,' she says.

'It's only slander if it's untrue,' you say.

Jasmine snorts. She picks up her cup, hand trembling a little. 'Whatever happened to him, he deserved it.'

'I knew it was you,' Bruce says.

He really didn't, you think, but hold your tongue.

'After potentially killing your first two husbands and getting away with it, it makes sense that you were sanguine about adding a third.'

At the mention of her previous husbands, Jasmine shakily places her cup on the coffee table, spilling the remnants. Her face, already a sickly pallor, grows paler.

'But it was all for nothing, Jasmine.'

'What do you mean?'

'By the time Bruce blundered into the desk at ten o'clock, causing the ball and chain to fall and the boxes of books to cascade to the floor like dominoes, Shao was already as good as dead. And not by your hand.'

'What!?'

Part Four – PAIGE

Finally, you turn to Paige. A master of similar fictional situations, she knows what's coming. She looks a combination of worried, puzzled and indignant.

'And then there's you, Paige,' you say as everyone's eyes lock onto her, 'ostensibly Shao's long-time editor, but in reality so much more. Your acquaintance goes back to your time at Sydney University. A young woman from country Tasmania, you scored a scholarship to the big smoke, studied literature and creative writing, and met the handsome, charismatic and egotistical Shao T. Mann in creative writing class before he became famous.'

You may be embellishing a little, but after the morning you've had you feel entitled to unfold the tale dramatically. 'You proceed to fall for Shao–'

'I knew it,' Jasmine spits.

'–while Bruce also finds his best-friend-turned-nemesis and,' your eyes flick to the bedraggled old lush, 'perhaps Bruce falls for you too, Paige.'

Grey hairs in Bruce's rough stubble catch glints of light as he shakes his head in denial.

'Either way,' you say, 'the three of you are locked in some kind of triangle – overlapping romance, work and friendship of a sort – which carries you forward on intertwined paths to success and hurt.'

'Some of it was good,' Paige says in a quiet voice.

You focus on her and force yourself not to even glance at Hudson. 'You help Shao with his course work, all but doing it for him, and by the time you've all graduated…'

Paige blanches and it tugs your heartstrings. Should you let it rest? Give her a chance to tell Hudson about her pregnancy herself? As a police detective you trampled all over complex family relationships, but that's not your job now. It comes as a relief to back off and allow Paige to reveal the truth to her son in her own time.

You nod to yourself before continuing. 'And then, when Shao returns from his travels he calls up his old University enabler in the hope she'll help him again, this time with a novel. You give in to his charms and begin a career as his ghostwriter.'

'No,' Bruce shakes his head vehemently. 'No.'

'What?' says Hudson with a shocked expression.

'Fast forward to the present,' you plough on, 'and with about thirty novels to his name Shao is one of Australia's most successful writers. Shao preens, the fans flock, but it's all smoke and mirrors.'

'I'll say,' Jasmine says glumly.

Paige sits as straight-backed as ever, appearing resolved to shoulder any criticisms from the others.

'But Paige finally grows weary of the arrangement and Shao's cruelty. At last, after three long decades, she decides to move on by killing off the lead character in the series.'

Paige nods slightly.

'Knowing Shao would discover this any day now–'

'And could have at any time,' Paige says, 'if he'd bothered to read the manuscripts.'

'–last night you went to your regular meeting with him, saw him enter the library just ahead of you, but realised he was already meeting with someone else. For a moment you hovered at the door and heard Shao offer your job to Hudson. You were shocked and angry that he would try to dupe another young, talented writer into the same awful arrangement he trapped you in.'

Paige nods again.

'Then Hudson stormed out and you stormed in to confront Shao. You exchanged terse words but Shao backed off, appeared chastened, and asked you to make him a cup of tea. Relieved, you headed to the kitchen, leaving your handbag in the library with Shao. And–'

Bruce leans forward. 'And?'

'–by my count there were three attempted murders in the library last night.'

'You outlined one involving the ants, one with the ball and chain, and…' Bruce looks at Paige in horror. 'You? No, I can't believe that.'

Paige remains silent but shakes her head in denial.

'You've jumped to the wrong conclusion, Bruce,' you say. 'I said there were three murder attempts in the library last night. I didn't say Shao was the target of them all.'

'Okay,' says Hudson. 'Now I'm lost.'

'Paige didn't try to harm anyone,' you say.

'Then what do you think I–' she begins.

'You were the target of an attempted murder,' you tell her, then watch her eyes grow wide with fear.

You reach out with a comforting hand to pat her shoulder. 'The threat has passed,' you say.

Part Five – FINAL REVEAL

SHAO

This is it, your favourite moment in any investigation: your chance to explain the false starts, cul-de-sacs and dead ends you've negotiated to reach your conclusions. You understand why Agatha Christie gave Monsieur Poirot his satisfying denouement scenes at the end of every novel – revealing your solution to the mystery is thrilling.

'I'll begin by stepping through the complicated dance of visitors in and out of the library last night,' you say. 'It's crucial to understanding what happened.'

Bruce rolls his eyes and flaps the end of his squalid scarf at you. 'Hurry up then.'

It's easy to see why his five wives left him.

'Shh.' Hudson reaches out with one leg and kicks the side of Bruce's chair. Bruce glares in response.

'After my visit at 8.30 pm,' you say, 'Shao's next visitor was Jasmine at 9 pm.'

She shrugs, jewellery gleaming in the firelight.

'When you realised Shao hadn't written the Carl Kuphem series and decided to literally leave him for dead, the items at your disposal were limited. It became obvious this morning that you assumed he died from a blow to the head. Knowing the scene, the only weapons available to you at 9 pm were his typewriter, the boxes of books and the old ball and chain.'

'I'm hardly physically capable of using any of those things as a weapon,' she says.

'But you kept mentioning the ball and chain. I wondered if you could have wielded it, but after handling it yesterday afternoon I didn't think so. It was difficult to control, like a twisting snake, and too heavy. Then Paige related the story of your professor who died from an antique cannonball rolling off a shelf onto his head.'

Had Jasmine visited that professor the day he died?

'It became clear to me you could have moved the ball and chain along the shelf to position it over Shao's head as he sat at the desk.'

'You can't be charged for moving knickknacks on shelves,' she says.

You'd felt slightly anxious about that part of your theory; now you are certain it is correct.

'At the same time you realised Shao wasn't the creator of Carl Kuphem, Shao realised Paige was ending their arrangement. That left him with no future books to sell, and if you also left him, no financial support. While you plotted his death, he came up with a plan for his own grifting.'

'Me,' says Hudson.

You nod. 'Indeed. When you arrived at 9.10 pm to talk to Shao he had just decided to ask you to be his new ghostwriter. His approach was rushed, overdone, and failed. He deeply insulted you on many levels,' here it's Hudson's turn to nod, 'and you decided to retaliate, to teach him some respect for you and for Tasmanians more generally.'

'I'm sorry, I really am,' Hudson says. 'I just saw red.'

'Shao left the library briefly to steal the vintage book from the museum, and at the same time you stole one of the new Carl Kuphem books intending to fill it with jack jumper ants. Shao returned with the antique book tucked inside his jacket, while you had a copy of *High Time* tucked inside yours. The two of you argued again then you left.'

'And I heard part of the argument,' says Paige.

'Yes,' you say. 'You and Hudson then passed each other in the library doorway at 9.20 pm as he left. Shao placed the vintage green book on the desk as you arrived – you said you saw him putting something down – but with his back to you, you couldn't tell what it was. So it looked to you like the green book was there before Hudson left the room.'

'Huh,' they both say with a similar inflection.

'Paige and Shao then argued about the end of Carl Kuphem and Shao's ghostwriting offer to Hudson. Shao said he felt unwell and asked Paige to make him a cup of tea. Paige obliged.'

'He really had quite a hold on you, didn't he?' Bruce interjects.

Paige looks to be on the verge of tears. 'Change is difficult, even if it's change for the better.'

'While Paige was out of the room, Shao took the opportunity to rifle through her handbag, as he had apparently done many times before.'

'Why would a rich man do that?' Hudson says.

'Rich,' Jasmine snorts. 'Free with other people's money more like it.'

'From the handbag he took a plastic bag of gummies and Paige's red Mont Blanc pen. He tampered with the pen then replaced it, but in the wrong compartment in the handbag.'

'What do you mean tampered with the pen?' asks Paige.

'I'll get to that,' you answer. 'By then the time was approximately 9.25 pm. You returned with his tea, he drank it, then turned his back on you and stopped interacting.'

'You poisoned his tea!' blurts Jasmine.

'Don't be ridiculous,' Paige says dismissively.

'No,' you say, 'I thought of that and ruled it out – it didn't fit with the rest of the evidence. So, it's now going on for half past nine. Paige leaves, taking the cup and saucer and her handbag with her, and Bruce enters a minute or two later.'

'My heart alarm went off at 9.25 pm.'

You suspect Bruce isn't keeping up with the conversation and is trying to draw attention to himself. 'Yes, your alarm went off a few minutes earlier. Then you went to the library and saw Shao sitting in the chair, back to you, putting the plastic bag on the table, although you were unsure what it was. He didn't speak, just sat there in silence, head resting on the palm of one hand, elbow on the table. The more you talked and he continued to ignore you, the more infuriated you became.'

'So bloody rude.' Bruce takes a swig from his flask of salty wine.

'In reconstructing the events of last night, by this point I knew when and how the green book and the plastic bag joined the other items on the table, but the pen wasn't there. It had entered the library in Paige's handbag then left again.'

'Who cares?' says Jasmine petulantly.

'You should,' you say. 'The first time someone noticed it on the desk was when Hudson returned at 9.50 pm. Although you lied about it initially, Jasmine, you also returned to the library before Hudson at around 9.40 pm, and you took Paige's pen with you.'

'Nuh-uh.' She is as transparent as glass to you now you know when she's lying. How could you have been taken in by her act last night?

'You entered Paige's room and stole the pen from her handbag while she was in the shower.'

'Sorry, hang on a minute: Jasmine also stole my pen from my handbag last night?' Paige glances at Jasmine but keeps her attention on you. 'What on earth for? You could afford to buy a Mont Blanc every day.'

'She took it to the library sometime between 9.40 pm and 9.50 pm. Shao appeared to be passed out, or comatose. She moved the ball and chain closer to his head to further her attempt to kill him, and she placed the pen on the desk in a rather lame attempt to cast suspicion on you, Paige. She was so infuriated by Shao's continued silence that she then kicked his chair hard enough to crack the bamboo leg, injuring her foot.'

'Absolutely none of this would hold up in a court in any real country,' says Jasmine.

You raise an eyebrow at her then decide to ignore the bait and move on.

'Hudson has already confessed to leaving the mutilated copy of *High Time* containing the jack jumpers on the desk at 9.50 pm, and Shao was still sitting at the desk in his chair. So the chair leg must have finally given way after that,' you surmise.

'That leaves only Bruce who stumbled back into the library at ten o'clock, blind drunk. Bleary-eyed and fed up he had another good shout at Shao, was shocked by the typewriter, then bumped into the desk and bookshelf while trying to steady himself.'

With no objection from Bruce, you continue. 'That initiated the chain reaction which saw the ball and chain roll off the shelf, bouncing off and scattering the boxes of books. It also struck Shao in his chair, which was enough to finally break the chair leg completely and topple it and Shao to the floor,' you say, shaking your head in bemusement. 'And that fully explains the unexpected and frankly bizarre scene that confronted me in the library this morning.'

'Look, that's a very impressive timeline,' says Hudson, nodding. 'But you're obviously holding something back. How did Shao actually die? And how'd the ants die? Paige looks like she might pass out – put us out of our misery.'

Now that you examine Paige closely you notice her pale complexion and shallow breathing. Hudson is right, she is barely holding her nerve.

'Okay, you're right. I said before that there were three attempts at murder in the library last night. Jasmine, with the ball and chain.'

'You'll never prove it,' she says, sniffing with contempt.

'Then me with the ants, although it was more like attempted assault,' says Hudson. 'I'm such an idiot.'

You nod, unsure of how to acknowledge his continued confession. 'And finally Shao himself.'

'You said Paige was the target of the third attempt before,' says Bruce.

You glance at Paige, trying to find a gentle way to say this. 'In Australia, the most common motive for homicide is killing a woman trying to escape a relationship with you.'

'Sorry?' says Bruce, befuddled.

'Maybe knock off the cooking wine, old man,' says Hudson. 'The detective is saying Shao tried to kill–'

Paige lets out an involuntary groan as she realises you're saying the man she loved all her adult life tried to kill her last night. She sways in her seat; Hudson reaches out a hand to steady her.

'How could I have misjudged him so badly?' Paige bites on the knuckles of a closed fist.

'When Shao told Hudson that Paige wouldn't be around much longer, I don't think he meant because she was leaving,' you say. 'I think he meant because he'd decided to kill her.'

'Just like that?' Paige's voice breaks.

'I think the museum tour, and finding the arsenic-coated green book, reminded him of the mode of death in *High Ground*.'

'Oh,' she says, a catch in her voice.

'He stole the book from the museum, then took your pen from your handbag and rubbed it on the arsenic, using your plastic gummy bear bag to protect his hand. Then he replaced your pen, expecting you to be poisoned when you used it over the next day or so.'

'Hang on,' Jasmine croaks, 'the pen was poisoned?'

'The signs of arsenic poisoning include a rash where it contacts the skin, and vomiting, stomach cramps, tremors and even death if ingested.'

Jasmine's mouth hangs open as she stares at you. 'My husband tried to kill her?'

'Yes,' you smile at her, 'and you took the proverbial bullet.'

'This is outrageous,' she says.

You couldn't agree more.

'Getting me to a hospital should be everyone's priority.'

No-one acknowledges her demand.

'I still don't get it,' says Bruce. 'How did Mann die?'

'Ohhh,' says Paige. 'I understand now. My handbag.'

You can see she's reached the same conclusion as you.

'In the few minutes Paige was in the kitchen making Shao his tea, I think he opened her handbag, saw the bag of orange gummy bears and decided to use the plastic bag to hold her pen while he poisoned it. Mr Sweet-tooth emptied the whole bag of bears into his mouth – leaving a stray one behind – chewed and swallowed them while he was poisoning her pen and replacing it in her bag.'

'But they weren't sweets,' Paige says, 'they were ibuprofen gummies. Why would he eat them all in one go like that?'

'He had to dispose of them in order to use the bag,' you answer. 'He didn't test one to see if he liked them, just assumed they would be sweet.'

'How many were in the bag?' Hudson asks in a hushed tone.

'Perhaps twenty-five or thirty,' Paige says.

'Oh,' he says.

'He must have started to feel the effects soon after he swallowed. He was alive when Bruce entered at 9.30 pm, when he dropped the plastic bag on the desk and settled into the position you described, Bruce, with his head in one hand and elbow on the desk. Drowsiness is a symptom of an ibuprofen overdose. After that he stayed upright until you knocked him over at 10 pm.'

'But when did he die?' Bruce says.

'Perhaps in the half hour between 9.30 pm and 10 pm, possibly even after you knocked him to the ground. The farting and belching could have been someone who was unconscious, or gas escaping a corpse. Either way, without rapid access to a hospital, Shao was dead the moment he ate those gummies.'

Bruce splutters, then shakes his head. 'So, let me get this straight, are you saying Mann died because he ate some orange jelly teddy bears?'

You sigh. 'Yes.' You can see the headline now: Copper's Fail – World Famous Author Dies from Bears as Ex-detective Naps.

Jasmine begins to laugh, a horrendous, bone chilling chortle. 'Europe's lovely at this time of year,' she says.

Jasmine Quill would not be escaping to Europe any time soon if you had any say in the matter. You may be retired, but you still have friends in every branch of law enforcement.

Next to you, Paige is shaking and begins to dry retch.

You recognise her symptoms. 'Paige,' you say gently, 'you're going into shock. Hudson and I will take care of you.'

Hudson looks panicked. 'What do we do?'

'We're going to keep the room warm and quiet and make sure she has liquids and some sugar. Put the kettle on and bring in a bowl of sugar and a spoon, honey would be better. Then find some spare blankets and bring in more firewood.'

Bruce stands up. 'I'll get the blankets.'

'Thanks,' you nod and walk to the door with him. 'Jasmine can't go anywhere, but help me keep an eye on her, okay?'

'Of course,' says Bruce and heads up the hallway to fetch blankets.

As you move about the sitting room rearranging things to ensure Paige is warm, comfortable and being looked after, you notice flashing lights out the window, presumably an emergency service patrol on the river checking on people isolated by the floods. You rub Paige's arm and say, 'You're going to be okay.'

You wonder what the festival organisers will make of this morning's events and the inevitable publicity. Will you be invited back again, or banned forever? Either way, you have some interesting grist for a novel, and there are plenty of other festivals out there.

If the festival hadn't invited Shao T. Mann, and by extension Paige, along with their long-hidden son Hudson, Shao might still be alive today. Almost a year ago their coincidental invitation had lit a fuse that last night detonated thirty years of secrets, lies, frustration and resentment. Quite a confluence of events indeed.

Once you're home, perhaps you can begin a new manuscript and capture the essence of this weekend – the characters, clues, twists and turns – and write a bestseller. Who knows? Someday you might even win a Devil in the Detail Award for the murder you wrote.

Where to next?

Choose from 1, 2 or 3.

1. Did you solve the mystery before the end? You can celebrate being one of the best amateur sleuths to read mystery fiction!
2. Did you miss some clues? Turn back to Chapter 1, *Your Body in the Library* by Z.E. Davidson, and choose a different path.
3. If you think you identified the fastest pathway through the book and solved the mystery in just ten chapters – Chapter 1 plus nine other chapters before this hidden chapter – you can email a list of the chapters and clues to ljmowen@gmail.com to check your findings against the solution.

We hope you enjoyed investigating this case.

CONTRIBUTOR BIOGRAPHIES

L.J.M. Owen, Commissioning Editor

Dr L.J. Owen escaped dark days as a public servant for a sunnier profession – inventing murder. A multi-award winning writer, L.J.'s novels include the chilling *The Great Divide*, longlisted for the 2020 Ngaio Marsh Award, and three books in the Dr Pimms archaeological mystery series: *Egyptian Enigma, Mayan Mendacity,* and *Olmec Obituary*. At the 2020 Scarlet Stilettos, L.J.'s historical thriller and legal mystery short stories won three awards. L.J. also writes under the pen names Carys King, Elaine Kelso, Jack Cainery (*il est francais*) and Doc Rowen.

In 2019, with her trademark disregard for sleep, L.J. founded the Terror Australis Readers and Writers Festival (TARWF), Australia's southern-most literary festival. L.J. is the current Director of TARWF, the Convenor of TARWF's annual Children's Mystery Short Story Competition, and the Convenor of the Tasmanian chapter of Sisters in Crime Australia.

A passionate supporter of emerging, disabled, and regional writers, and literacy for adults, L.J.'s guiding principles are kindness, integrity, and finding joy in the unexpected. She holds degrees in archaeology, forensic science, and librarianship, speaks five languages, and travelled the world before disability struck. Now sharing a home in the bush with Tasmanian devils, L.J. serves a co-op of rescue cats, entrenched chickens, and grifter possums. She is currently in trouble with at least one of them.

Zoe Davidson, Developmental Editor

Writing as Z. E. Davidson, Zoe Davidson is an award winning writer of short fiction with a novel in the works. She was the developmental editor for this anthology.

Zoe began volunteering with the Terror Australis Readers and Writers Festival in 2022, after several years of attending, briefly served on the Board secretariat. Zoe lives in southern Tasmania, and can be found reading or cycling. She has yet to master doing both at once.

Alison Alexander

Born and bred in Hobart, Dr Alison Alexander is a former lecturer in History at the University of Tasmania. She has written 34 books about Tasmanian history, on topics ranging from the battle to end convict transportation to the Clarence Football Club. She has also written award-winning biographies of Jane Franklin and, closer to home, Hobart artist Patricia Giles.

Alison is the Matron of the Terror Australis Readers and Writers Festival in southern Tasmania. As a complete change from her regular writing practice, she greatly enjoyed contributing a chapter to the present exciting project.

Sarah Barrie

Sarah Barrie is the author of nine novels including her bestselling print debut *Secrets of Whitewater Creek*, the Hunters Ridge trilogy, the Tasmanian-set Calico Mountain trilogy and a new crime series starring Constable Lexi Winter. In a past life, Sarah worked as a teacher, a vet nurse, a horse trainer and a magazine editor, before deciding she wanted to write novels. About the only thing that has remained constant is her love of all things crime.

Her favourite place in the world is the family property, where she writes her stories overlooking mountains crisscrossed with farmland, bordered by the beauty of the Australian bush, and where, at the end of the day, she can spend time with family, friends, a good Irish whiskey and a copy of her next favourite book.

Karen Brooks

Formerly an officer in the Australian Army, Dr Karen Brooks has written 15 books, with her historical fiction, *The Good Wife of Bath: A Mostly True Story, The Brewer's Tale, The Locksmith's Daughter, The Chocolate Maker's Wife*, and *The Darkest Shore* published to critical and popular acclaim here and internationally. With a Ph.D. in English/Cultural Studies, she's also widely published on popular culture, education and social psychology and was an award winning lecturer.

Karen's latest novel, *The Escapades of Tribulation Johnson: or, A Woman Writes Back*, explores the heady, dangerous world of Restoration Theatre and the deadly politics of a bygone era.

She lives in a remarkable convict-built house in Hobart with her husband and furbabies, and when not writing is working in their brewstillery, Captain Bligh's.

Alan Carter

Dr Alan Carter lives just south of Hobart, is a current Committee Member of the Australian Crime Writers Association, and works with writing students at the University of Tasmania.

As well as swimming in icy cold water for fun, he is the author of five Cato Kwong novels – *Prime Cut, Getting Warmer, Bad Seed, Heaven Sent* and *Crocodile Tears* – and the Nick Chester novels *Marlborough Man* and *Doom Creek*, set in New Zealand.

Prime Cut won a Ned Kelly Award for Best Debut Crime in 2011 and *Marlborough Man* won the Ngaio Marsh for Best Crime Novel in 2018. Alan's novels have been translated into French, German and Spanish.

R.B. Cole

Barbie Robinson and Richard Scherer are co-Principals of Living Arts Canberra, a not for profit website, podcast platform and internet radio station. Together, they support a wide array of arts festivals and events in NSW and Victoria, as well as the Terror Australis Readers and Writers Festival in southern Tasmania.

Barbie is an arts journalist, arts advocate, photographer, writer and designer. She is the author/designer of three children's picture books, three solo books of poetry, two joint photography and poetry publications marking the 2003 Canberra Firestorm, and was both a writer and designer for the 2008 group community writing project, between the lines, stories of 11 women.

Following a career in newspaper journalism and communications, Richard has mastered an impressive array of broadcast and digital technical skills. He is expanding his creative practice to include writing fiction.

Together, Richard and Barbie are R. B. Cole.

Natalie Conyer

Dr Natalie Conyer is a crime writer and the author of *Present Tense*, which won the Ned Kelly award for the best debut crime novel of 2020, was shortlisted for the Davitt Award and nominated as one of 2020's best reads by *The Australian*.

Her short stories have won several awards in the Sisters in Crime Australia annual Scarlet Stiletto Competition; they are being published as a collection. She also has a story in the anthology, *Dark Deeds Downunder 2*. Sydney based, Natalie is a swimmer, a TV addict, a world-class procrastinator, and a crime fiction tragic who loves the genre so much she did a doctorate on it.

Craig Cormick

Dr Craig Cormick OAM is an award-winning author of over 40 works of fiction and non-fiction, for adults and children. In 2016 he won the Tasmanian Writers' Prize for the story *No Man is an Island*. He is a former Chair of the ACT Writers Centre and has been a writer in residence in Malaysia and in Antarctica – travelling to the icy continent from Hobart. He has a been a guest at several writing festivals in Tasmania and his creative PhD, *The Last Supper*, was on the creation and recreation of the 'Cannibal Convict' Alexander Pearce of Van Diemen's Land.

Craig loves messing with history in his work, almost as much as history loves messing with him. His most recent book is *On A Barbarous Coast*, an alternate telling of Captain Cook's visit to the east coast of Australia, cowritten with indigenous author Harold Ludwick.

E.K. Cutting

Writer, librarian, and literary award judge, Em Cutting grew up in a world of words. Writing as E.K. Cutting, she has published short fiction in a range of genres though she recently settled on a life of crime. She was the in-house line editor for this anthology.

Em is a member of the Terror Australis Readers and Writers Festival (TARWF) Board, helps run the Tasmanian chapter of Sisters in Crime Australia, has worked in a number of Tasmanian libraries, judges the national Aurelius Awards and TARWF Children's Mystery Short Story Competition. She loves to craft.

Jo Dixon

Jo Dixon moved from suburban Brisbane to rural Tasmania over a decade ago. Since then, she's been wrangling an ever-growing collection of animals, bringing up two sons, and attempting to transform blackberry-infested paddocks into beautiful gardens.

Now, she also writes full-time, creating twisty, suspenseful stories that feature flawed characters who've made mistakes, but who turn out to be stronger than they think.

Jo's debut novel, *The House of Now and Then*, was released by Harlequin/HarperCollins in 2023. Her second novel is due for release in 2024. Both books are set in southern Tasmania. She is currently working on her third book.

Jacq Ellem

Jacq Ellem is a bibliophile, copywriter, occasional broadcaster, and an internationally award-winning podcaster, including Best Writing and Best Performance for *Tales from Three Corners*.

She hosts *Murder Mondays* for Sisters in Crime Australia, is the Podcast Wrangler for NZ Webfest, and holds the title of Chief Cat Herder & Senior Creative for an Audio Production Company in the cloud.

She lives an ordinary life in an ordinary cottage, which includes cold swimming, jam making, a small amount of chainsawing, and is an awesome auntie to seven Grott Monsters. Comfortable chaos is her superpower.

Jason Franks

Jason Franks is the author of the novels *Faerie Apocalypse, Bloody Waters,* and *Shadowmancy*, and the writer of the Sixsmiths graphic novels. His work has been short-listed for Aurealis, Ditmar and Ledger awards. Franks' short fiction has been published in *Deathlings, Aurealis, Midnight Echo*, and many other magazines and anthologies, including IFWG's Cthulhu *Deep Down Under.*

Jason lives in Melbourne with his family and three electric guitars that his wife refuses to acknowledge.

E.V. Scott

Kew Gibson, writing as E.V. Scott, is the bestselling author of Australian rural romcoms such as *Lonely in Longreach* and *Meet Me in Bendigo.* A life-long storyteller, Kew lived in Britain and Papua New Guinea before coming home to Australia to train as a cultural anthropologist. She now lives amongst vineyards and orchards in rural Tasmania, with her husband and son, two cats and a cocker spaniel.

Narrelle M. Harris

Narrelle M. Harris writes crime, horror, fantasy and romance. Her 40+ works include vampire novels, erotic spy adventures, het and queer romance, and Holmes/Watson mysteries. Her ghost/crime story 'Jane' won the Body in the Library prize at the 2017 Scarlet Stiletto Awards and her collection *Scar Tissue and Other Stories* was nominated for the 2019 Aurealis Awards.

Among her many creative endeavours, Narrelle coaches writers living with autism, as well as other emerging writers and editors. She was the commissioning editor for *The Only One in the World: A Sherlock Holmes Anthology* (2021); and *Clamour and Mischief* (2022) which was shortlisted for an Aurealis Awards for best anthology. In 2023, she is co-editing two more anthologies, along with writing more fiction. Her next novel, with Clan Destine Press, is *The She-Wolf of Baker Street.*

Angela Meyer

Dr Angela Meyer has worked in the book industry for almost two decades, including as a bookseller, book journalist, Books+Publishing editor, commissioning editor and publisher, freelance editor, literary award judge, and author.

She is currently a lecturer in the Master of Writing and Publishing at RMIT.

Her debut novel, *A Superior Spectre*, was shortlisted for an Aurealis Award, the MUD Literary Prize, an ABIA, the Readings Prize and a Saltire Literary Society Award. She is the author of a novella, *Joan Smokes*, which won the inaugural Mslexia Novella Award (UK), and a book of flash fiction, *Captives*. Her second novel, *Moon Sugar*, was released in October 2022.

A supporter of regional and emerging writers, Angela is the inaugural Chair of the Terror Australis Readers and Writers Festival Board.

Allison Mitchell

Allison Mitchell lives in Tasmania where she has spent most of her life. She's inspired to write by family stories from the 1950s and by spending time in Tasmania's wild places, such as Tullah and Liawenee.

Allison was a finalist in the Tasmanian Writers' Prize in 2018 and 2022 and shortlisted for the 2022 Scarlet Stiletto Awards. In 2023, Allison perfected a work-life balance, spending three days a week working for 26TEN, Tasmania's campaign for adult literacy, and the rest of the week studying and writing for a degree in Honours in Creative Writing at the University of Tasmania.

David Owen

David Owen is the author of 19 books of fiction and nonfiction, including the famed Pufferfish series, with two more novels scheduled for publication in 2023-4. Revised editions of his natural history books on the Thylacine and Tasmanian Devil will be published at the end of 2023.

A Librarian by profession, David has been employed at Government House since 2009, initially as Deputy and then as Official Secretary from 2012. Previously he was employed by Arts Tasmania, and the University of Tasmania. He offers occasional courses in crime fiction writing, and is a former Editor of Tasmania's *Island* magazine.

Livia Day

Dr Tansy Rayner Roberts writes prolifically across a number of genres, including gaslamp fantasy, science fiction, critical essays and magical mysteries. Writing as Livia Day, she is the author of cozy, crafty & cafe-themed Hobart-set crime novels such as *A Trifle Dead* and *Dyed & Buried*.

Tansy is also a writing teacher, an award-winning podcaster, an untamed quilter, and in her copious spare time she is a sales manager for a company that builds and restores grave monuments. She lives in southern Tasmania with her family.

Matthew D. Ruffin

A former university lecturer in sustainability and a home energy efficiency guru, Matt Ruffin has abandoned all pretence of capitalist respectability and now spends his days caring for humans, animals, and manuscripts. He was the line editor for this anthology.

Marion Stoneman

Marion Stoneman has enjoyed writing from a young age, especially poetry. She worked at the Tasmanian Writers Centre for nine years, assisting writers and helping to present the Tasmanian Readers and Writers Festival. In 2006 she founded the Eastern Shore Writers Group with poet Lyn Reeves and continues to convene the group, having co-edited two group anthologies: *I Want You to be the Victim* (2019) and *Corrosion* (2022). She was also the in-house structural editor for this anthology.

In 2019 Marion joined the team to present the inaugural Terror

Australis Readers and Writers Festival in the Huon Valley and has continued her involvement, most recently as part of the festival Board. She is a keen sailor and soon plans to cast off into the wide blue yonder in search of more great stories.

Maggie Veness

Maggie Veness discovered the joy of fiction writing after her fourth child left the nest. Flash and short length stories suit her attention span best. She finds people intriguing. Show her an idiosyncrasy or peccadillo and she'll engage you with a story that reveals her quirky, raw, or irreverent sensibility. Her contemporary stories get to the mad heart of things, which isn't always comfortable. She resolutely avoids self-publication.

Maggie has enjoyed seeing dozens of her stories published across many counties. Preferring the tactile experience of a bound book, the vast majority of her work has been print-published.

Sarah White

Sarah White writes novels and short stories inspired by stories found in the pages of history books, where settings are so atmospheric that they could be called characters in their own right. She holds a Master of History, and BA in Journalism and Literary Studies and her work has previously been published in both a local anthology and a national academic journal.

When she's not writing, or getting lost in the archives, or volunteering for the Terror Australis Readers and Writers Festival, she lives with her husband and daughter in Tasmania's Huon Valley.

ACKNOWLEDGEMENTS

I would like to acknowledge all the writers who have helped to shape the idea of the isolated country house murder mystery, the writers who create interactive stories, and the authors who write books suitable for both their usual fans and emerging adult readers. Your work inspired us.

I would also like to acknowledge the traditional custodians of the land on which I live and write, the Melukerdee people of the south east nations, and offer my thanks and respect to their elders past and present.

This book was made possible by a grant from Arts Tasmania that allowed me, as the commissioning editor, to pay all the contributing writers appropriately.

It was also made possible by the extraordinary contribution of the anthology's developmental editor, Z.E. Davidson.

This story reads as one continuous narrative thanks to the impressive structural editing of E.K. Cutting and Marion Stoneman, and essential line editing of Matt Ruffin. My thanks also to inspirational external editor Angela Meyer and marvellous proofreaders Karen Brooks, Natalie Conyer and Kew Gibson.

My deepest thanks to Lindy Cameron, CEO of Clan Destine Press, for creating a space in which to bring my experimental single-story novel anthology to life, and Judith Rossell for transforming my rough sketches (the roughest!) into beautiful artwork.

Likewise, my thanks to all the contributing writers – emerging and established – for undertaking this journey with me, for helping each other, for being willing to try something new, remixing ideas, writing for two audiences at once, and for working in the second-person point of view. Your enthusiasm, creativity and patience were fundamental to this undertaking.

And finally, as writers, our whole anthology team would like to acknowledge our readers. This book, like all our work, exists because of you.

Printed in Australia
Ingram Content Group Australia Pty Ltd
AUHW022130021023
384439AU00001B/1

9 781922 904522